Ross Richie CEO & Founder
Matt Gagnon Editor-In-Chief
Filip Sablik President of Publishing & Marketing
Stephen Christy President of Development
Lance Kreiter VP of Licensing & Merchandising
Phil Barbaro VP of Finance
Bryce Carlson Managing Editor
Mel Caylo Marketing Manager
Scott Newman Production Design Manager
Irene Bradish Operations Manager
Christine Dinh Brand Communications Manager
Sierra Hahn Senior Editor
Dafna Pleban Editor
Shannon Watters Editor
Eric Harburn Editor
Ian Brill Editor
Whitney Leopard Associate Editor
Jasmine Amiri Associate Editor
Chris Rosa Associate Editor
Alex Galer Assistant Editor
Cameron Chittock Assistant Editor
Mary Gumport Assistant Editor
Kelsey Dieterich Production Designer
Jillian Crab Production Designer
Kara Leopard Production Designer
Michelle Ankley Production Design Assistant
Devin Funches E-Commerce & Inventory Coordinator
Aaron Ferrara Operations Coordinator
José Meza Sales Assistant
Elizabeth Loughridge Accounting Assistant
Stephanie Hocutt Marketing Assistant
Hillary Levi Executive Assistant
Kate Albin Administrative Assistant
James Arriola Mailroom Assistant

FEATHERS, December 2015. Published by Archaia, a division of Boom Entertainment, Inc. Feathers is ™ and © 2015 Jorge Corona. All rights reserved. Originally published in single magazine form as FEATHERS No. 1-6. ™ & © 2015 Jorge Corona. All Rights Reserved. Archaia™ and the Archaia logo are trademarks of Boom Entertainment, Inc., registered in various countries and categories. All characters, events, and institutions depicted herein are fictional. Any similarity between any of the names, characters, persons, events, and/or institutions in this publication to actual names, characters, and persons, whether living or dead, events, and/or institutions is unintended and purely coincidental.

BOOM! Studios, 5670 Wilshire Boulevard, Suite 450, Los Angeles, CA 90036-5679.

Printed in China. First Printing.

ISBN: 978-1-60886-753-0, eISBN: 978-1-61398-424-6

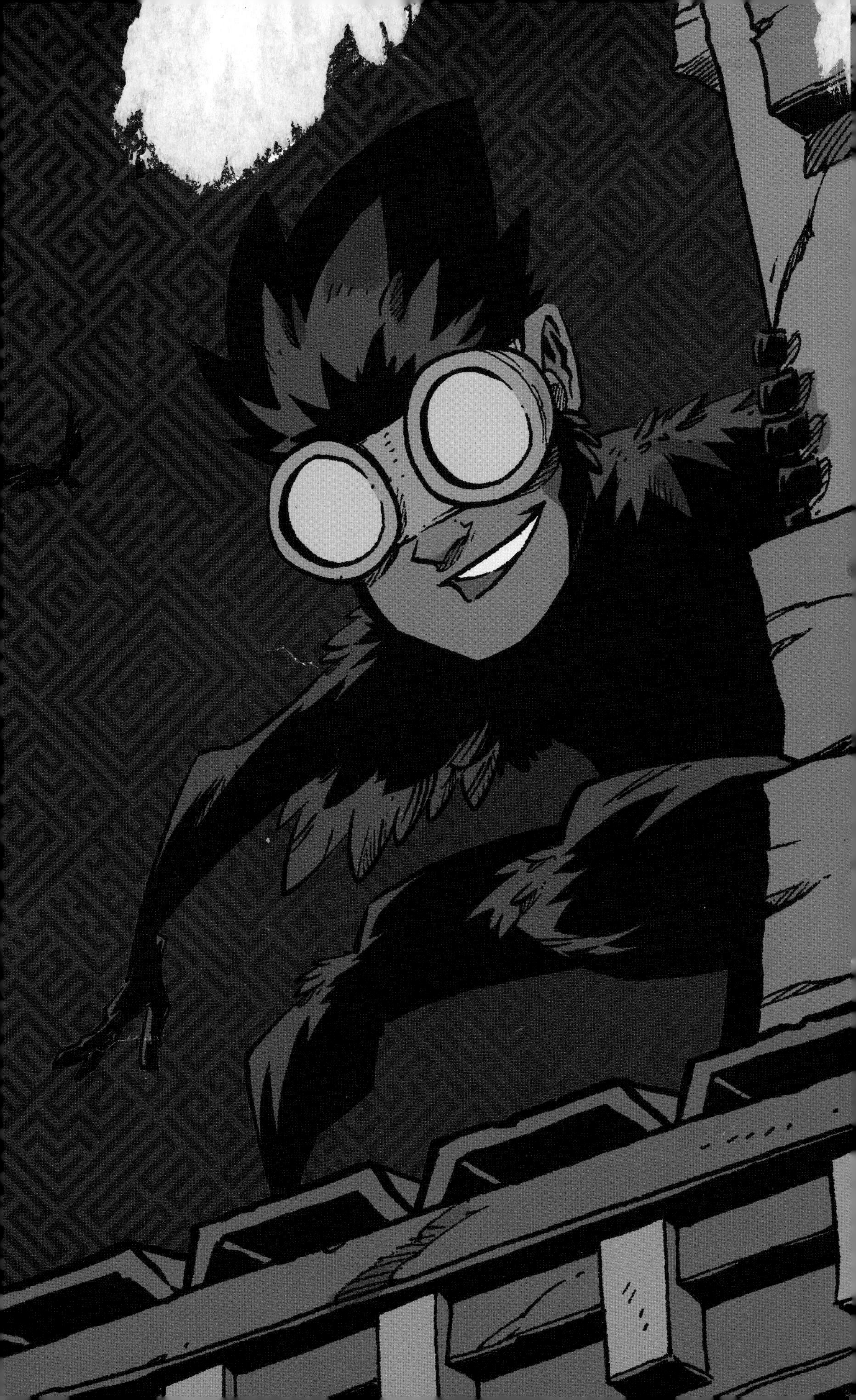

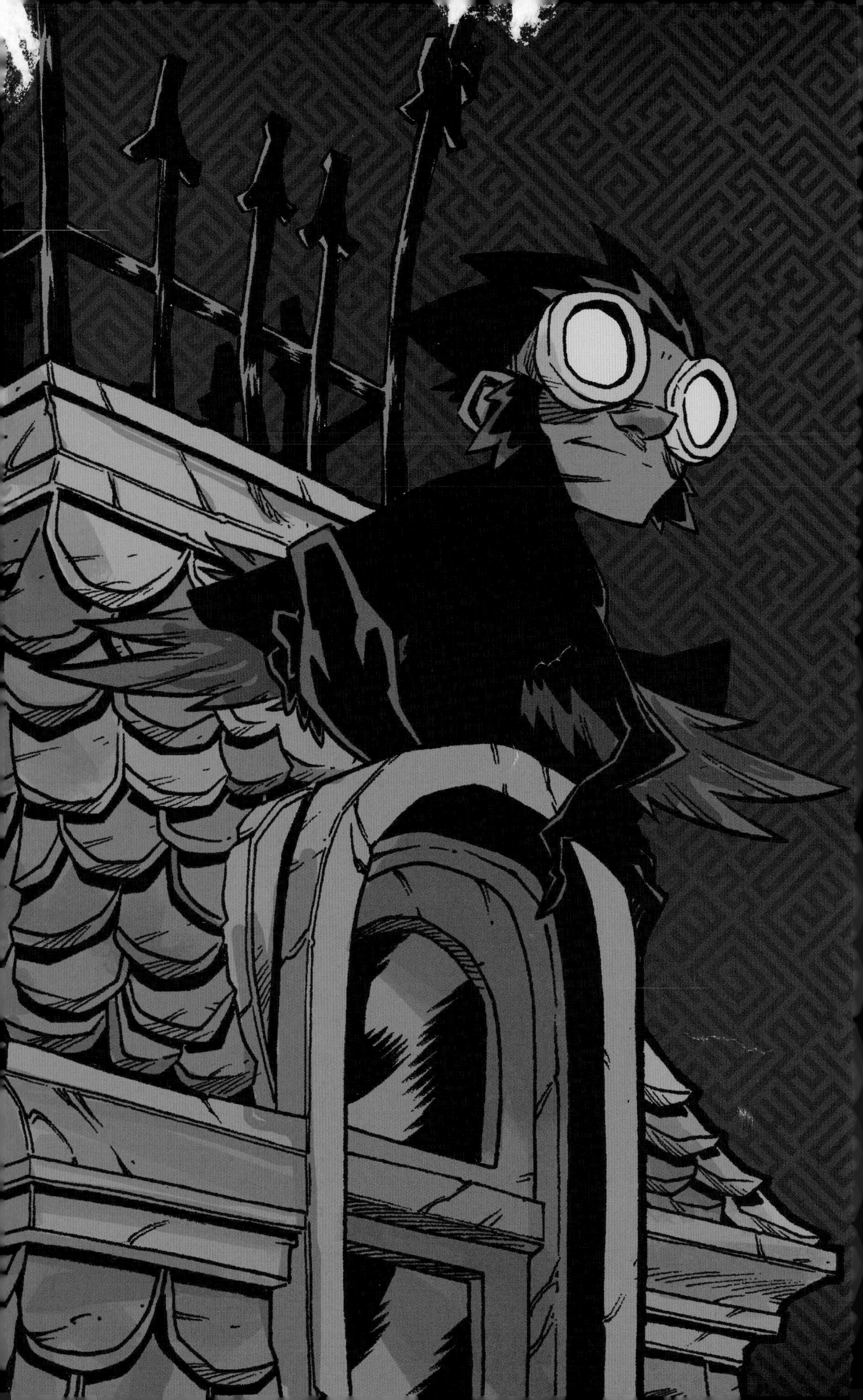

WRITTEN & ILLUSTRATED BY
JORGE CORONA

COLORS BY
JEN HICKMAN

LETTERS BY
DERON BENNETT

COVER BY
JORGE CORONA

DESIGNER **JILLIAN CRAB**
ASSISTANT EDITOR **MARY GUMPORT**
ORIGINAL SERIES EDITOR **REBECCA TAYLOR**
COLLECTION EDITOR **IAN BRILL**

CREATED BY **JORGE CORONA**

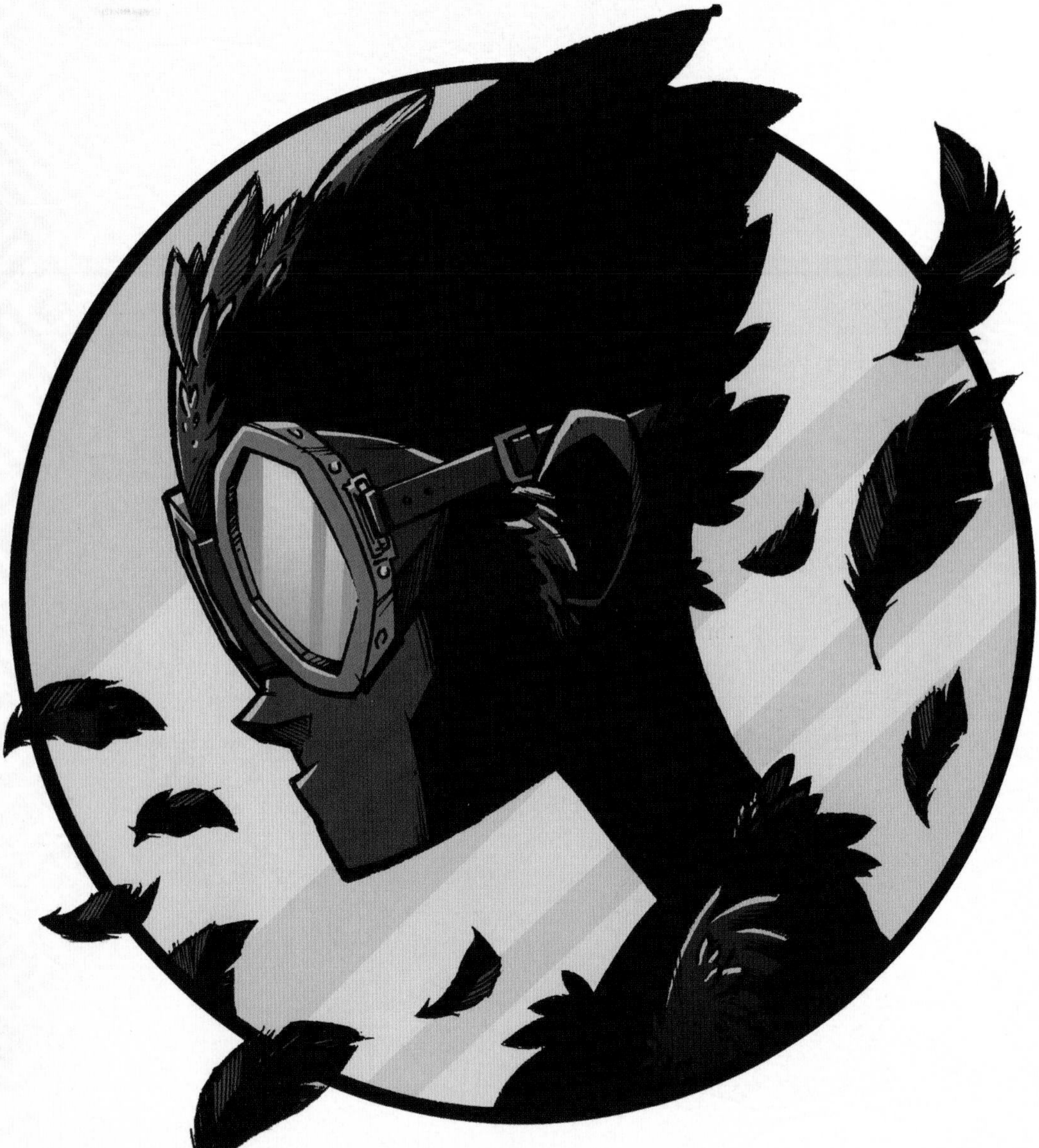

FOREWORD

The story of *Feathers* is a perfect example of an idea that took a life of its own. It started as a personal storytelling exercise of a *Beauty and the Beast* type of narrative, the tale of a boy and a girl forming a friendship against all odds in a world that would oppose it. That core idea remained, but little by little the concepts and surroundings expanded, shaping the world and the story you now hold in your hands.

The story of Poe and Bianca is one about duality, about the meeting of opposites, and about coexistence. In a world that keeps pushing for extremes, where everything is black or white, their story tries to find a middle ground.

Thank you for picking up this book, let yourself get lost in the Maze, and tag along with its ghosts, discovering a world bigger than what our characters expected, but a world that fits within each and every one of us.

Special thanks to my parents, Elisa Quijano and Heberto Corona, and to Morgan Beem, for their support, inspiration, and company while creating this world. Thanks to Rebecca Taylor and Mary Gumport for their tireless dedication and complete trust in shaping together this book. And last but not least, thanks to Jen Hickman, Deron Bennett, and Jillian Crab for helping me bring to life the story you're about to read.

Jorge Corona
Maracaibo, 2015

CHAPTER
ONE

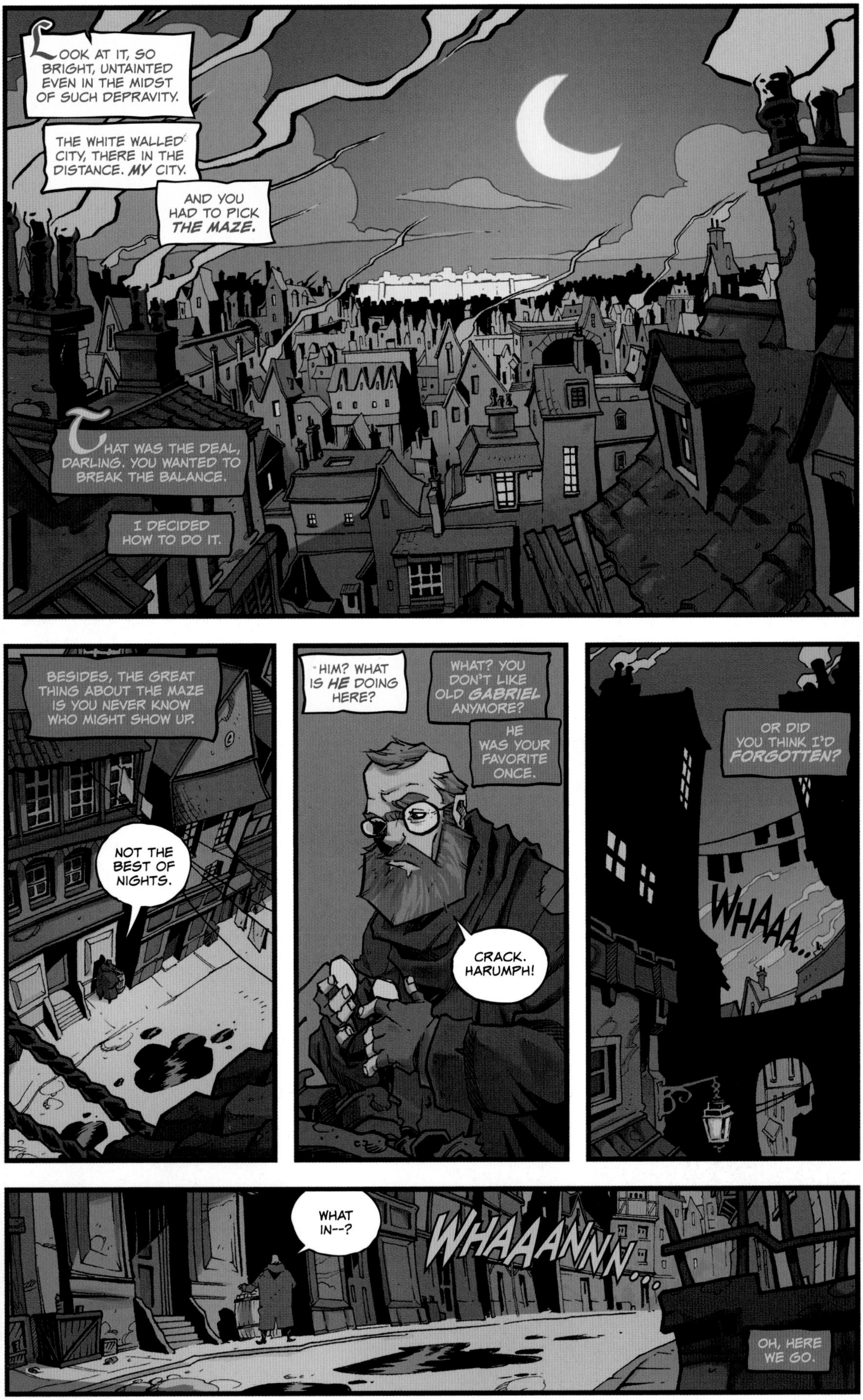
LOOK AT IT, SO BRIGHT, UNTAINTED EVEN IN THE MIDST OF SUCH DEPRAVITY.
THE WHITE WALLED CITY, THERE IN THE DISTANCE. MY CITY.
AND YOU HAD TO PICK THE MAZE.
THAT WAS THE DEAL, DARLING. YOU WANTED TO BREAK THE BALANCE.
I DECIDED HOW TO DO IT.
BESIDES, THE GREAT THING ABOUT THE MAZE IS YOU NEVER KNOW WHO MIGHT SHOW UP.
NOT THE BEST OF NIGHTS.
HIM? WHAT IS HE DOING HERE?
WHAT? YOU DON'T LIKE OLD GABRIEL ANYMORE?
HE WAS YOUR FAVORITE ONCE.
CRACK. HARUMPH!
OR DID YOU THINK I'D FORGOTTEN?
WHAAA...
WHAT IN--?
WHAAANNN...
OH, HERE WE GO.

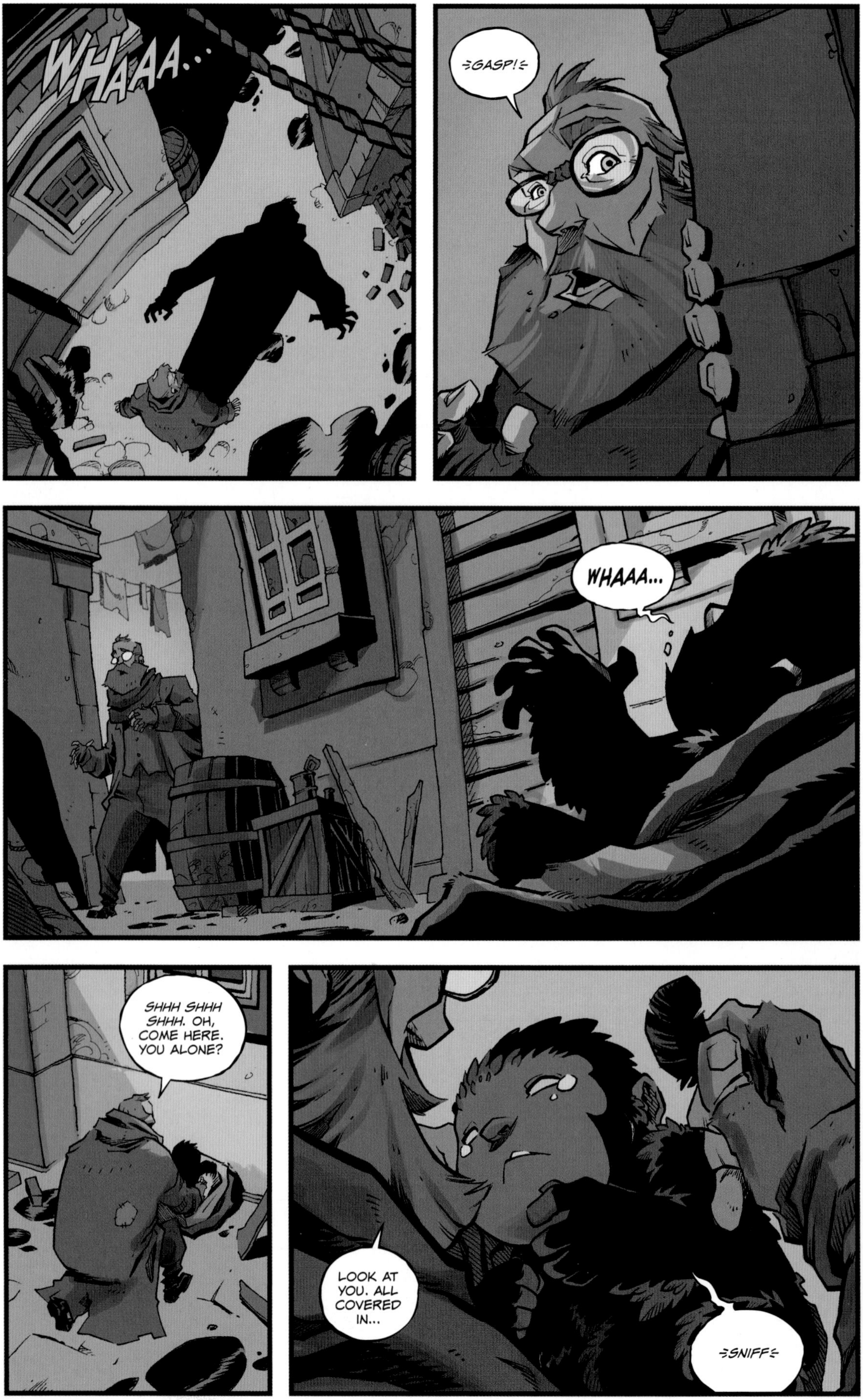
WHAAA...
GASP!
WHAAA...
SHHH SHHH SHHH. OH, COME HERE. YOU ALONE?
LOOK AT YOU. ALL COVERED IN...
SNIFF

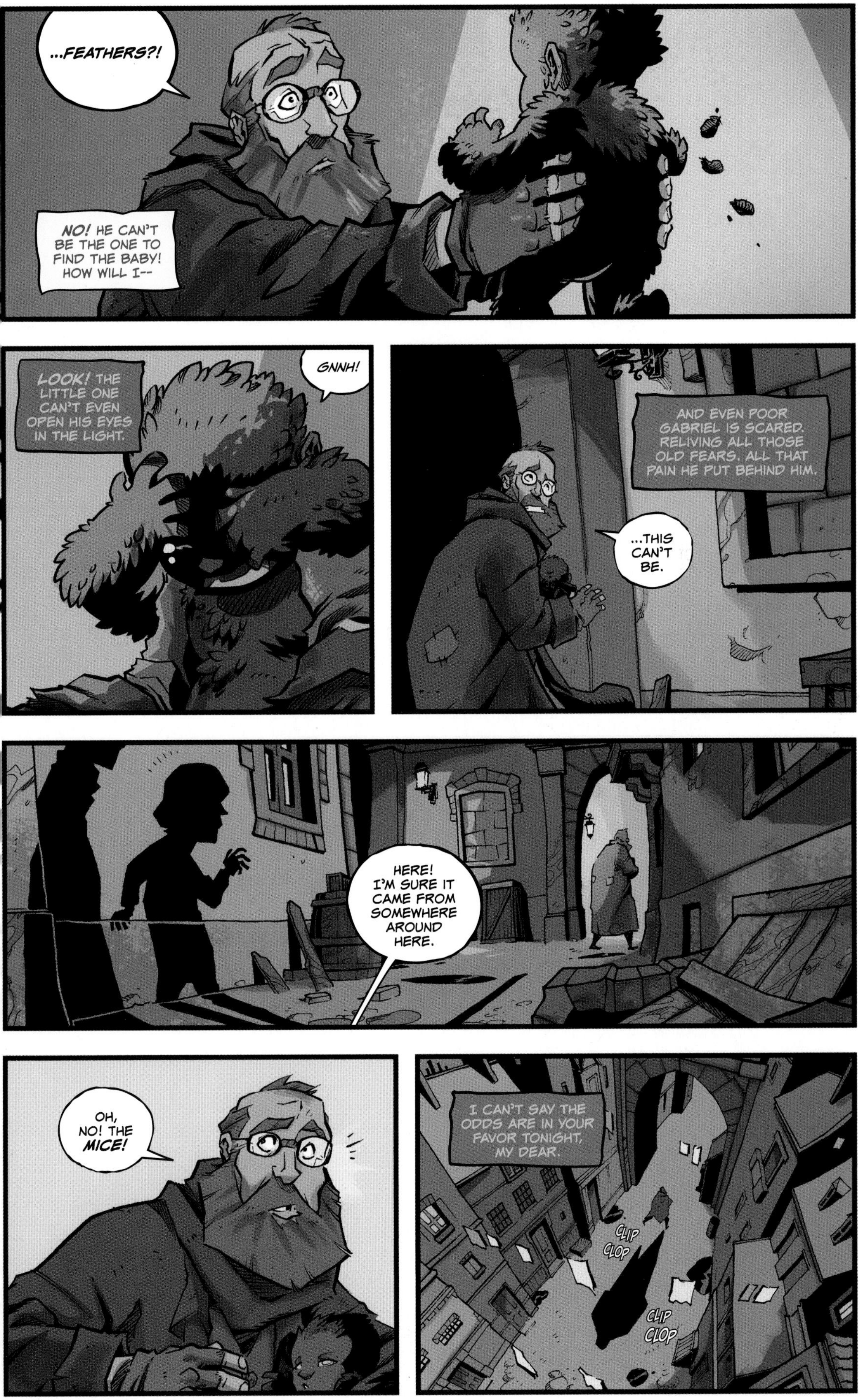
...FEATHERS?!
NO! HE CAN'T BE THE ONE TO FIND THE BABY! HOW WILL I--
LOOK! THE LITTLE ONE CAN'T EVEN OPEN HIS EYES IN THE LIGHT.
GNNH!
AND EVEN POOR GABRIEL IS SCARED. RELIVING ALL THOSE OLD FEARS. ALL THAT PAIN HE PUT BEHIND HIM.
...THIS CAN'T BE.
HERE! I'M SURE IT CAME FROM SOMEWHERE AROUND HERE.
OH, NO! THE MICE!
I CAN'T SAY THE ODDS ARE IN YOUR FAVOR TONIGHT, MY DEAR.
CLIP CLOP
CLIP CLOP

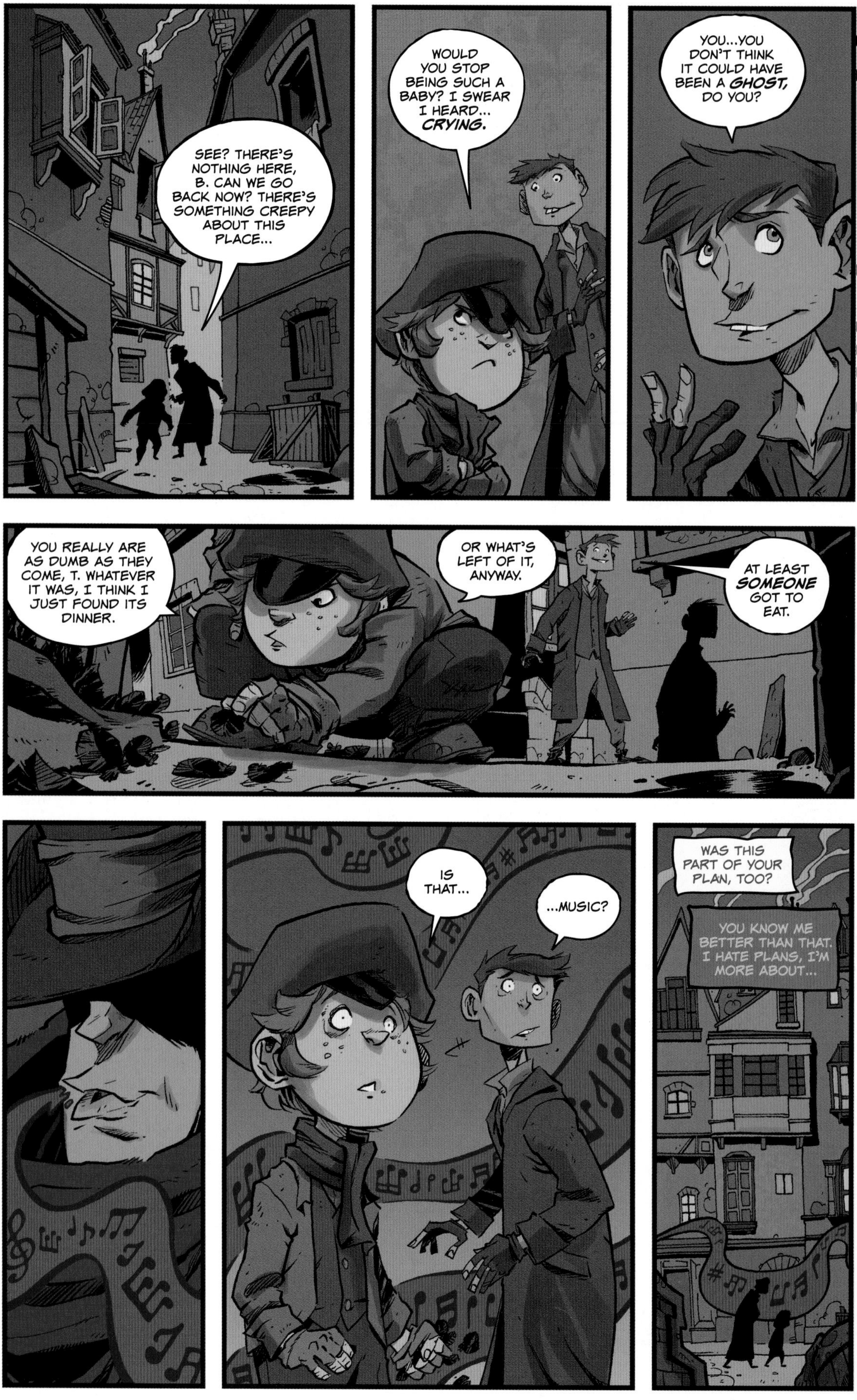
SEE? THERE'S NOTHING HERE, B. CAN WE GO BACK NOW? THERE'S SOMETHING CREEPY ABOUT THIS PLACE...
WOULD YOU STOP BEING SUCH A BABY? I SWEAR I HEARD... CRYING.
YOU...YOU DON'T THINK IT COULD HAVE BEEN A GHOST, DO YOU?
YOU REALLY ARE AS DUMB AS THEY COME, T. WHATEVER IT WAS, I THINK I JUST FOUND ITS DINNER.
OR WHAT'S LEFT OF IT, ANYWAY.
AT LEAST SOMEONE GOT TO EAT.
IS THAT...
...MUSIC?
WAS THIS PART OF YOUR PLAN, TOO?
YOU KNOW ME BETTER THAN THAT. I HATE PLANS, I'M MORE ABOUT...

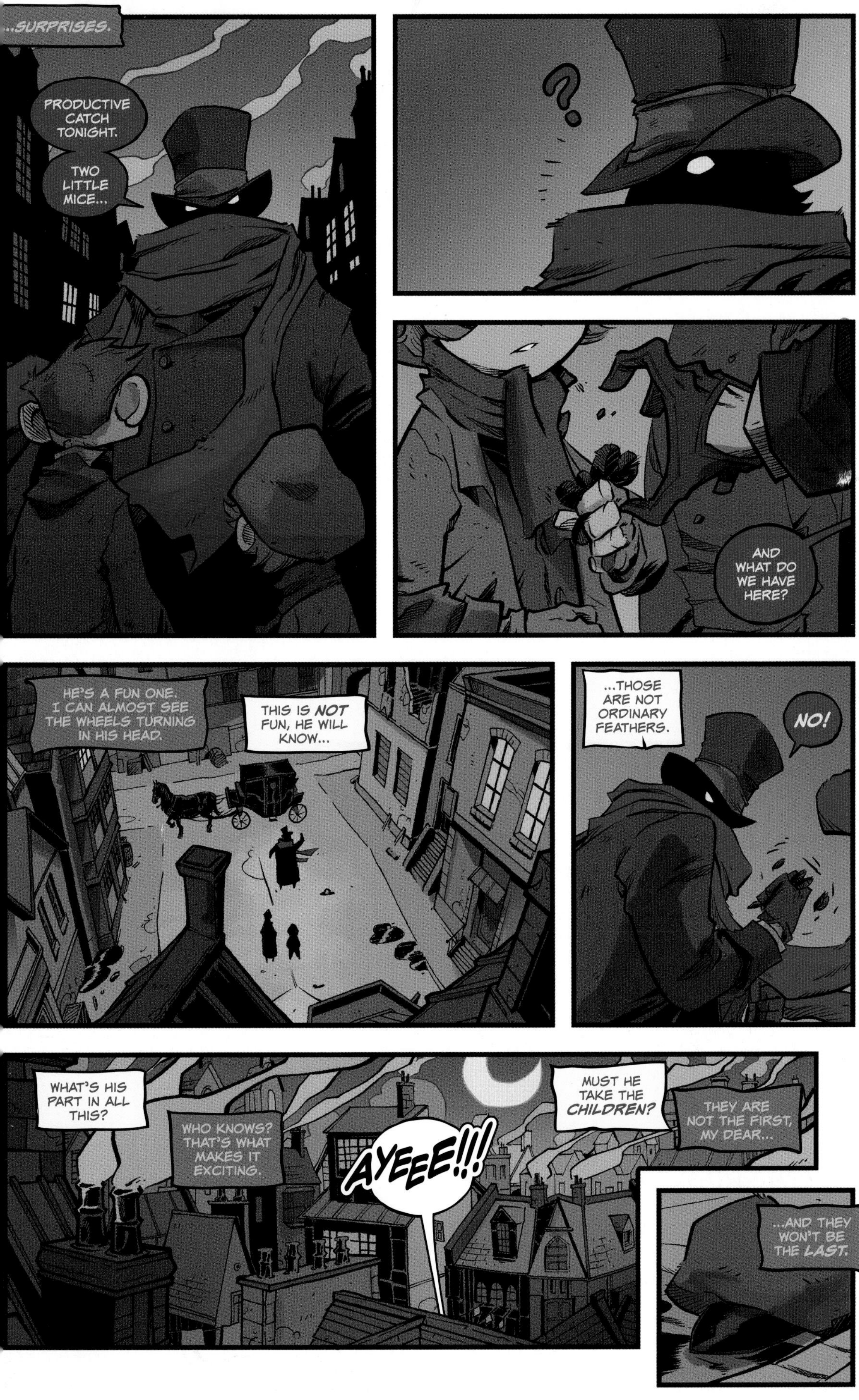
...SURPRISES.
PRODUCTIVE CATCH TONIGHT.
TWO LITTLE MICE...
?
AND WHAT DO WE HAVE HERE?
HE'S A FUN ONE. I CAN ALMOST SEE THE WHEELS TURNING IN HIS HEAD.
THIS IS NOT FUN, HE WILL KNOW...
...THOSE ARE NOT ORDINARY FEATHERS.
NO!
WHAT'S HIS PART IN ALL THIS?
WHO KNOWS? THAT'S WHAT MAKES IT EXCITING.
AYEEE!!!
MUST HE TAKE THE CHILDREN?
THEY ARE NOT THE FIRST, MY DEAR...
...AND THEY WON'T BE THE LAST.

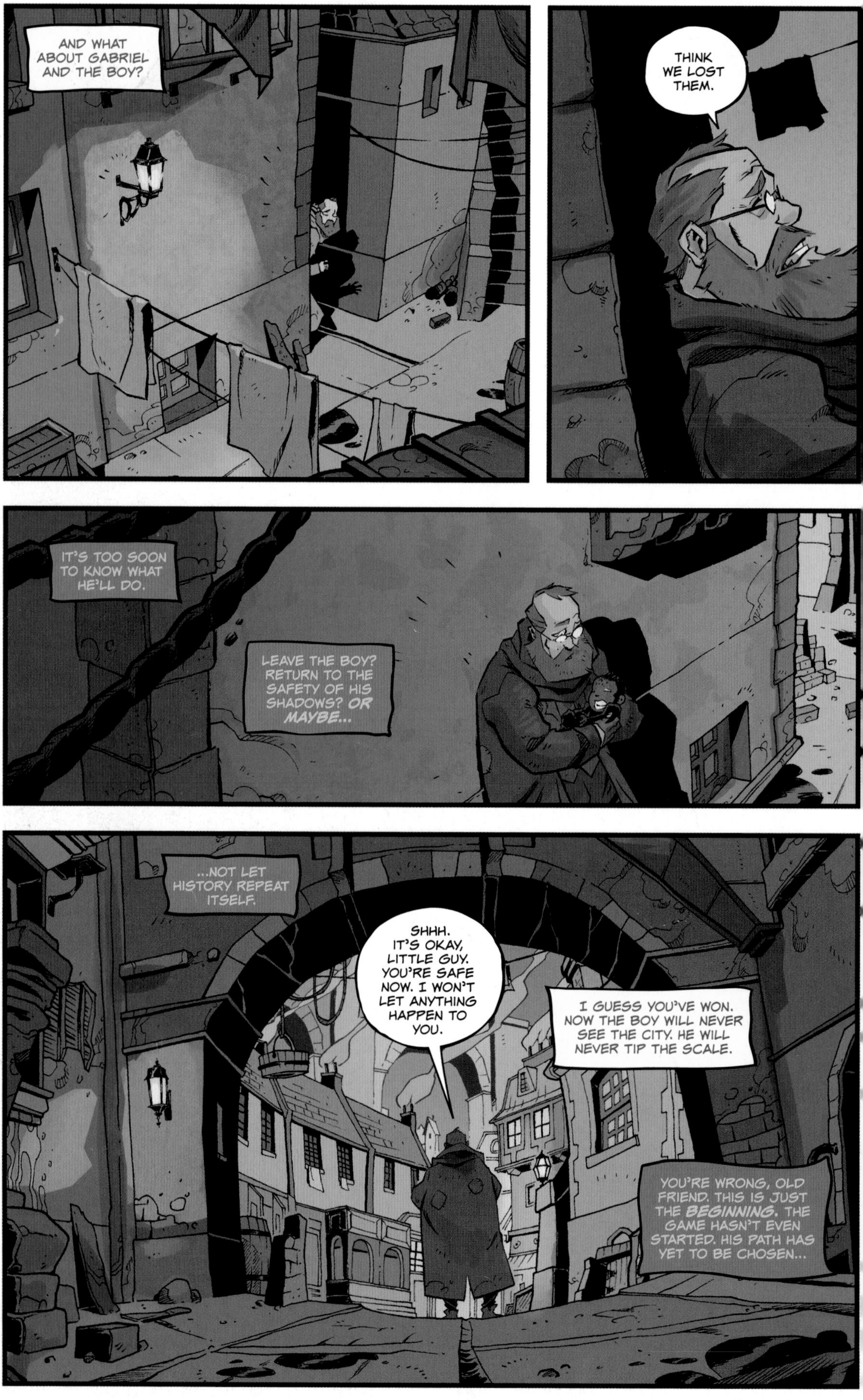
AND WHAT ABOUT GABRIEL AND THE BOY?
THINK WE LOST THEM.
IT'S TOO SOON TO KNOW WHAT HE'LL DO.
LEAVE THE BOY? RETURN TO THE SAFETY OF HIS SHADOWS? OR MAYBE...
...NOT LET HISTORY REPEAT ITSELF.
SHHH. IT'S OKAY, LITTLE GUY. YOU'RE SAFE NOW. I WON'T LET ANYTHING HAPPEN TO YOU.
I GUESS YOU'VE WON. NOW THE BOY WILL NEVER SEE THE CITY. HE WILL NEVER TIP THE SCALE.
YOU'RE WRONG, OLD FRIEND. THIS IS JUST THE BEGINNING. THE GAME HASN'T EVEN STARTED. HIS PATH HAS YET TO BE CHOSEN...

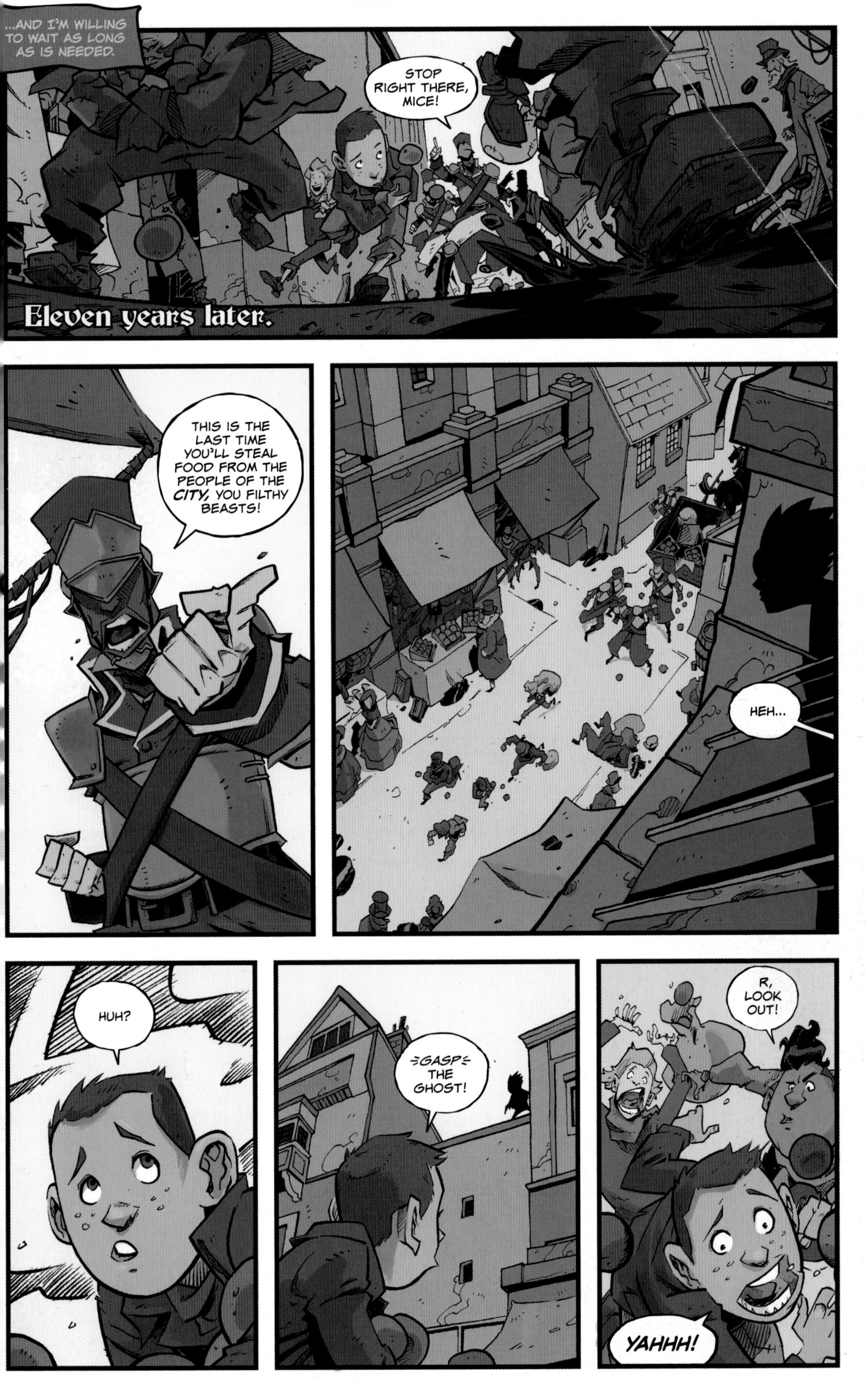
...AND I'M WILLING TO WAIT AS LONG AS IS NEEDED.
STOP RIGHT THERE, MICE!
Eleven years later.
THIS IS THE LAST TIME YOU'LL STEAL FOOD FROM THE PEOPLE OF THE *CITY,* YOU FILTHY BEASTS!
HEH...
HUH?
GASP THE GHOST!
R, LOOK OUT!
YAHHH!

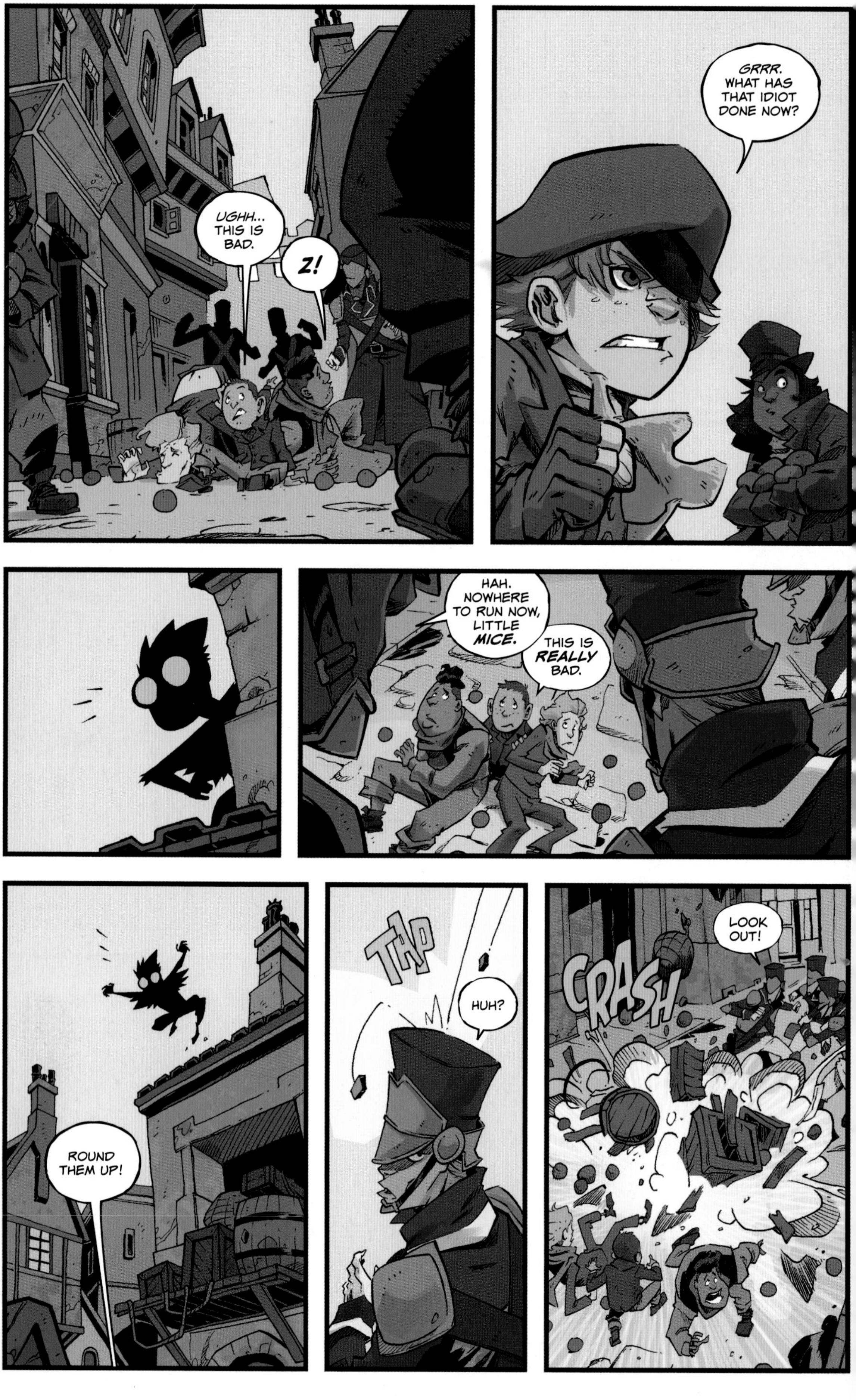
UGHH... THIS IS BAD.
Z!
GRRR. WHAT HAS THAT IDIOT DONE NOW?
HAH. NOWHERE TO RUN NOW, LITTLE MICE.
THIS IS REALLY BAD.
ROUND THEM UP!
TAP
HUH?
CRASH
LOOK OUT!

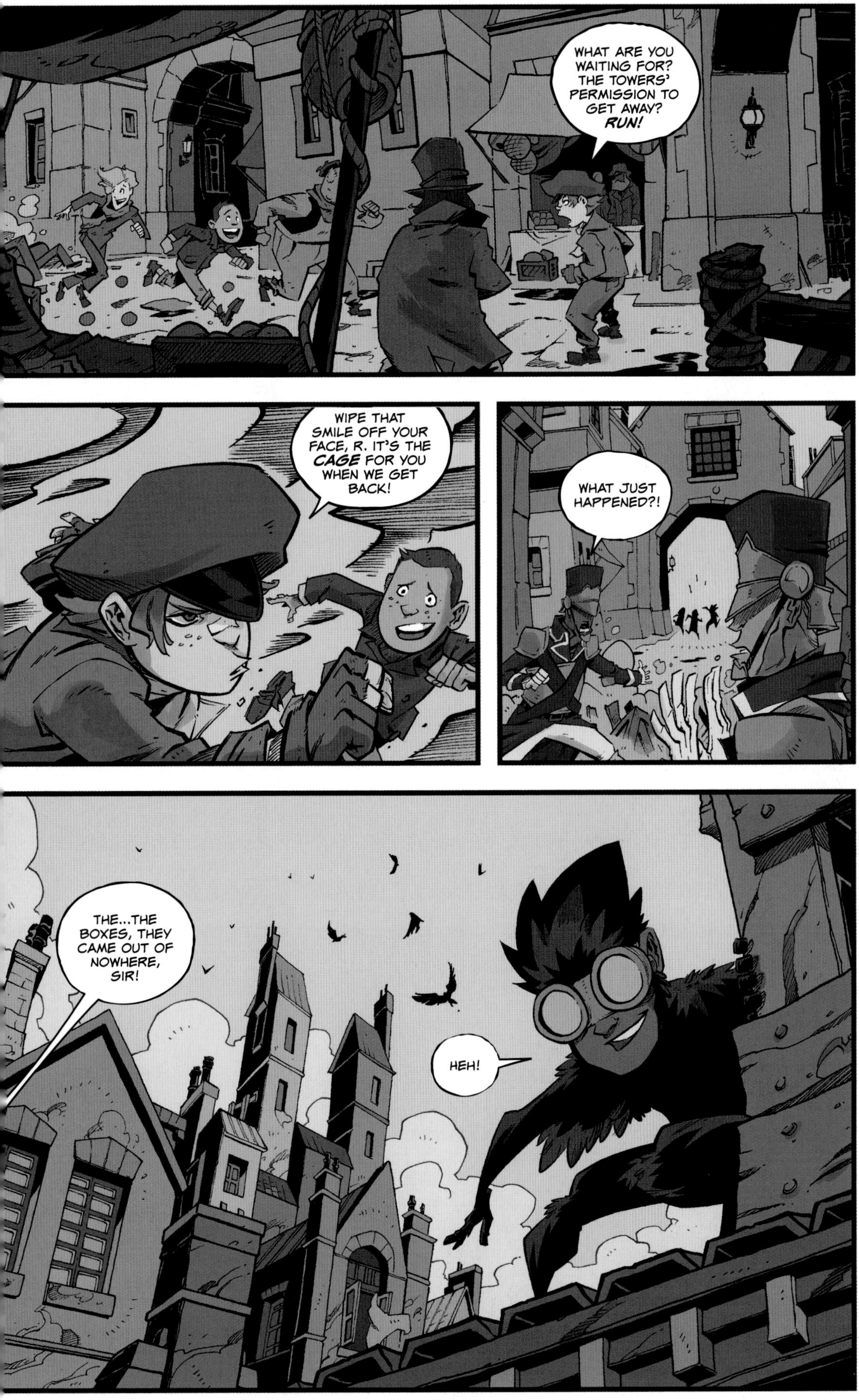
WHAT ARE YOU WAITING FOR? THE TOWERS' PERMISSION TO GET AWAY? RUN!
WIPE THAT SMILE OFF YOUR FACE, R. IT'S THE CAGE FOR YOU WHEN WE GET BACK!
WHAT JUST HAPPENED?!
THE...THE BOXES, THEY CAME OUT OF NOWHERE, SIR!
HEH!

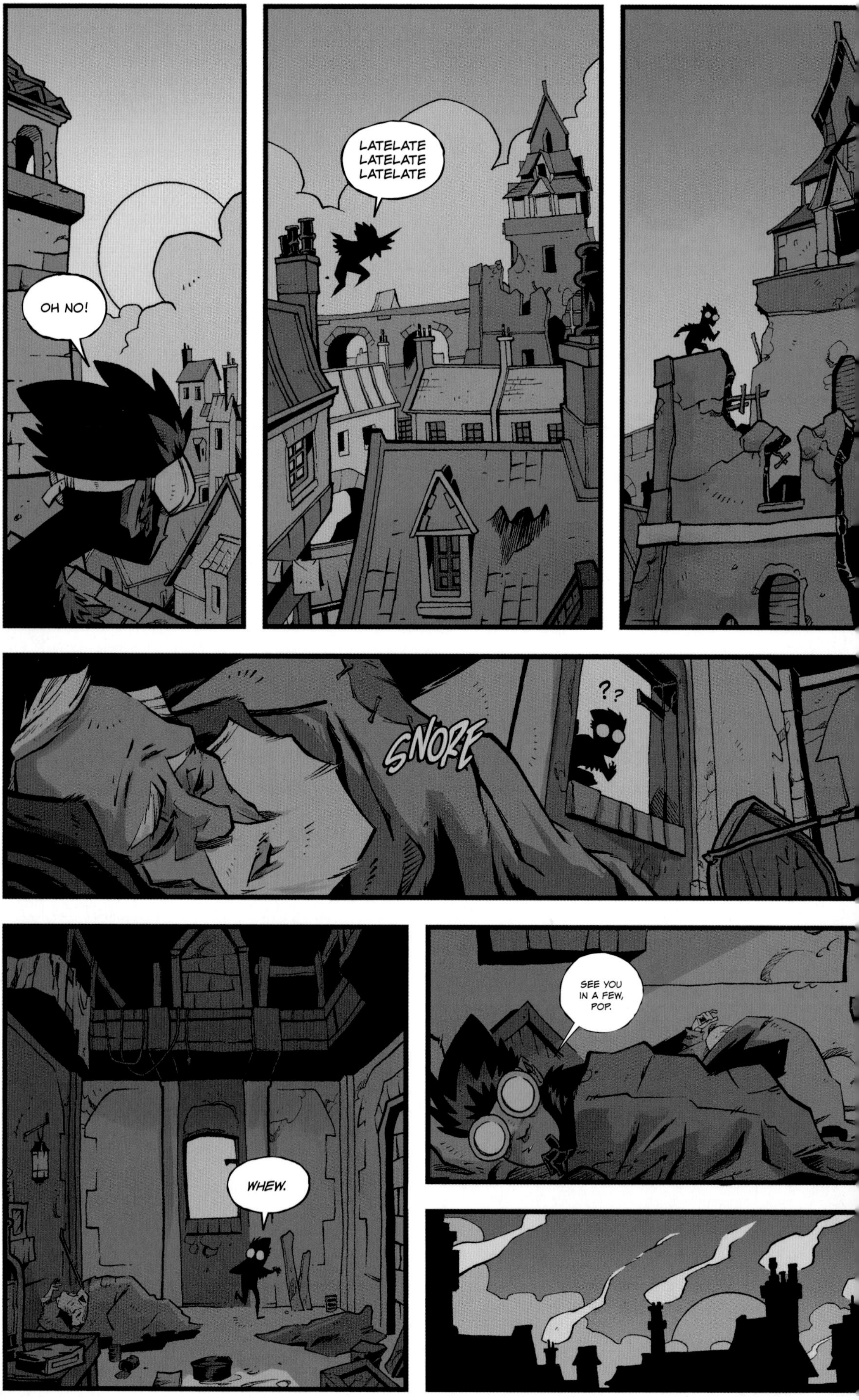
OH NO!
LATELATE
LATELATE
LATELATE
??
SNORE
WHEW.
SEE YOU
IN A FEW,
POP.

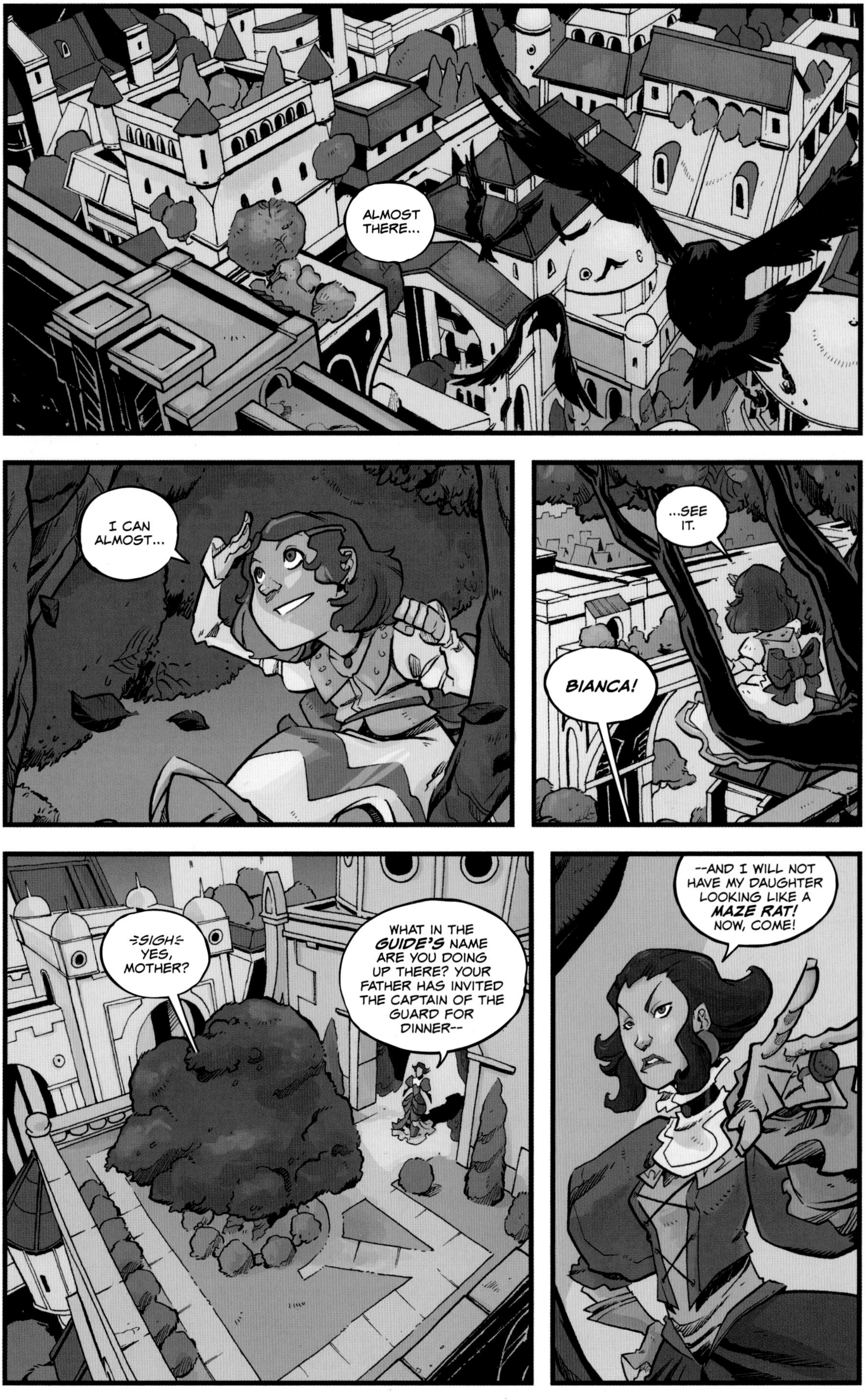
ALMOST THERE...
I CAN ALMOST...
...SEE IT.
BIANCA!
=SIGH= YES, MOTHER?
WHAT IN THE GUIDE'S NAME ARE YOU DOING UP THERE? YOUR FATHER HAS INVITED THE CAPTAIN OF THE GUARD FOR DINNER--
--AND I WILL NOT HAVE MY DAUGHTER LOOKING LIKE A MAZE RAT! NOW, COME!

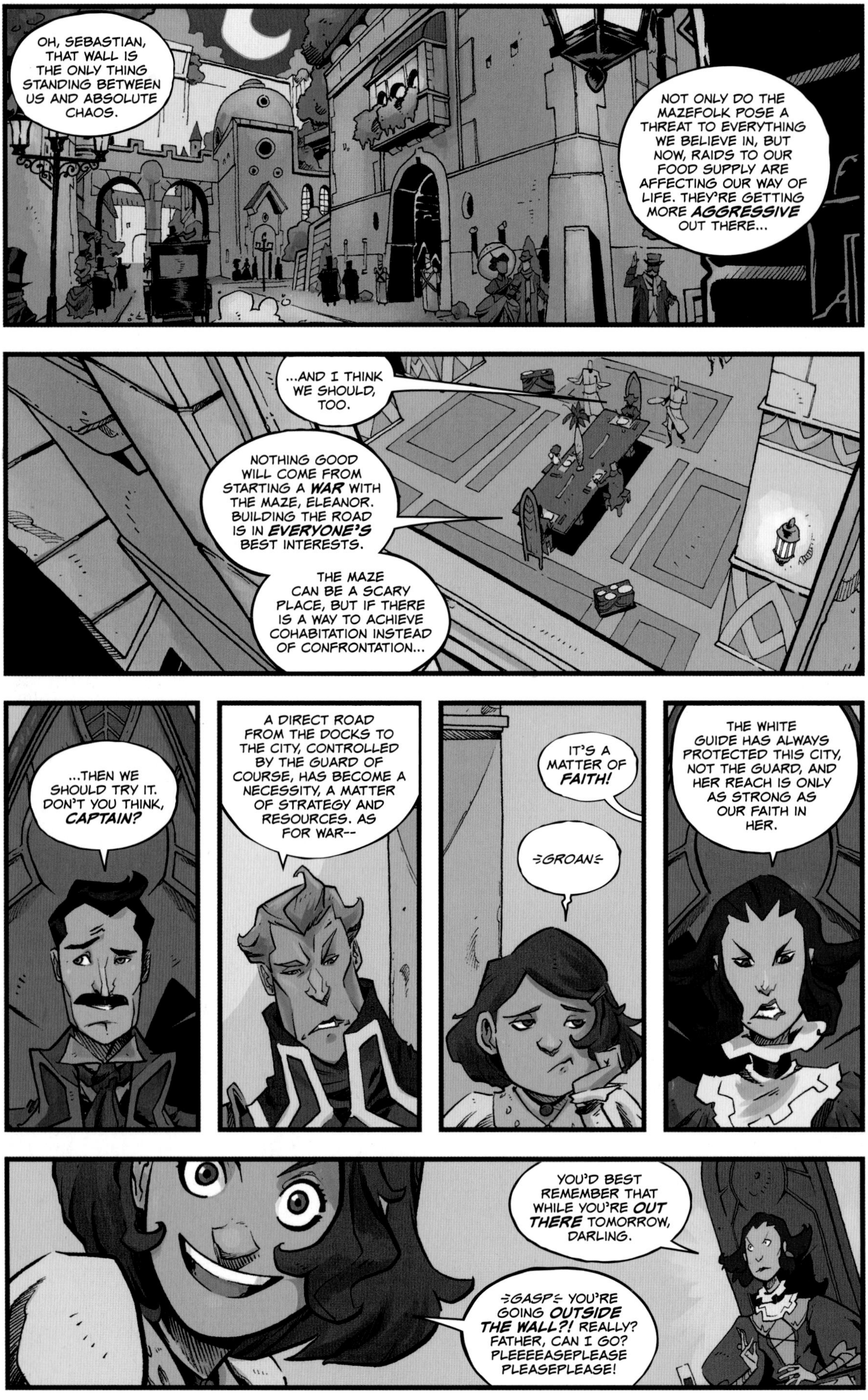
OH, SEBASTIAN, THAT WALL IS THE ONLY THING STANDING BETWEEN US AND ABSOLUTE CHAOS.
NOT ONLY DO THE MAZEFOLK POSE A THREAT TO EVERYTHING WE BELIEVE IN, BUT NOW, RAIDS TO OUR FOOD SUPPLY ARE AFFECTING OUR WAY OF LIFE. THEY'RE GETTING MORE AGGRESSIVE OUT THERE...
...AND I THINK WE SHOULD, TOO.
NOTHING GOOD WILL COME FROM STARTING A WAR WITH THE MAZE, ELEANOR. BUILDING THE ROAD IS IN EVERYONE'S BEST INTERESTS.
THE MAZE CAN BE A SCARY PLACE, BUT IF THERE IS A WAY TO ACHIEVE COHABITATION INSTEAD OF CONFRONTATION...
...THEN WE SHOULD TRY IT. DON'T YOU THINK, CAPTAIN?
A DIRECT ROAD FROM THE DOCKS TO THE CITY, CONTROLLED BY THE GUARD OF COURSE, HAS BECOME A NECESSITY, A MATTER OF STRATEGY AND RESOURCES. AS FOR WAR--
IT'S A MATTER OF FAITH!
GROAN
THE WHITE GUIDE HAS ALWAYS PROTECTED THIS CITY, NOT THE GUARD, AND HER REACH IS ONLY AS STRONG AS OUR FAITH IN HER.
YOU'D BEST REMEMBER THAT WHILE YOU'RE OUT THERE TOMORROW, DARLING.
GASP YOU'RE GOING OUTSIDE THE WALL?! REALLY? FATHER, CAN I GO? PLEEEEASEPLEASE PLEASEPLEASE!

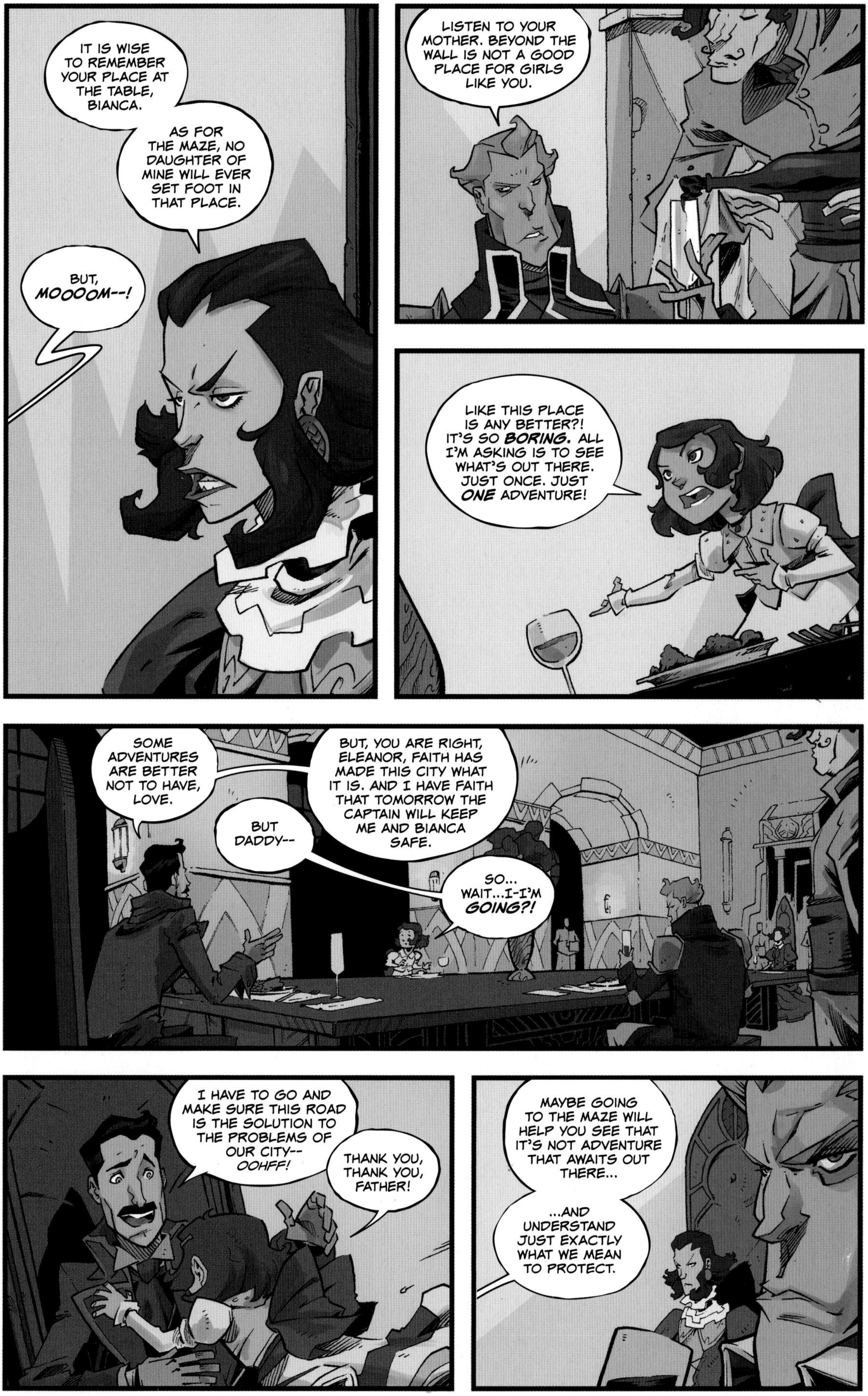
IT IS WISE TO REMEMBER YOUR PLACE AT THE TABLE, BIANCA.
AS FOR THE MAZE, NO DAUGHTER OF MINE WILL EVER SET FOOT IN THAT PLACE.
BUT, MOOOOM--!
LISTEN TO YOUR MOTHER. BEYOND THE WALL IS NOT A GOOD PLACE FOR GIRLS LIKE YOU.
LIKE THIS PLACE IS ANY BETTER?! IT'S SO BORING. ALL I'M ASKING IS TO SEE WHAT'S OUT THERE. JUST ONCE. JUST ONE ADVENTURE!
SOME ADVENTURES ARE BETTER NOT TO HAVE, LOVE.
BUT DADDY--
BUT, YOU ARE RIGHT, ELEANOR, FAITH HAS MADE THIS CITY WHAT IT IS. AND I HAVE FAITH THAT TOMORROW THE CAPTAIN WILL KEEP ME AND BIANCA SAFE.
SO... WAIT...I-I'M GOING?!
I HAVE TO GO AND MAKE SURE THIS ROAD IS THE SOLUTION TO THE PROBLEMS OF OUR CITY-- OOHFF!
THANK YOU, THANK YOU, FATHER!
MAYBE GOING TO THE MAZE WILL HELP YOU SEE THAT IT'S NOT ADVENTURE THAT AWAITS OUT THERE...
...AND UNDERSTAND JUST EXACTLY WHAT WE MEAN TO PROTECT.

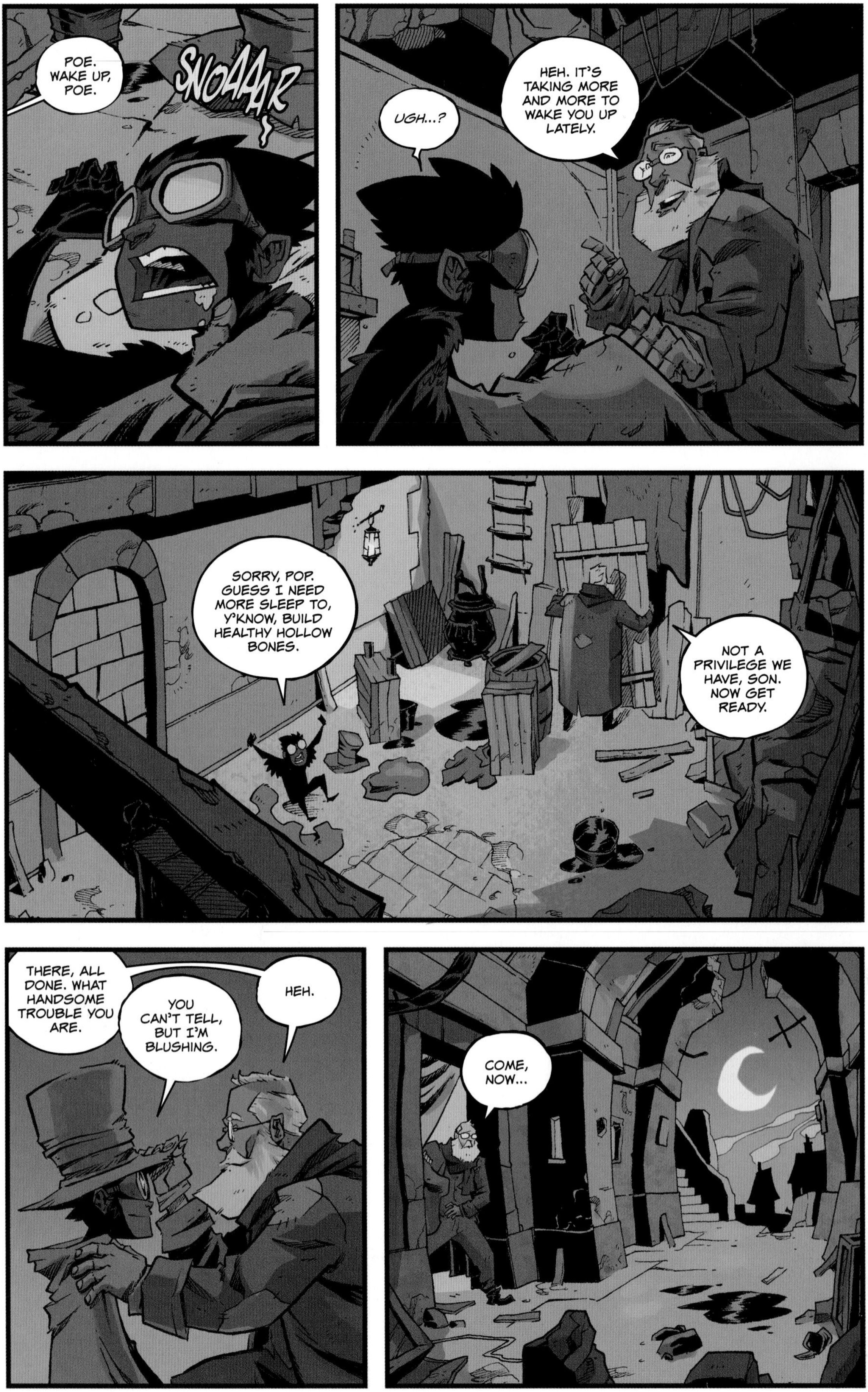
POE. WAKE UP, POE.
SNOAAAR
UGH...?
HEH. IT'S TAKING MORE AND MORE TO WAKE YOU UP LATELY.
SORRY, POP. GUESS I NEED MORE SLEEP TO, Y'KNOW, BUILD HEALTHY HOLLOW BONES.
NOT A PRIVILEGE WE HAVE, SON. NOW GET READY.
THERE, ALL DONE. WHAT HANDSOME TROUBLE YOU ARE.
YOU CAN'T TELL, BUT I'M BLUSHING.
HEH.
COME, NOW...

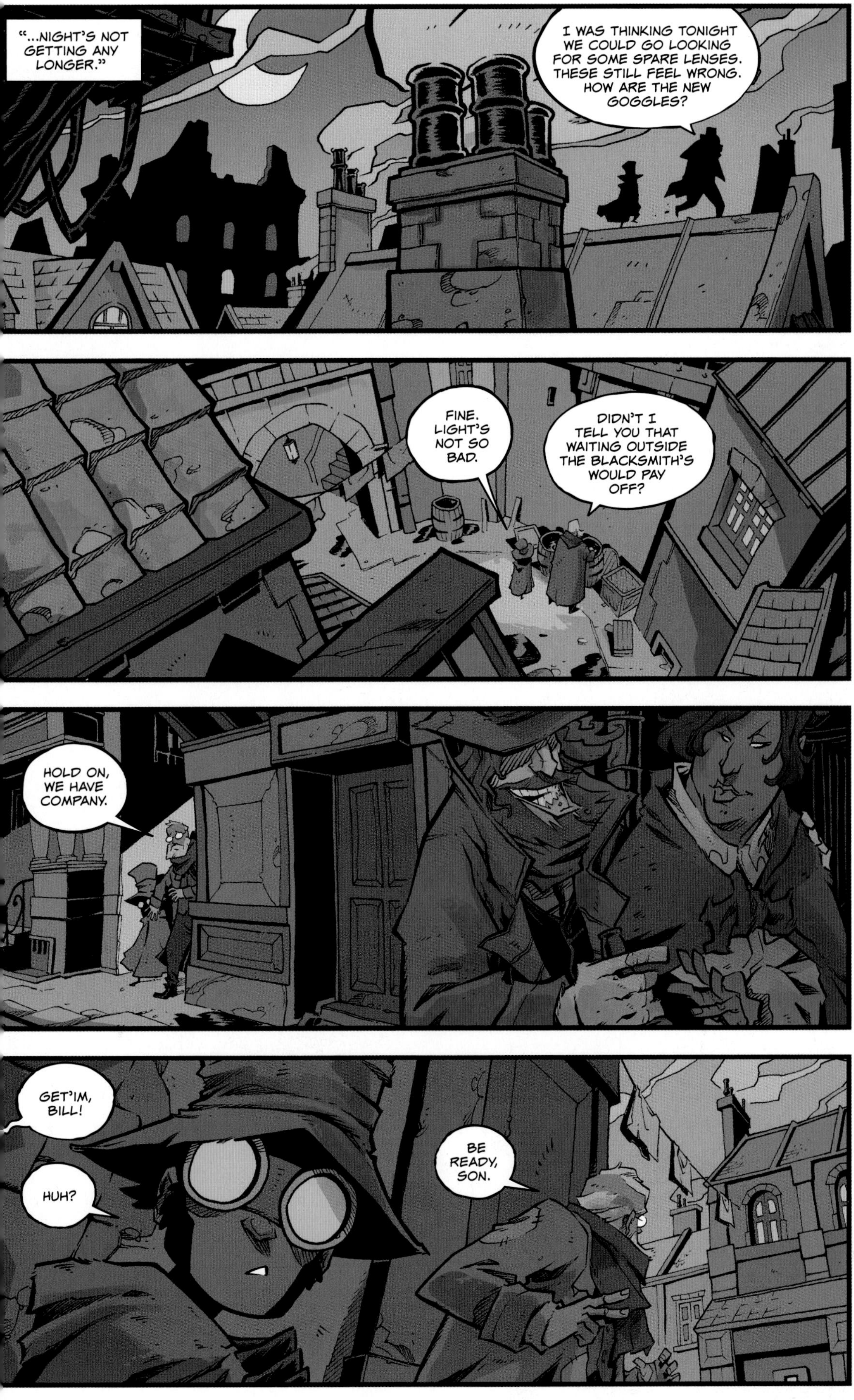
"...NIGHT'S NOT GETTING ANY LONGER."
I WAS THINKING TONIGHT WE COULD GO LOOKING FOR SOME SPARE LENSES. THESE STILL FEEL WRONG. HOW ARE THE NEW GOGGLES?
FINE. LIGHT'S NOT SO BAD.
DIDN'T I TELL YOU THAT WAITING OUTSIDE THE BLACKSMITH'S WOULD PAY OFF?
HOLD ON, WE HAVE COMPANY.
GET'IM, BILL!
HUH?
BE READY, SON.

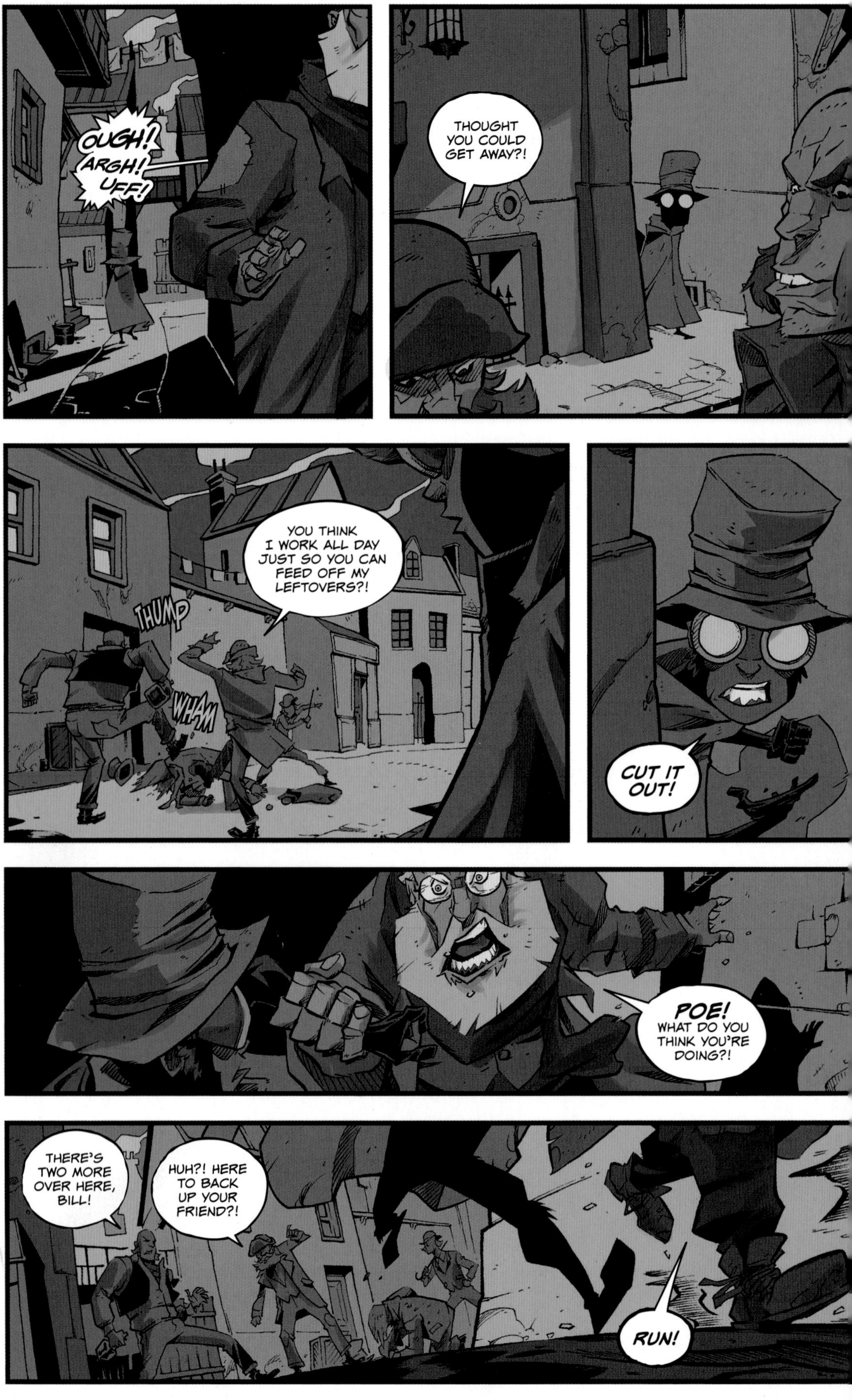
OUGH! ARGH! UFF!
THOUGHT YOU COULD GET AWAY?!
YOU THINK I WORK ALL DAY JUST SO YOU CAN FEED OFF MY LEFTOVERS?!
THUMP
WHAM
CUT IT OUT!
POE! WHAT DO YOU THINK YOU'RE DOING?!
THERE'S TWO MORE OVER HERE, BILL!
HUH?! HERE TO BACK UP YOUR FRIEND?!
RUN!

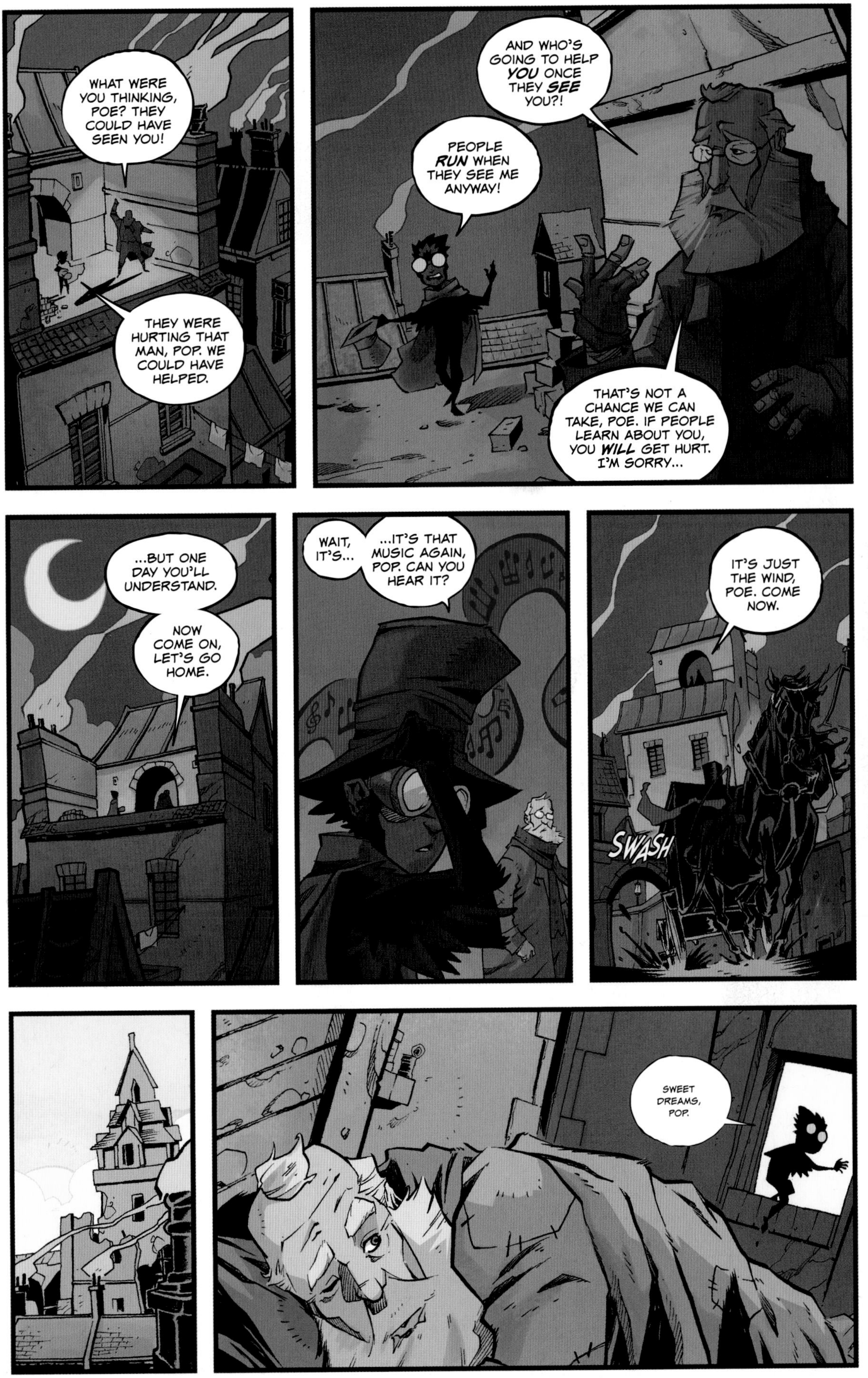
WHAT WERE YOU THINKING, POE? THEY COULD HAVE SEEN YOU!
THEY WERE HURTING THAT MAN, POP. WE COULD HAVE HELPED.
AND WHO'S GOING TO HELP YOU ONCE THEY SEE YOU?!
PEOPLE RUN WHEN THEY SEE ME ANYWAY!
THAT'S NOT A CHANCE WE CAN TAKE, POE. IF PEOPLE LEARN ABOUT YOU, YOU WILL GET HURT. I'M SORRY...
...BUT ONE DAY YOU'LL UNDERSTAND.
NOW COME ON, LET'S GO HOME.
WAIT, IT'S...
...IT'S THAT MUSIC AGAIN, POP. CAN YOU HEAR IT?
IT'S JUST THE WIND, POE. COME NOW.
SWASH
SWEET DREAMS, POP.

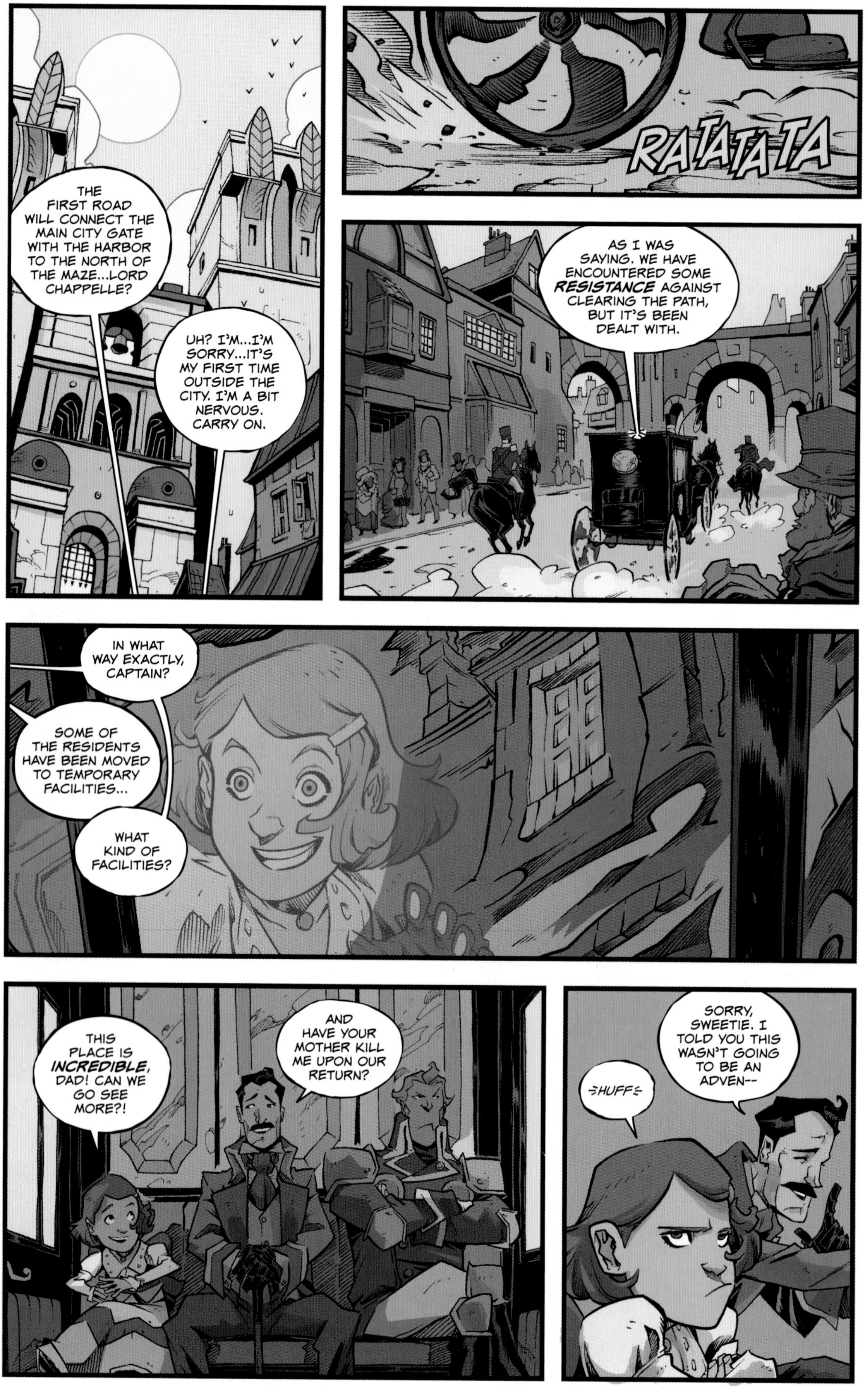
THE FIRST ROAD WILL CONNECT THE MAIN CITY GATE WITH THE HARBOR TO THE NORTH OF THE MAZE...LORD CHAPPELLE?
UH? I'M...I'M SORRY...IT'S MY FIRST TIME OUTSIDE THE CITY. I'M A BIT NERVOUS. CARRY ON.
RATATATA
AS I WAS SAYING. WE HAVE ENCOUNTERED SOME RESISTANCE AGAINST CLEARING THE PATH, BUT IT'S BEEN DEALT WITH.
IN WHAT WAY EXACTLY, CAPTAIN?
SOME OF THE RESIDENTS HAVE BEEN MOVED TO TEMPORARY FACILITIES...
WHAT KIND OF FACILITIES?
THIS PLACE IS INCREDIBLE, DAD! CAN WE GO SEE MORE?!
AND HAVE YOUR MOTHER KILL ME UPON OUR RETURN?
SORRY, SWEETIE. I TOLD YOU THIS WASN'T GOING TO BE AN ADVEN--
HUFF

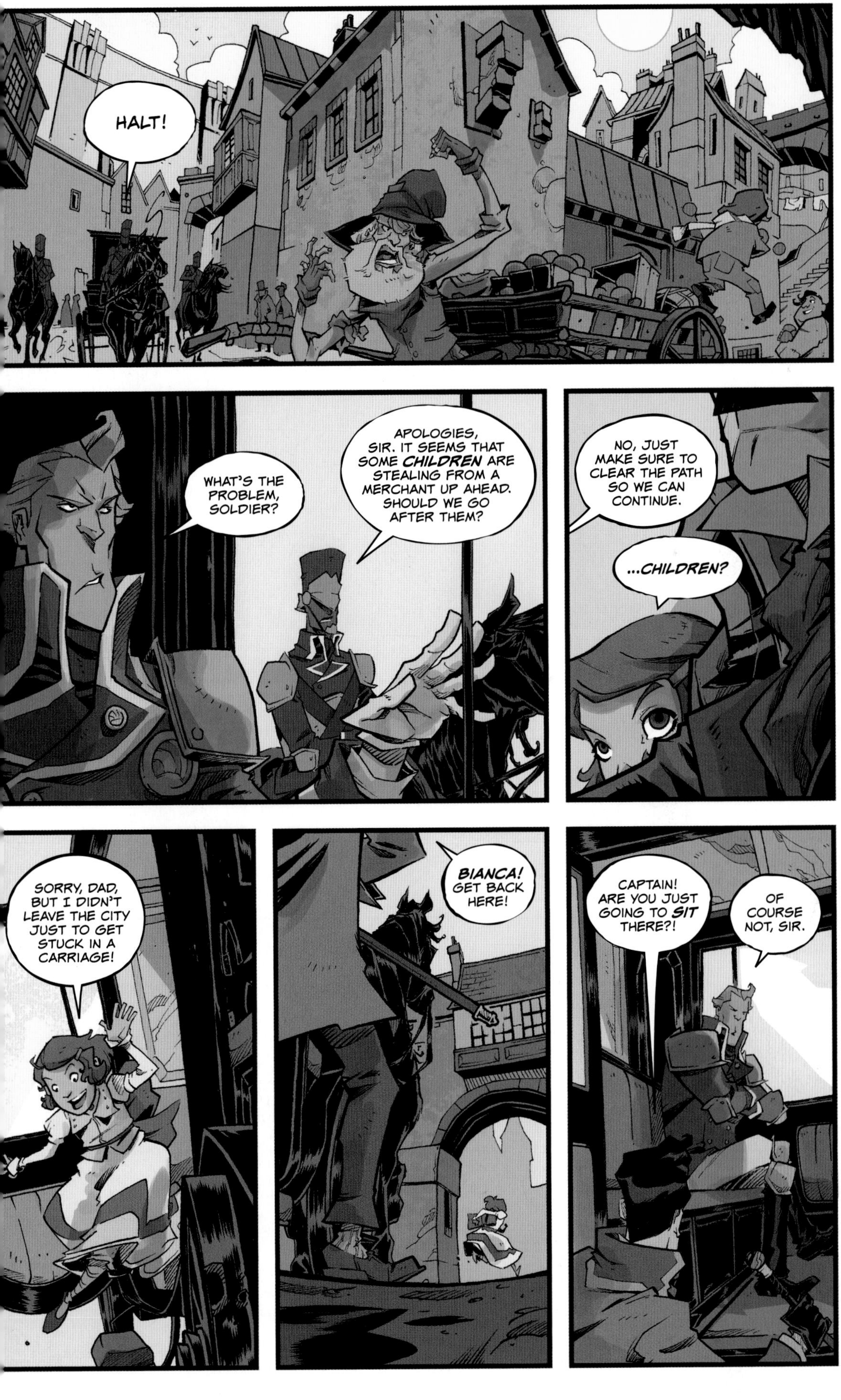
HALT!
WHAT'S THE PROBLEM, SOLDIER?
APOLOGIES, SIR. IT SEEMS THAT SOME CHILDREN ARE STEALING FROM A MERCHANT UP AHEAD. SHOULD WE GO AFTER THEM?
NO, JUST MAKE SURE TO CLEAR THE PATH SO WE CAN CONTINUE.
...CHILDREN?
SORRY, DAD, BUT I DIDN'T LEAVE THE CITY JUST TO GET STUCK IN A CARRIAGE!
BIANCA! GET BACK HERE!
CAPTAIN! ARE YOU JUST GOING TO SIT THERE?!
OF COURSE NOT, SIR.

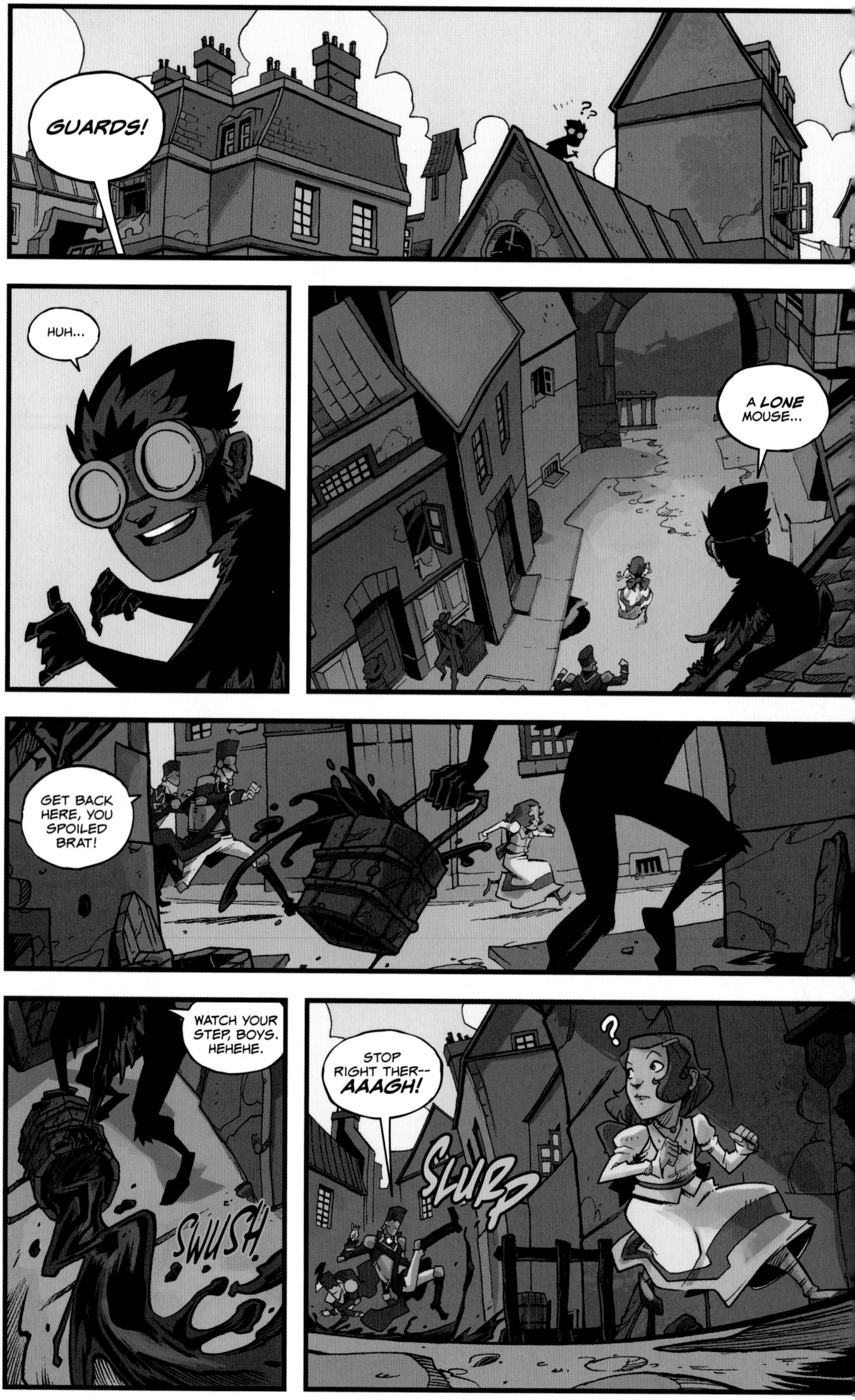
GUARDS!
??
HUH...
A LONE MOUSE...
GET BACK HERE, YOU SPOILED BRAT!
WATCH YOUR STEP, BOYS. HEHEHE.
SWUSH!
?
STOP RIGHT THER-- AAAGH!
SLURP

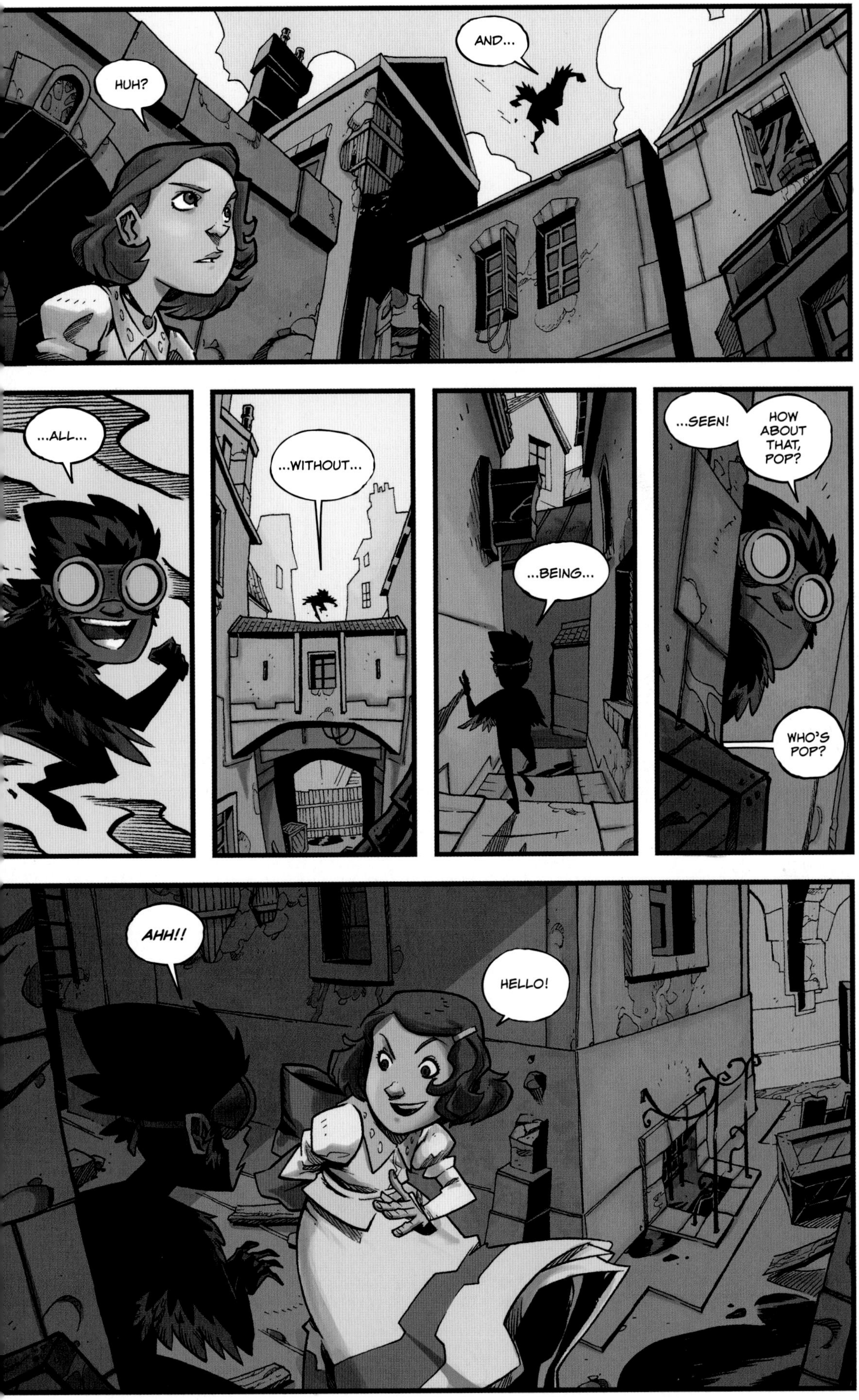
HUH?
AND...
...ALL...
...WITHOUT...
...BEING...
...SEEN!
HOW ABOUT THAT, POP?
WHO'S POP?
AHH!!
HELLO!

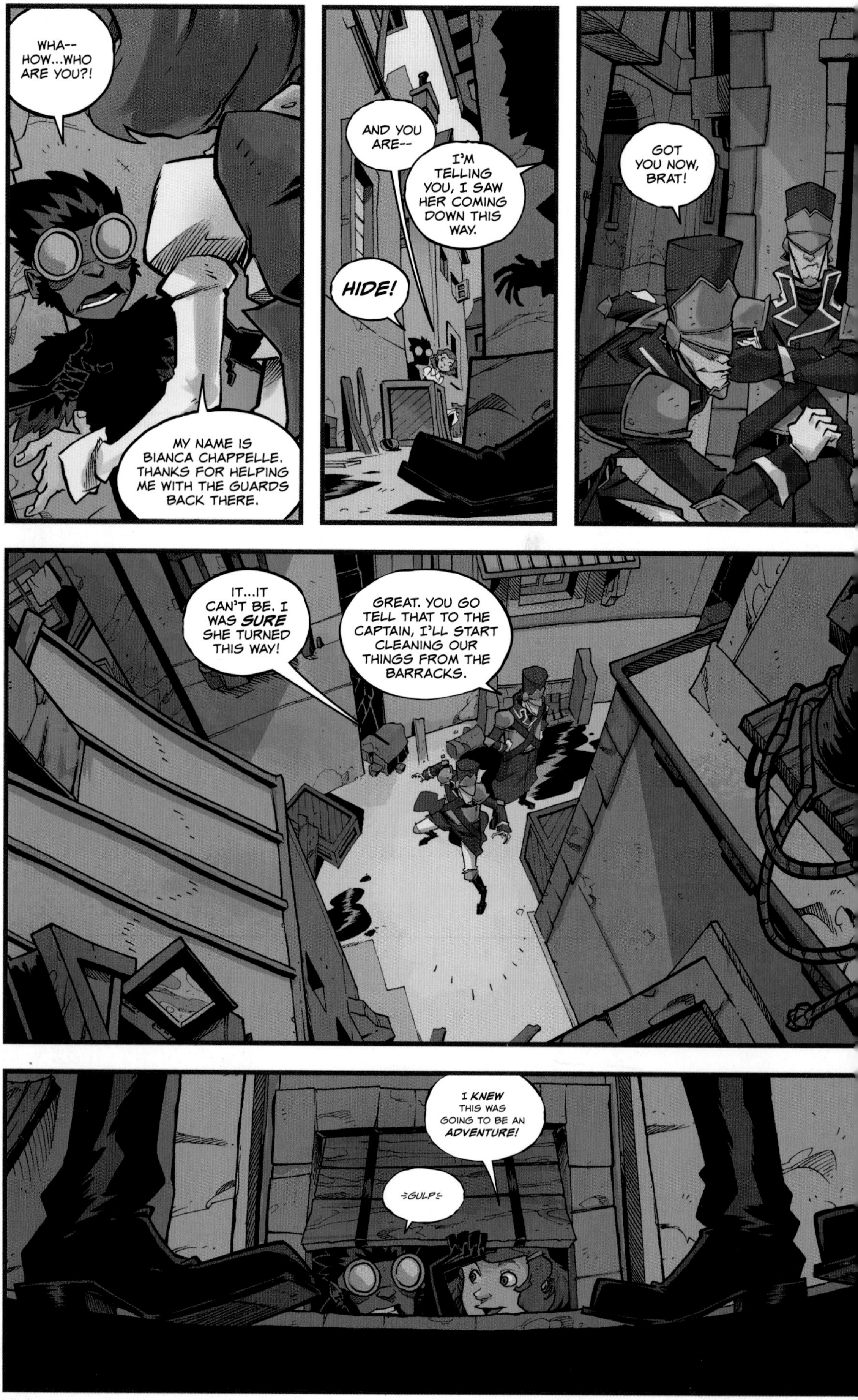
WHA-- HOW...WHO ARE YOU?!
MY NAME IS BIANCA CHAPPELLE. THANKS FOR HELPING ME WITH THE GUARDS BACK THERE.
AND YOU ARE--
I'M TELLING YOU, I SAW HER COMING DOWN THIS WAY.
HIDE!
GOT YOU NOW, BRAT!
IT...IT CAN'T BE. I WAS SURE SHE TURNED THIS WAY!
GREAT. YOU GO TELL THAT TO THE CAPTAIN, I'LL START CLEANING OUR THINGS FROM THE BARRACKS.
I KNEW THIS WAS GOING TO BE AN ADVENTURE!
GULP

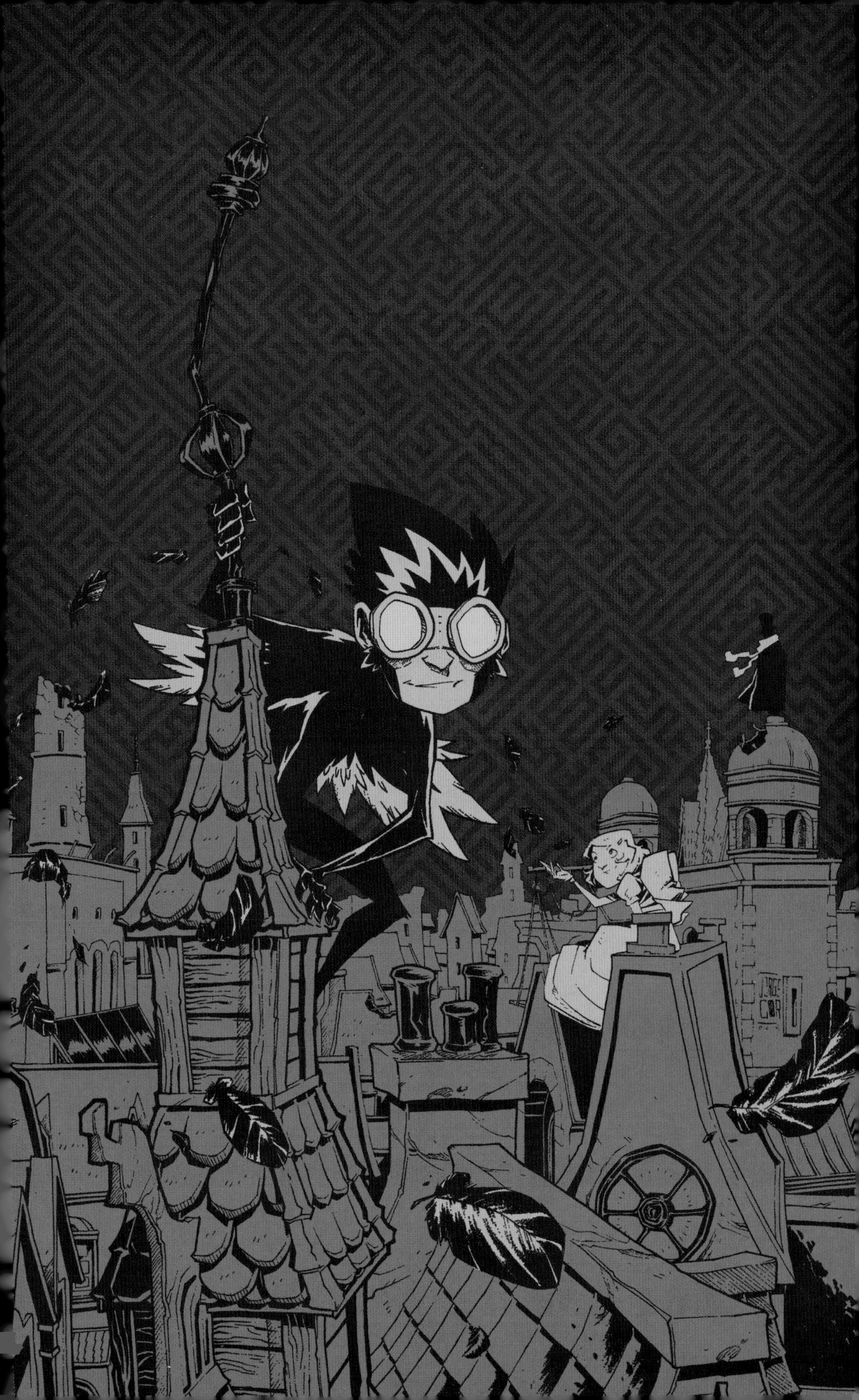

CHAPTER
TWO

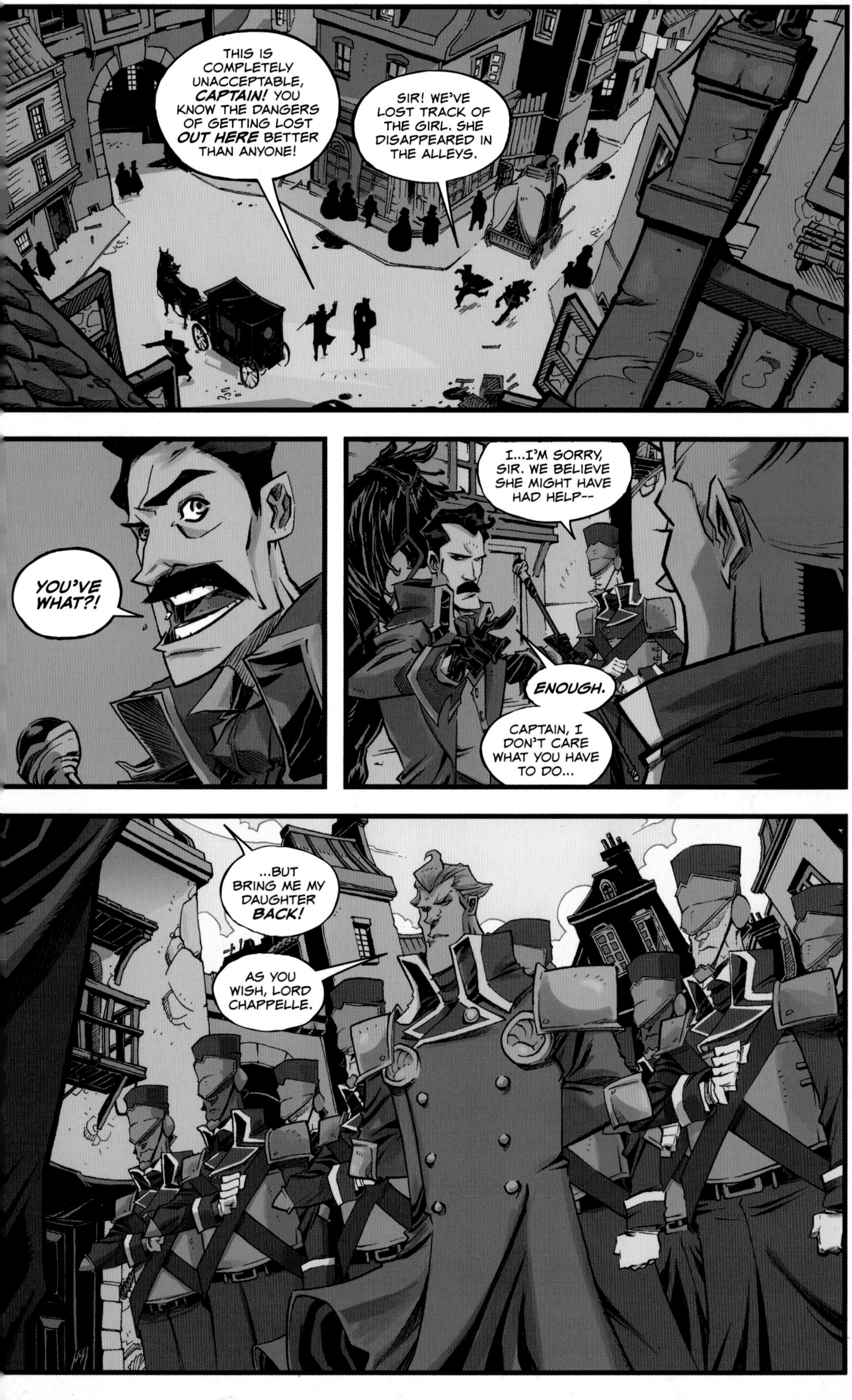
THIS IS COMPLETELY UNACCEPTABLE, CAPTAIN! YOU KNOW THE DANGERS OF GETTING LOST OUT HERE BETTER THAN ANYONE!
SIR! WE'VE LOST TRACK OF THE GIRL. SHE DISAPPEARED IN THE ALLEYS.
YOU'VE WHAT?!
I...I'M SORRY, SIR. WE BELIEVE SHE MIGHT HAVE HAD HELP--
ENOUGH.
CAPTAIN, I DON'T CARE WHAT YOU HAVE TO DO...
...BUT BRING ME MY DAUGHTER BACK!
AS YOU WISH, LORD CHAPPELLE.

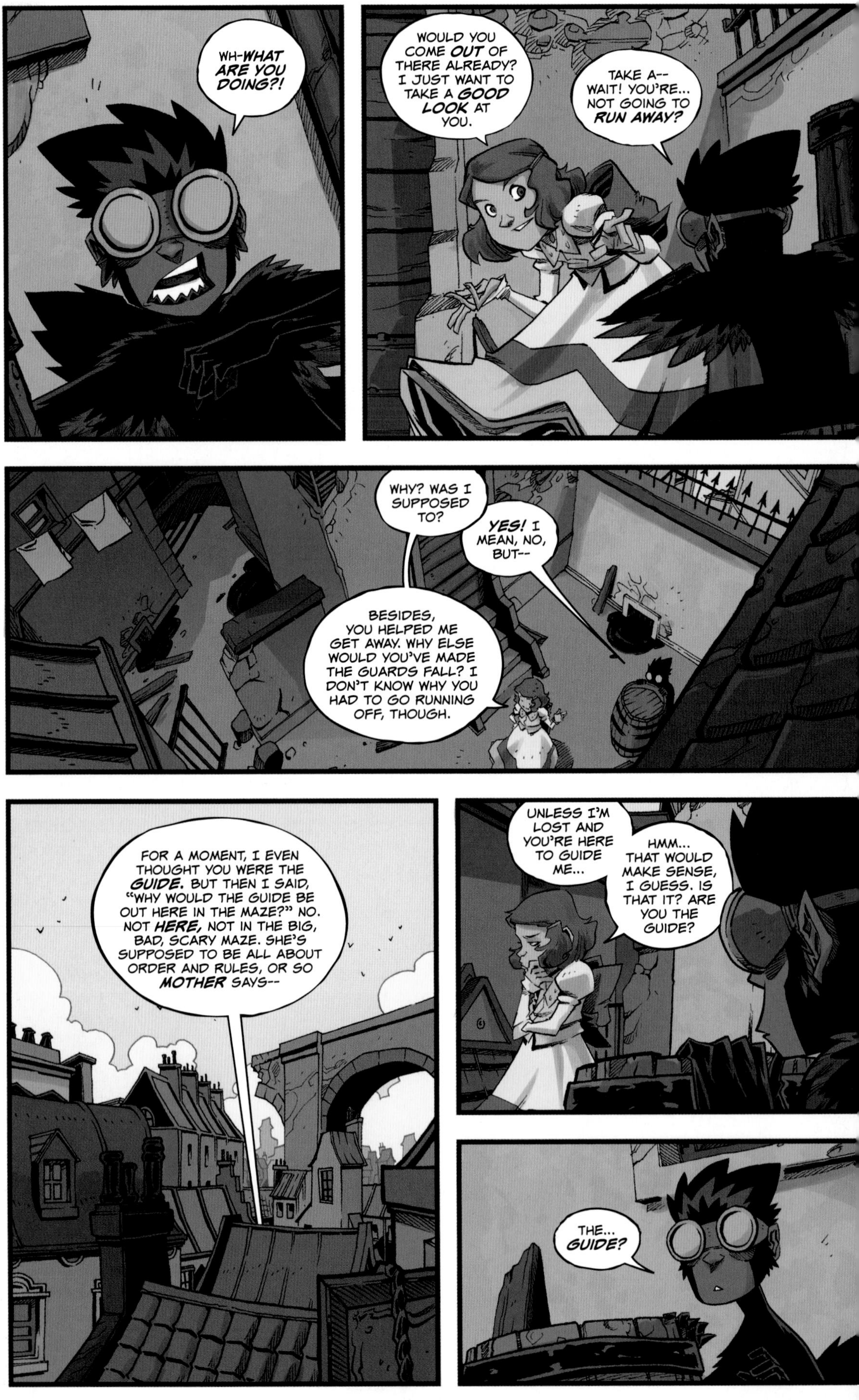

WH-WHAT ARE YOU DOING?!
WOULD YOU COME OUT OF THERE ALREADY? I JUST WANT TO TAKE A GOOD LOOK AT YOU.
TAKE A-- WAIT! YOU'RE... NOT GOING TO RUN AWAY?
WHY? WAS I SUPPOSED TO?
YES! I MEAN, NO, BUT--
BESIDES, YOU HELPED ME GET AWAY. WHY ELSE WOULD YOU'VE MADE THE GUARDS FALL? I DON'T KNOW WHY YOU HAD TO GO RUNNING OFF, THOUGH.
FOR A MOMENT, I EVEN THOUGHT YOU WERE THE GUIDE. BUT THEN I SAID, "WHY WOULD THE GUIDE BE OUT HERE IN THE MAZE?" NO. NOT HERE, NOT IN THE BIG, BAD, SCARY MAZE. SHE'S SUPPOSED TO BE ALL ABOUT ORDER AND RULES, OR SO MOTHER SAYS--
UNLESS I'M LOST AND YOU'RE HERE TO GUIDE ME...
HMM... THAT WOULD MAKE SENSE, I GUESS. IS THAT IT? ARE YOU THE GUIDE?
THE... GUIDE?

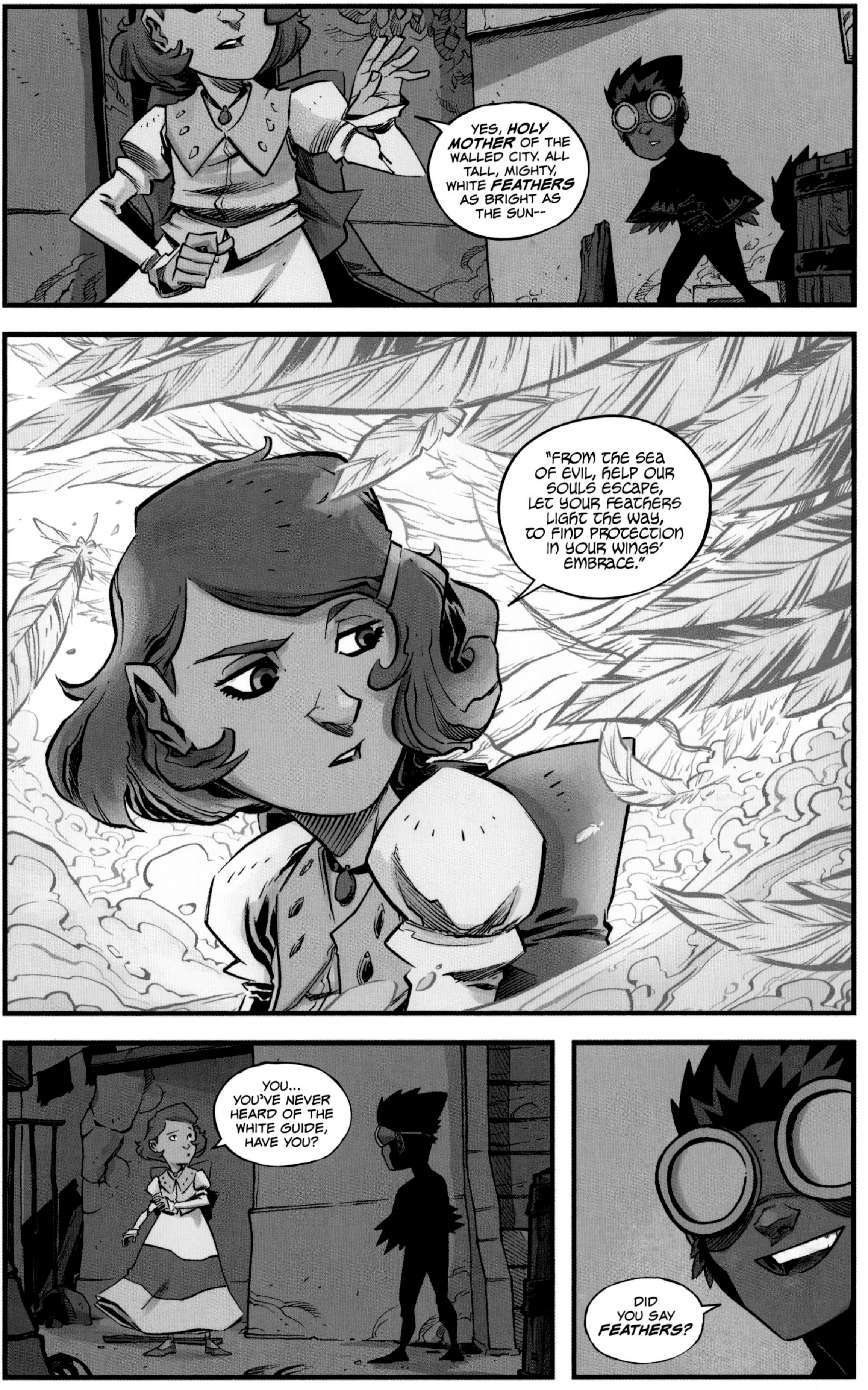
YES, HOLY MOTHER OF THE WALLED CITY. ALL TALL, MIGHTY, WHITE FEATHERS AS BRIGHT AS THE SUN--
"FROM THE SEA OF EVIL, HELP OUR SOULS ESCAPE, LET YOUR FEATHERS LIGHT THE WAY, TO FIND PROTECTION IN YOUR WINGS' EMBRACE."
YOU... YOU'VE NEVER HEARD OF THE WHITE GUIDE, HAVE YOU?
DID YOU SAY FEATHERS?

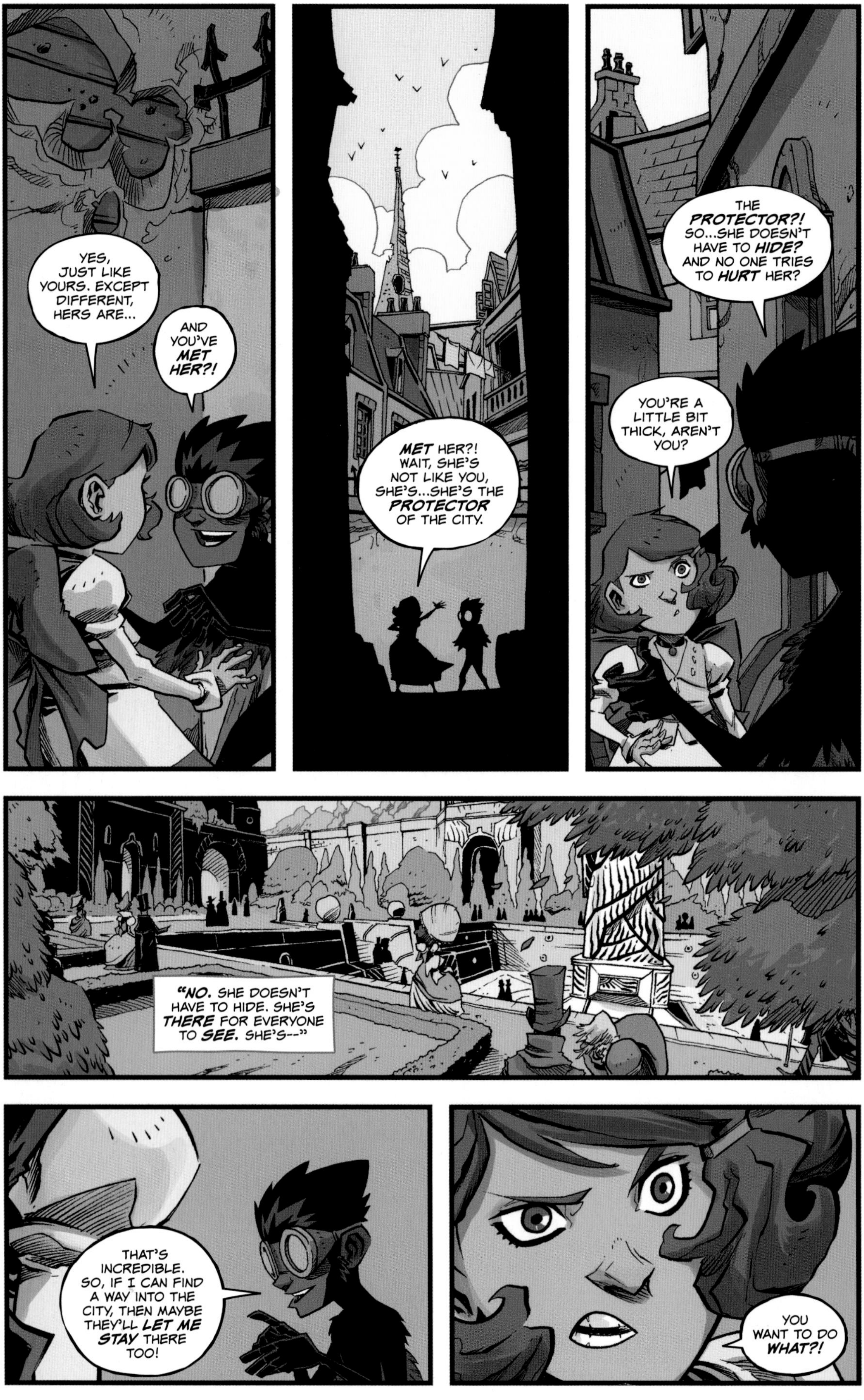
YES, JUST LIKE YOURS. EXCEPT DIFFERENT, HERS ARE...
AND YOU'VE MET HER?!
MET HER?! WAIT, SHE'S NOT LIKE YOU, SHE'S...SHE'S THE PROTECTOR OF THE CITY.
THE PROTECTOR?! SO...SHE DOESN'T HAVE TO HIDE? AND NO ONE TRIES TO HURT HER?
YOU'RE A LITTLE BIT THICK, AREN'T YOU?
"NO. SHE DOESN'T HAVE TO HIDE. SHE'S THERE FOR EVERYONE TO SEE. SHE'S--"
THAT'S INCREDIBLE. SO, IF I CAN FIND A WAY INTO THE CITY, THEN MAYBE THEY'LL LET ME STAY THERE TOO!
YOU WANT TO DO WHAT?!

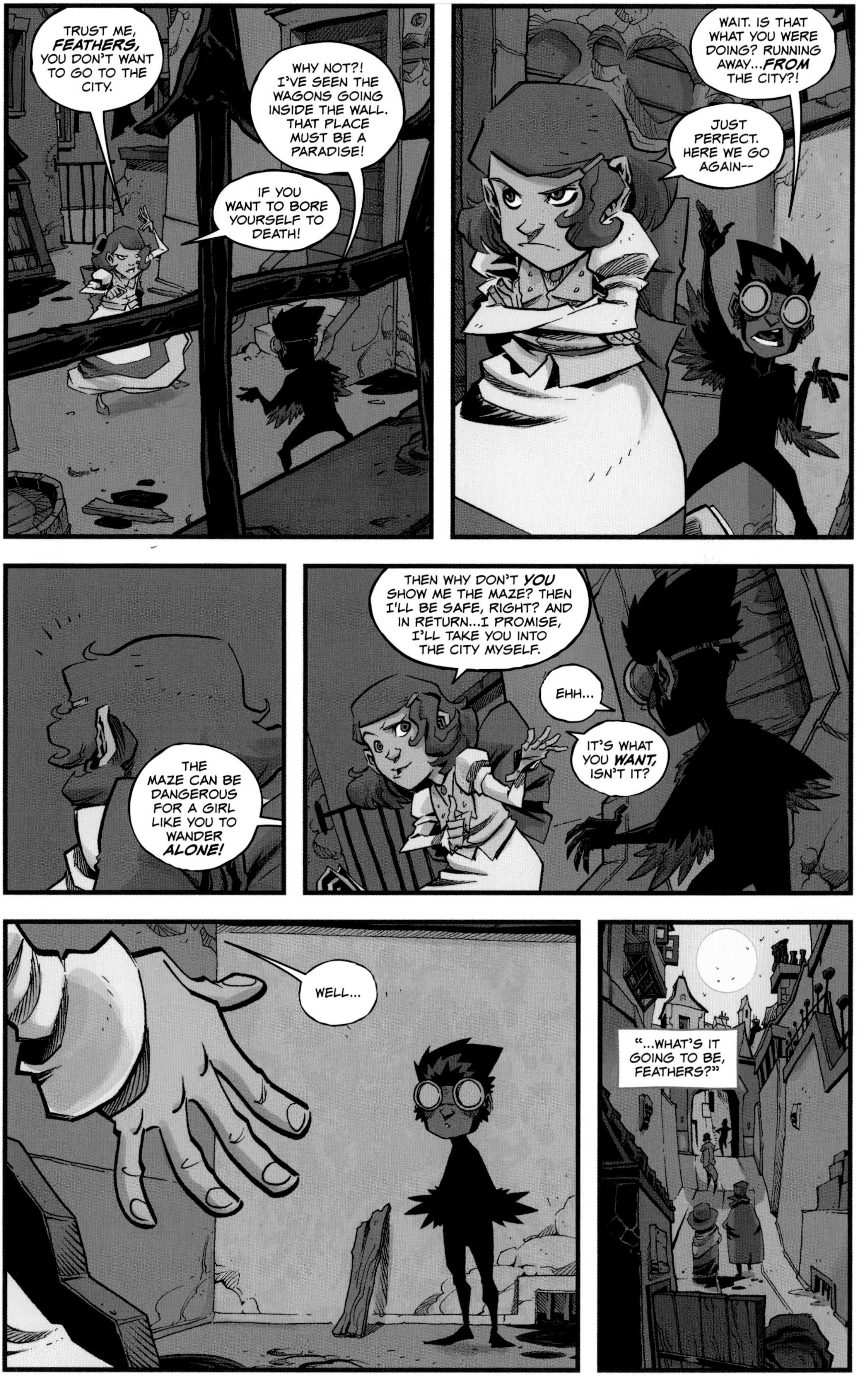
TRUST ME, **FEATHERS,** YOU DON'T WANT TO GO TO THE CITY.
WHY NOT?! I'VE SEEN THE WAGONS GOING INSIDE THE WALL. THAT PLACE MUST BE A PARADISE!
IF YOU WANT TO BORE YOURSELF TO DEATH!
WAIT. IS THAT WHAT YOU WERE DOING? RUNNING AWAY...**FROM** THE CITY?!
JUST PERFECT. HERE WE GO AGAIN--
THE MAZE CAN BE DANGEROUS FOR A GIRL LIKE YOU TO WANDER **ALONE!**
THEN WHY DON'T **YOU** SHOW ME THE MAZE? THEN I'LL BE SAFE, RIGHT? AND IN RETURN...I PROMISE, I'LL TAKE YOU INTO THE CITY MYSELF.
EHH...
IT'S WHAT YOU **WANT,** ISN'T IT?
WELL...
"...WHAT'S IT GOING TO BE, FEATHERS?"

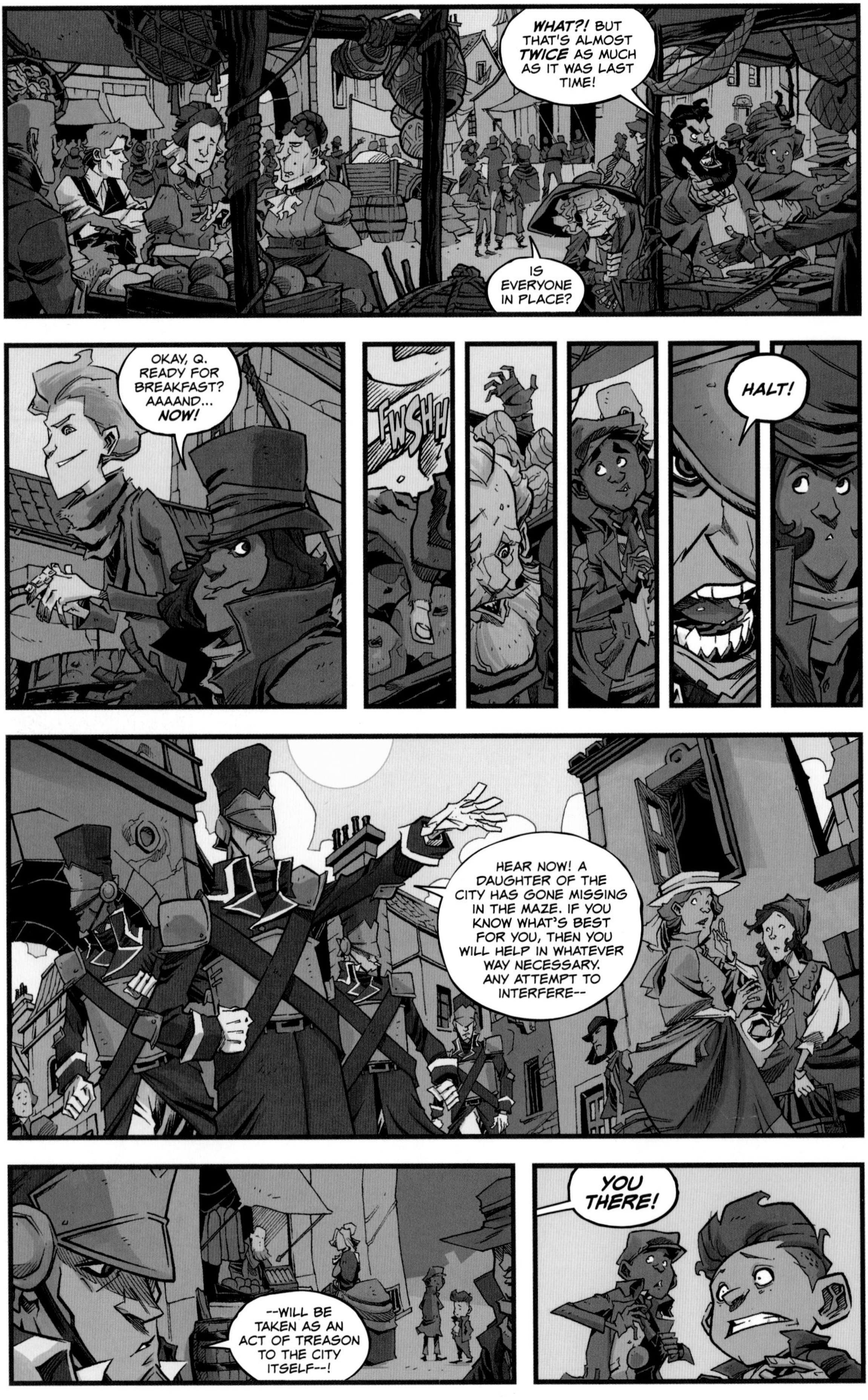
WHAT?! BUT THAT'S ALMOST TWICE AS MUCH AS IT WAS LAST TIME!
IS EVERYONE IN PLACE?
OKAY, Q. READY FOR BREAKFAST? AAAAND... NOW!
FWSHH
HALT!
HEAR NOW! A DAUGHTER OF THE CITY HAS GONE MISSING IN THE MAZE. IF YOU KNOW WHAT'S BEST FOR YOU, THEN YOU WILL HELP IN WHATEVER WAY NECESSARY. ANY ATTEMPT TO INTERFERE--
--WILL BE TAKEN AS AN ACT OF TREASON TO THE CITY ITSELF--!
YOU THERE!

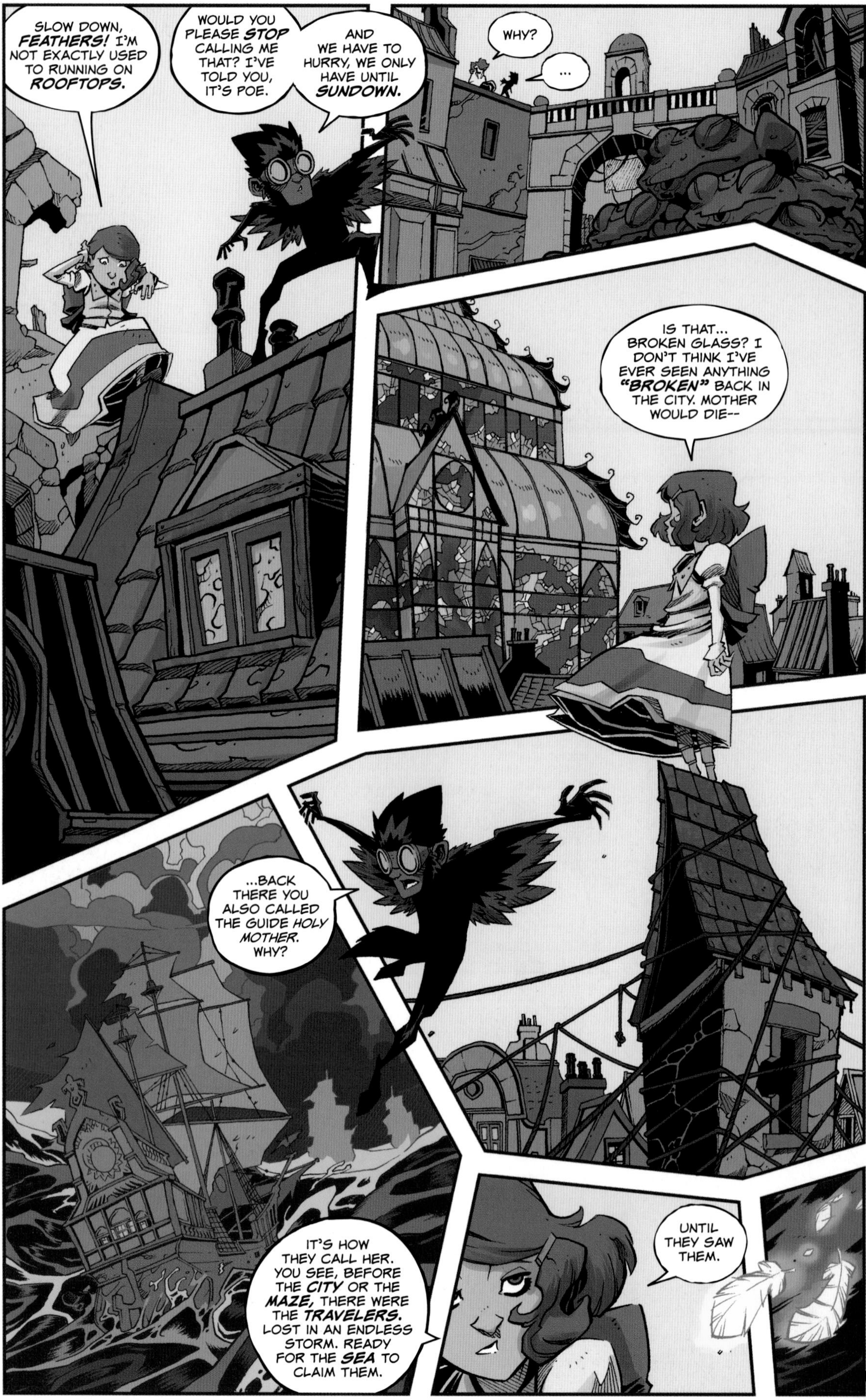
SLOW DOWN, **FEATHERS!** I'M NOT EXACTLY USED TO RUNNING ON **ROOFTOPS.**
WOULD YOU PLEASE **STOP** CALLING ME THAT? I'VE TOLD YOU, IT'S POE.
AND WE HAVE TO HURRY, WE ONLY HAVE UNTIL **SUNDOWN.**
WHY?
...
IS THAT... BROKEN GLASS? I DON'T THINK I'VE EVER SEEN ANYTHING **"BROKEN"** BACK IN THE CITY. MOTHER WOULD DIE--
...BACK THERE YOU ALSO CALLED THE GUIDE *HOLY MOTHER.* WHY?
IT'S HOW THEY CALL HER. YOU SEE, BEFORE THE **CITY** OR THE **MAZE,** THERE WERE THE **TRAVELERS.** LOST IN AN ENDLESS STORM. READY FOR THE **SEA** TO CLAIM THEM.
UNTIL THEY SAW THEM.

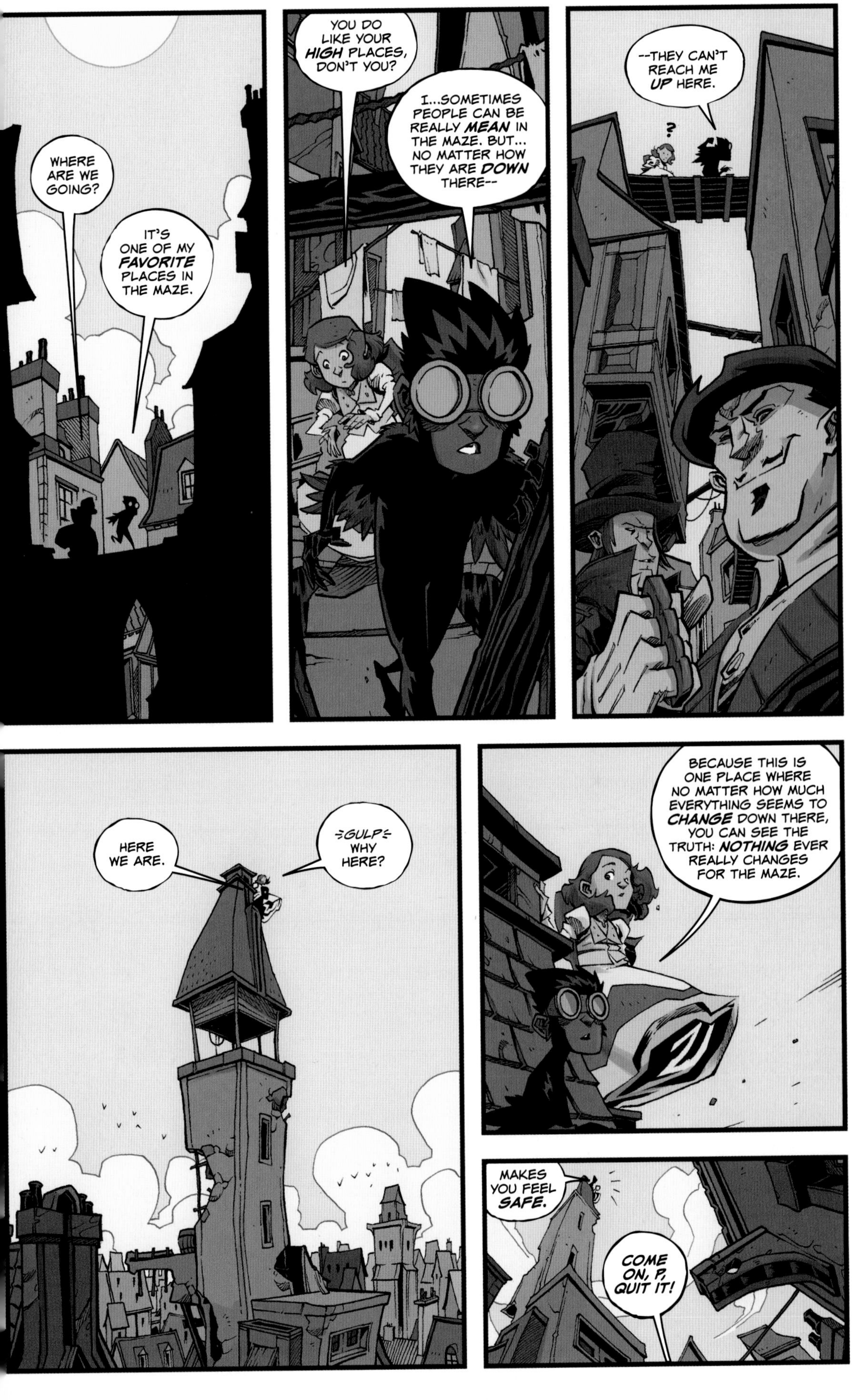

WHERE ARE WE GOING?
IT'S ONE OF MY *FAVORITE* PLACES IN THE MAZE.
YOU DO LIKE YOUR *HIGH* PLACES, DON'T YOU?
I...SOMETIMES PEOPLE CAN BE REALLY *MEAN* IN THE MAZE. BUT... NO MATTER HOW THEY ARE *DOWN* THERE--
--THEY CAN'T REACH ME *UP* HERE.
?
HERE WE ARE.
GULP WHY HERE?
BECAUSE THIS IS ONE PLACE WHERE NO MATTER HOW MUCH EVERYTHING SEEMS TO *CHANGE* DOWN THERE, YOU CAN SEE THE TRUTH: *NOTHING* EVER REALLY CHANGES FOR THE MAZE.
MAKES YOU FEEL *SAFE.*
COME ON, P, QUIT IT!

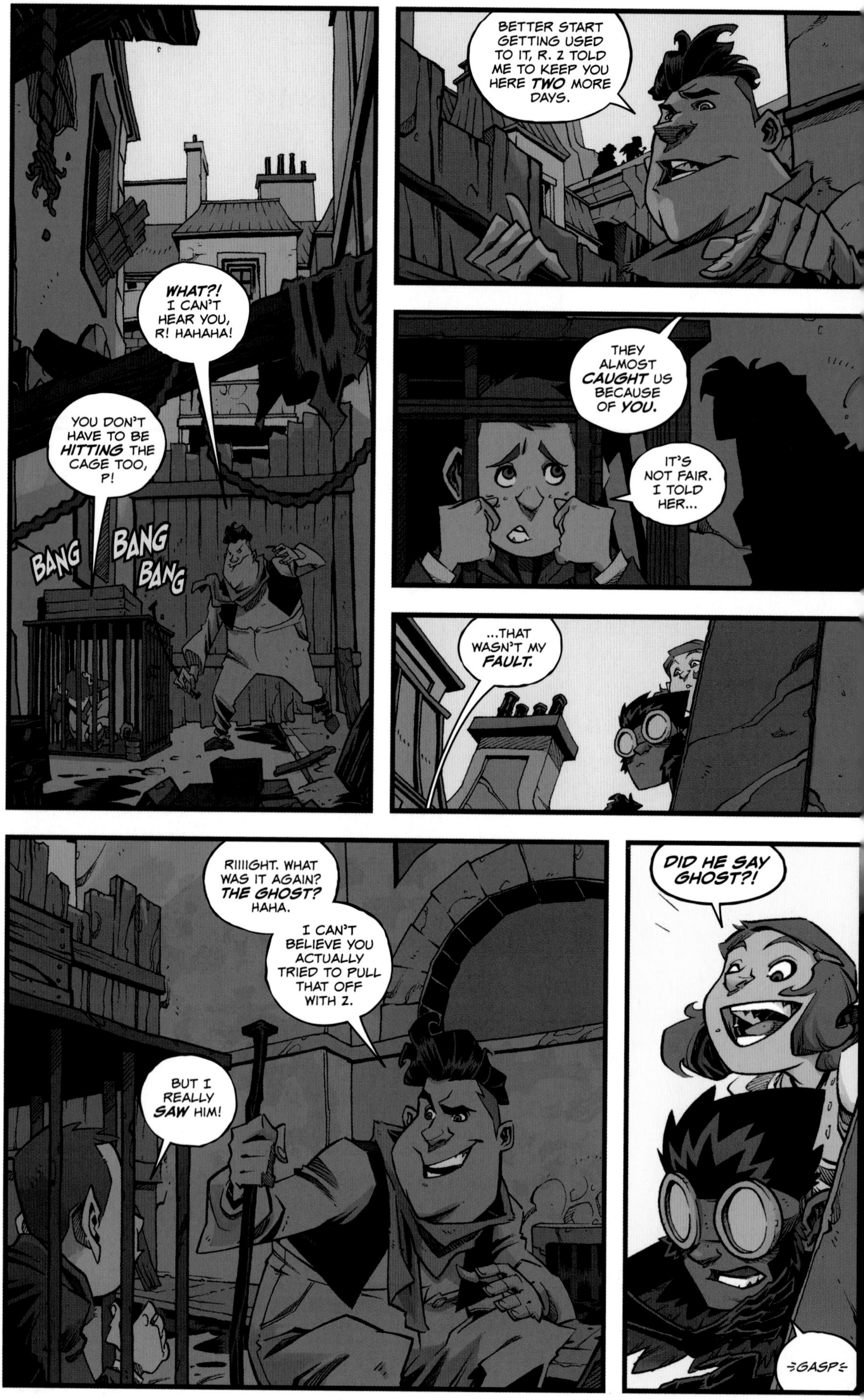
WHAT?! I CAN'T HEAR YOU, R! HAHAHA!
YOU DON'T HAVE TO BE HITTING THE CAGE TOO, P!
BANG
BANG
BANG
BETTER START GETTING USED TO IT, R. Z TOLD ME TO KEEP YOU HERE TWO MORE DAYS.
THEY ALMOST CAUGHT US BECAUSE OF YOU.
IT'S NOT FAIR. I TOLD HER...
...THAT WASN'T MY FAULT.
RIIIIGHT. WHAT WAS IT AGAIN? THE GHOST? HAHA.
I CAN'T BELIEVE YOU ACTUALLY TRIED TO PULL THAT OFF WITH Z.
BUT I REALLY SAW HIM!
DID HE SAY GHOST?!
GASP

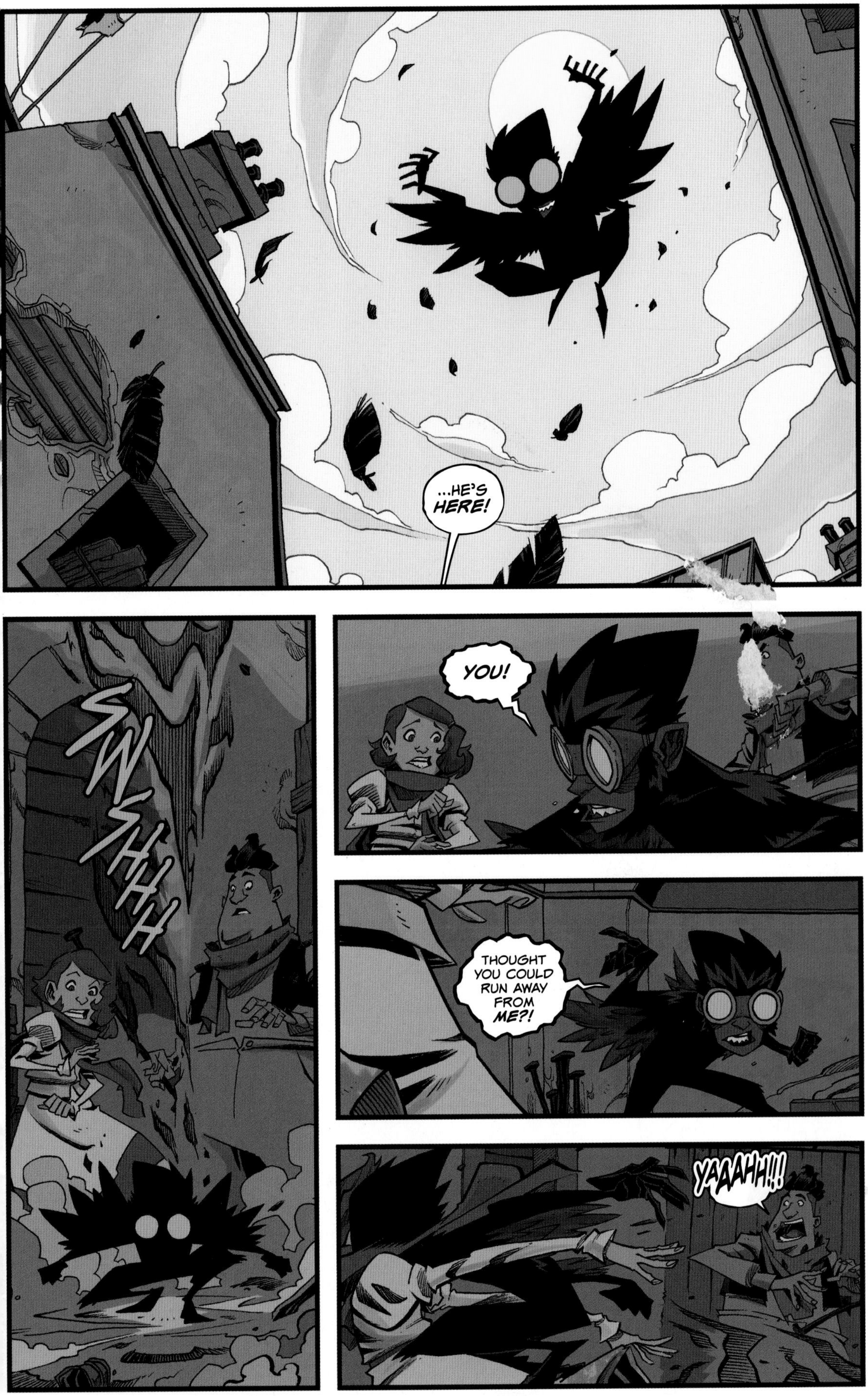
...HE'S HERE!
SWSHHH
YOU!
THOUGHT YOU COULD RUN AWAY FROM ME?!
YAAAHH!!!

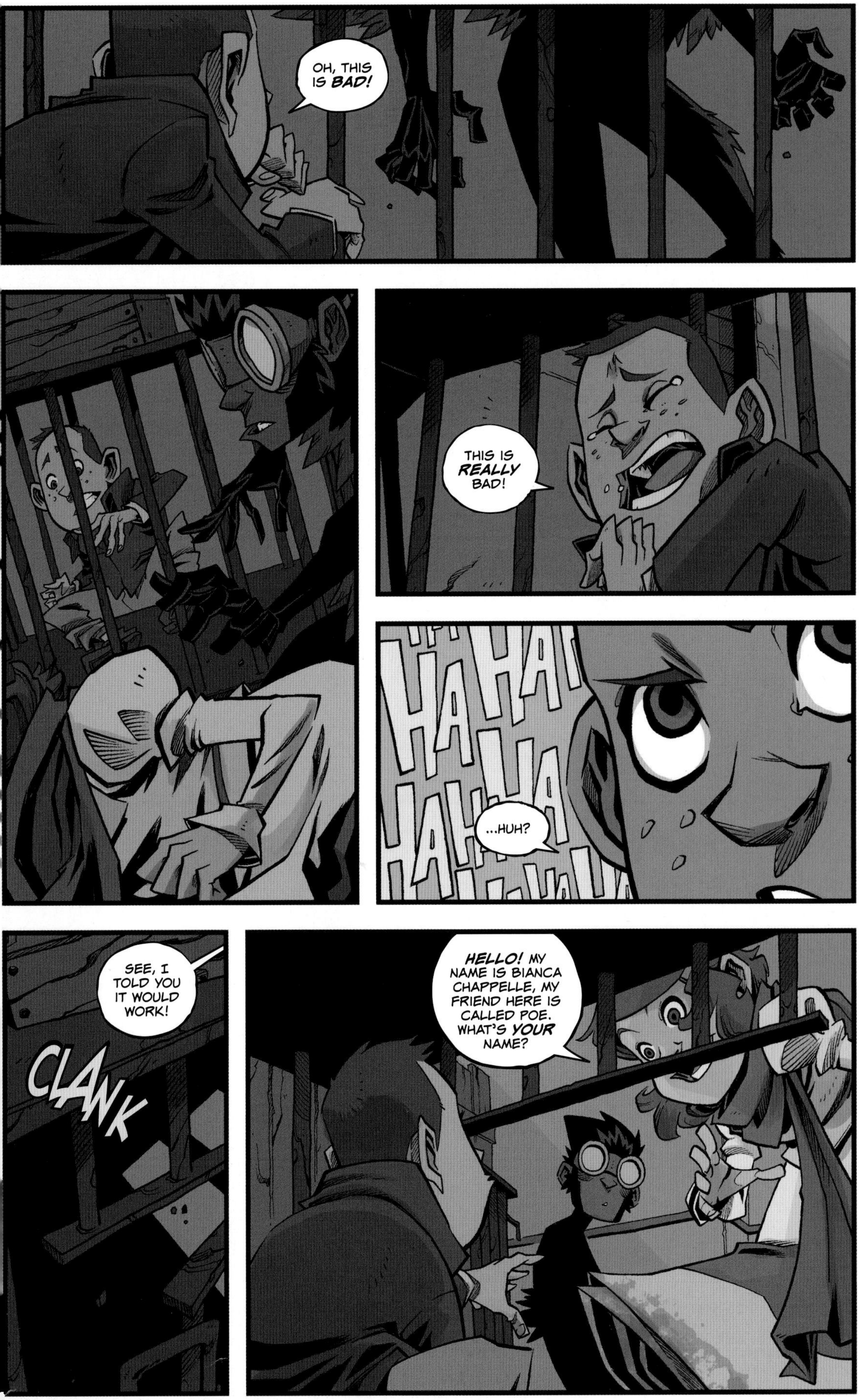
OH, THIS IS BAD!
THIS IS REALLY BAD!
HA HA HA HA HA HA
...HUH?
SEE, I TOLD YOU IT WOULD WORK!
CLANK
HELLO! MY NAME IS BIANCA CHAPPELLE, MY FRIEND HERE IS CALLED POE. WHAT'S YOUR NAME?

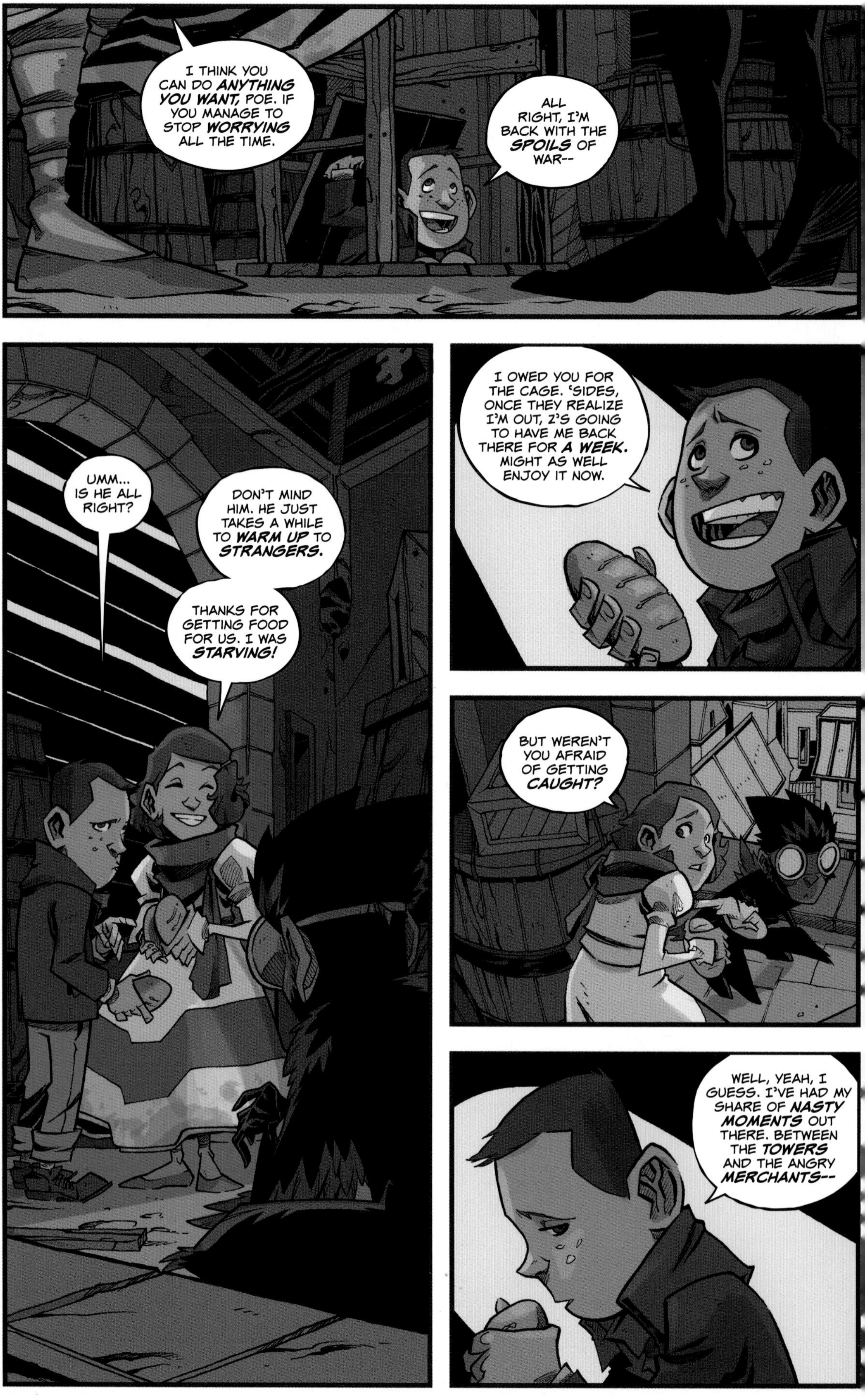

I THINK YOU CAN DO ANYTHING YOU WANT, POE. IF YOU MANAGE TO STOP WORRYING ALL THE TIME.
ALL RIGHT, I'M BACK WITH THE SPOILS OF WAR--
UMM... IS HE ALL RIGHT?
DON'T MIND HIM. HE JUST TAKES A WHILE TO WARM UP TO STRANGERS.
THANKS FOR GETTING FOOD FOR US. I WAS STARVING!
I OWED YOU FOR THE CAGE. 'SIDES, ONCE THEY REALIZE I'M OUT, Z'S GOING TO HAVE ME BACK THERE FOR A WEEK. MIGHT AS WELL ENJOY IT NOW.
BUT WEREN'T YOU AFRAID OF GETTING CAUGHT?
WELL, YEAH, I GUESS. I'VE HAD MY SHARE OF NASTY MOMENTS OUT THERE. BETWEEN THE TOWERS AND THE ANGRY MERCHANTS--

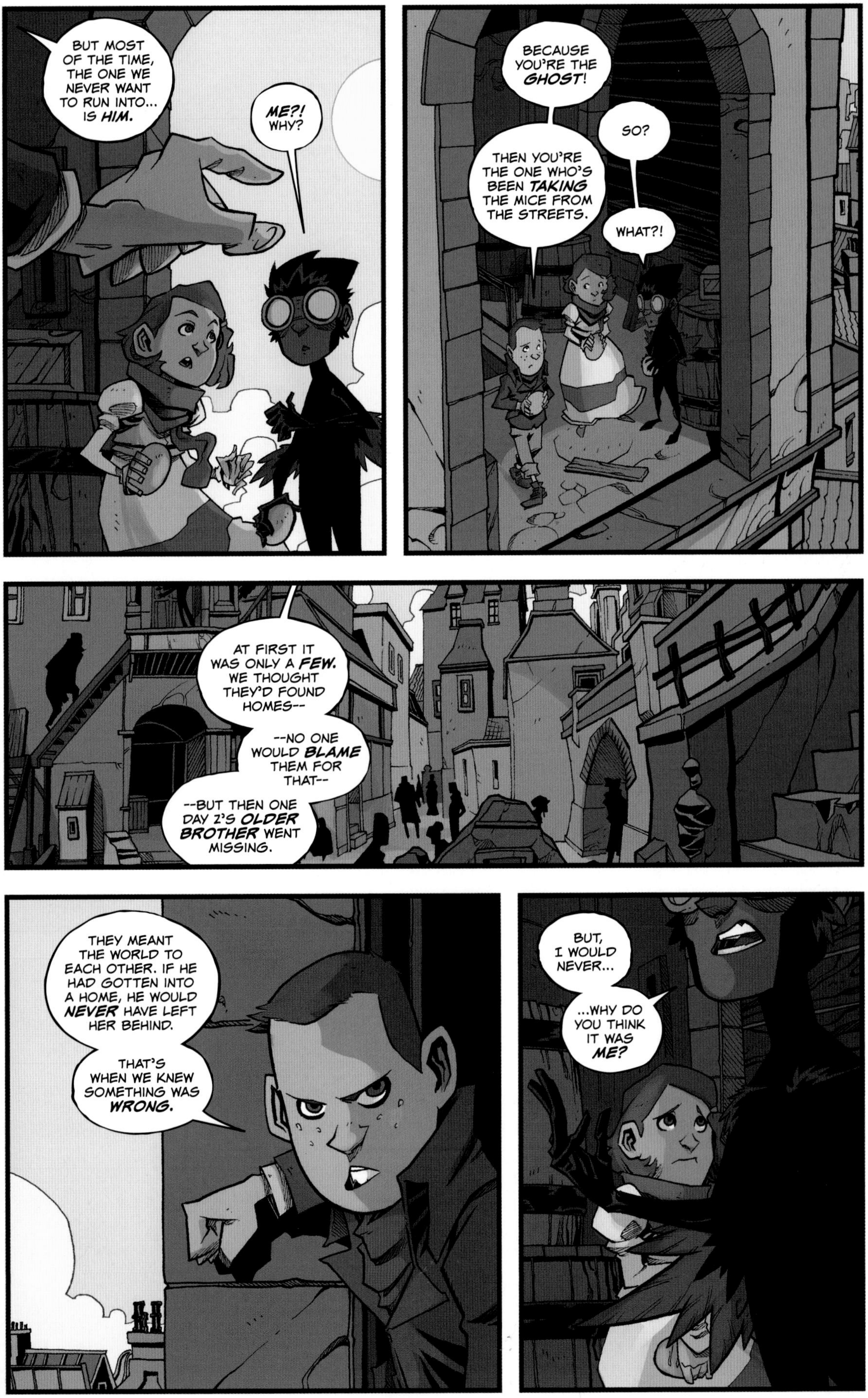

BUT MOST OF THE TIME, THE ONE WE NEVER WANT TO RUN INTO... IS **HIM.**
ME?! WHY?
BECAUSE YOU'RE THE **GHOST**!
SO?
THEN YOU'RE THE ONE WHO'S BEEN **TAKING** THE MICE FROM THE STREETS.
WHAT?!
AT FIRST IT WAS ONLY A **FEW.** WE THOUGHT THEY'D FOUND HOMES--
--NO ONE WOULD **BLAME** THEM FOR THAT--
--BUT THEN ONE DAY Z'S **OLDER BROTHER** WENT MISSING.
THEY MEANT THE WORLD TO EACH OTHER. IF HE HAD GOTTEN INTO A HOME, HE WOULD **NEVER** HAVE LEFT HER BEHIND.
THAT'S WHEN WE KNEW SOMETHING WAS **WRONG.**
BUT, I WOULD NEVER...
...WHY DO YOU THINK IT WAS **ME?**

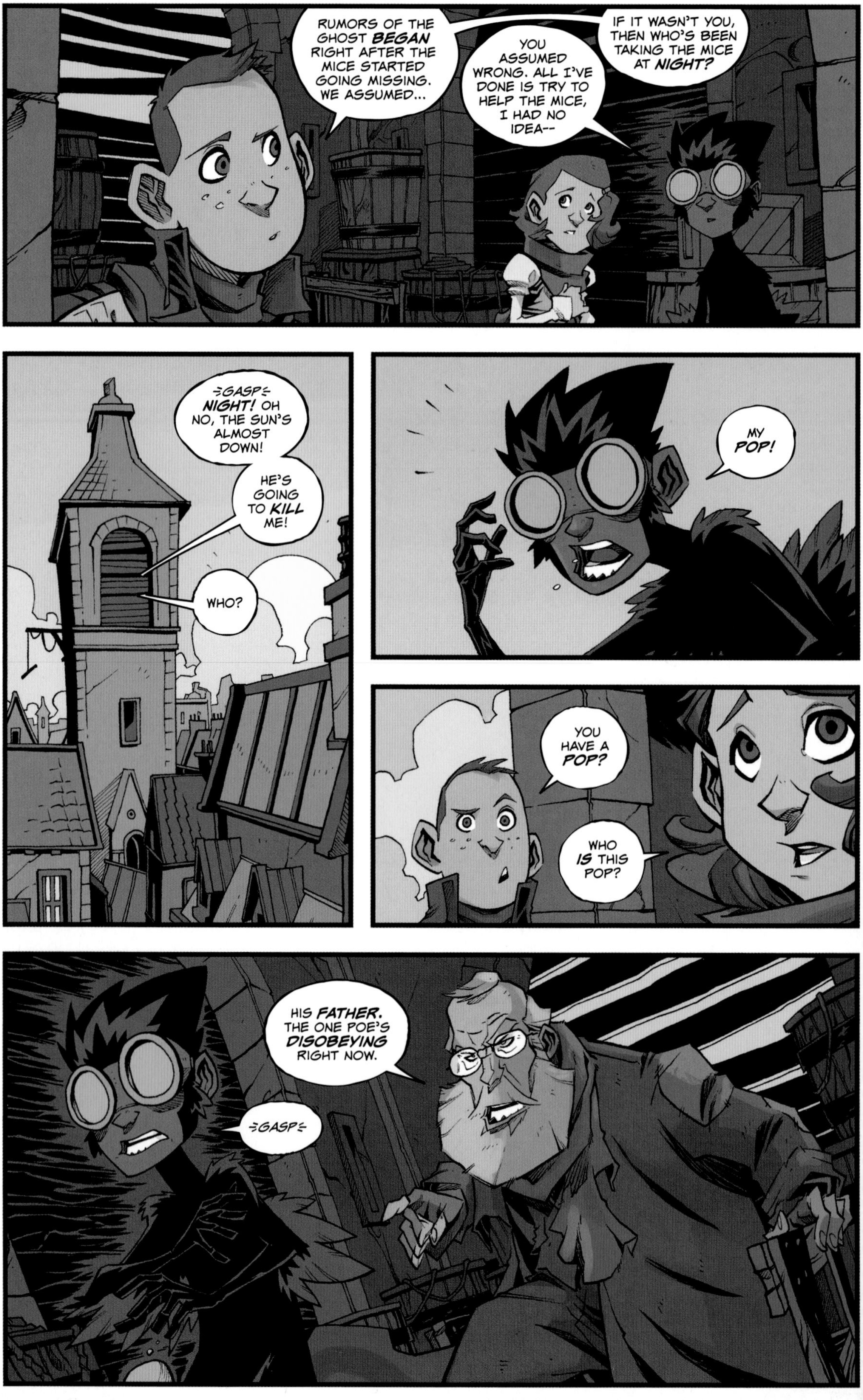
RUMORS OF THE GHOST BEGAN RIGHT AFTER THE MICE STARTED GOING MISSING. WE ASSUMED...
YOU ASSUMED WRONG. ALL I'VE DONE IS TRY TO HELP THE MICE, I HAD NO IDEA--
IF IT WASN'T YOU, THEN WHO'S BEEN TAKING THE MICE AT NIGHT?
=GASP= NIGHT! OH NO, THE SUN'S ALMOST DOWN!
HE'S GOING TO KILL ME!
WHO?
MY POP!
YOU HAVE A POP?
WHO IS THIS POP?
HIS FATHER. THE ONE POE'S DISOBEYING RIGHT NOW.
=GASP=

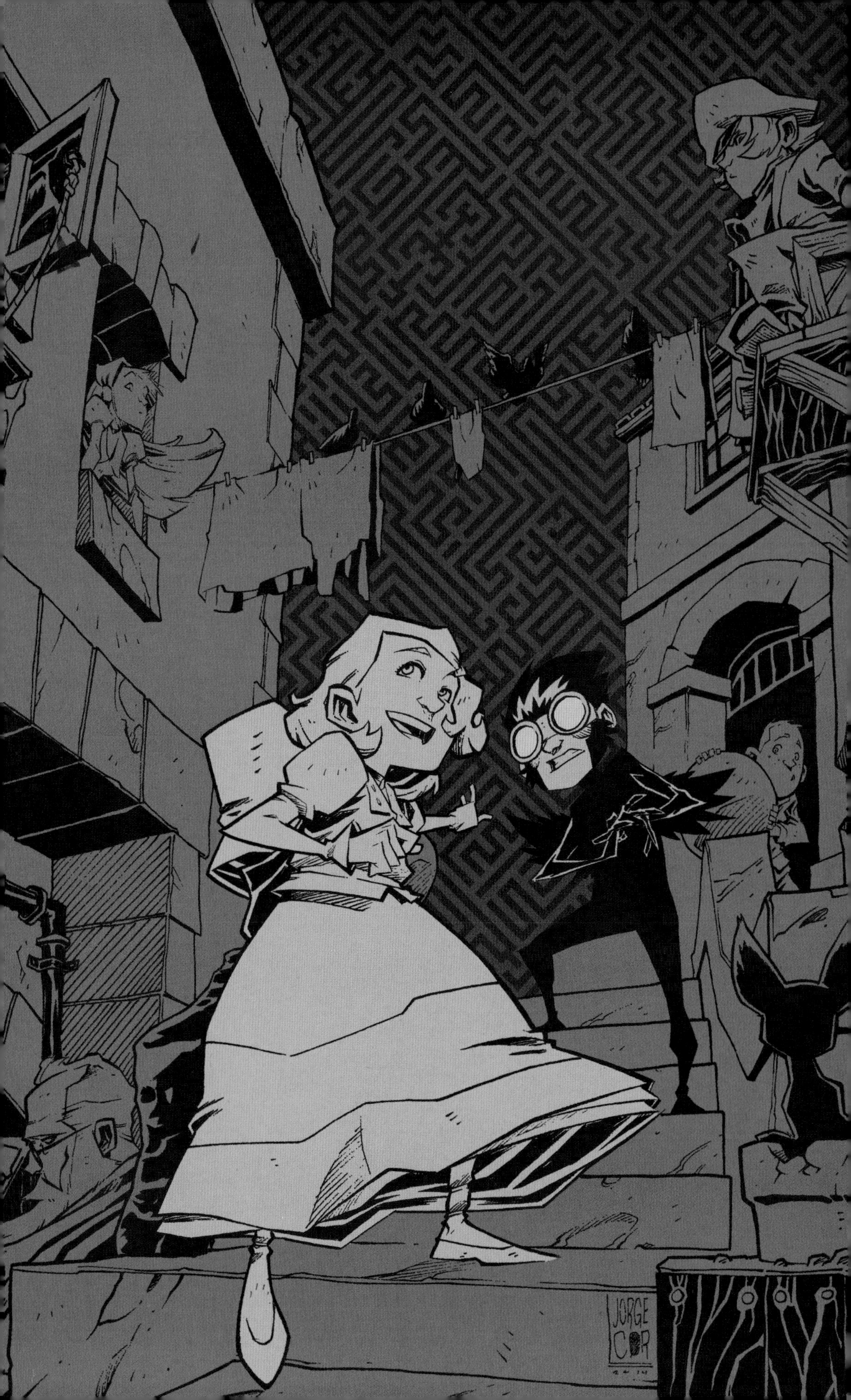
JORGE COR

CHAPTER
THREE

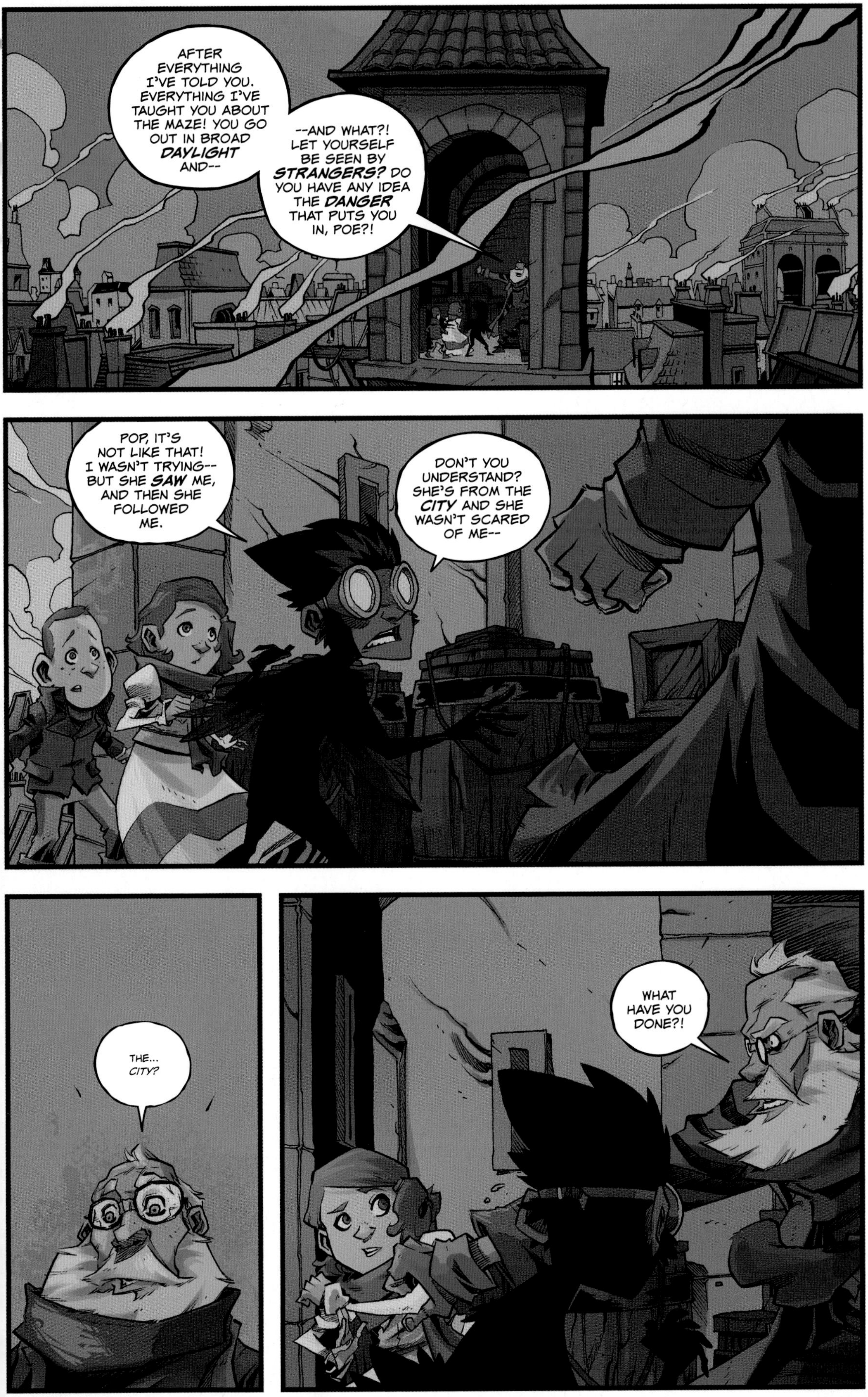
AFTER EVERYTHING I'VE TOLD YOU. EVERYTHING I'VE TAUGHT YOU ABOUT THE MAZE! YOU GO OUT IN BROAD DAYLIGHT AND--
--AND WHAT?! LET YOURSELF BE SEEN BY STRANGERS? DO YOU HAVE ANY IDEA THE DANGER THAT PUTS YOU IN, POE?!
POP, IT'S NOT LIKE THAT! I WASN'T TRYING-- BUT SHE SAW ME, AND THEN SHE FOLLOWED ME.
DON'T YOU UNDERSTAND? SHE'S FROM THE CITY AND SHE WASN'T SCARED OF ME--
THE... CITY?
WHAT HAVE YOU DONE?!

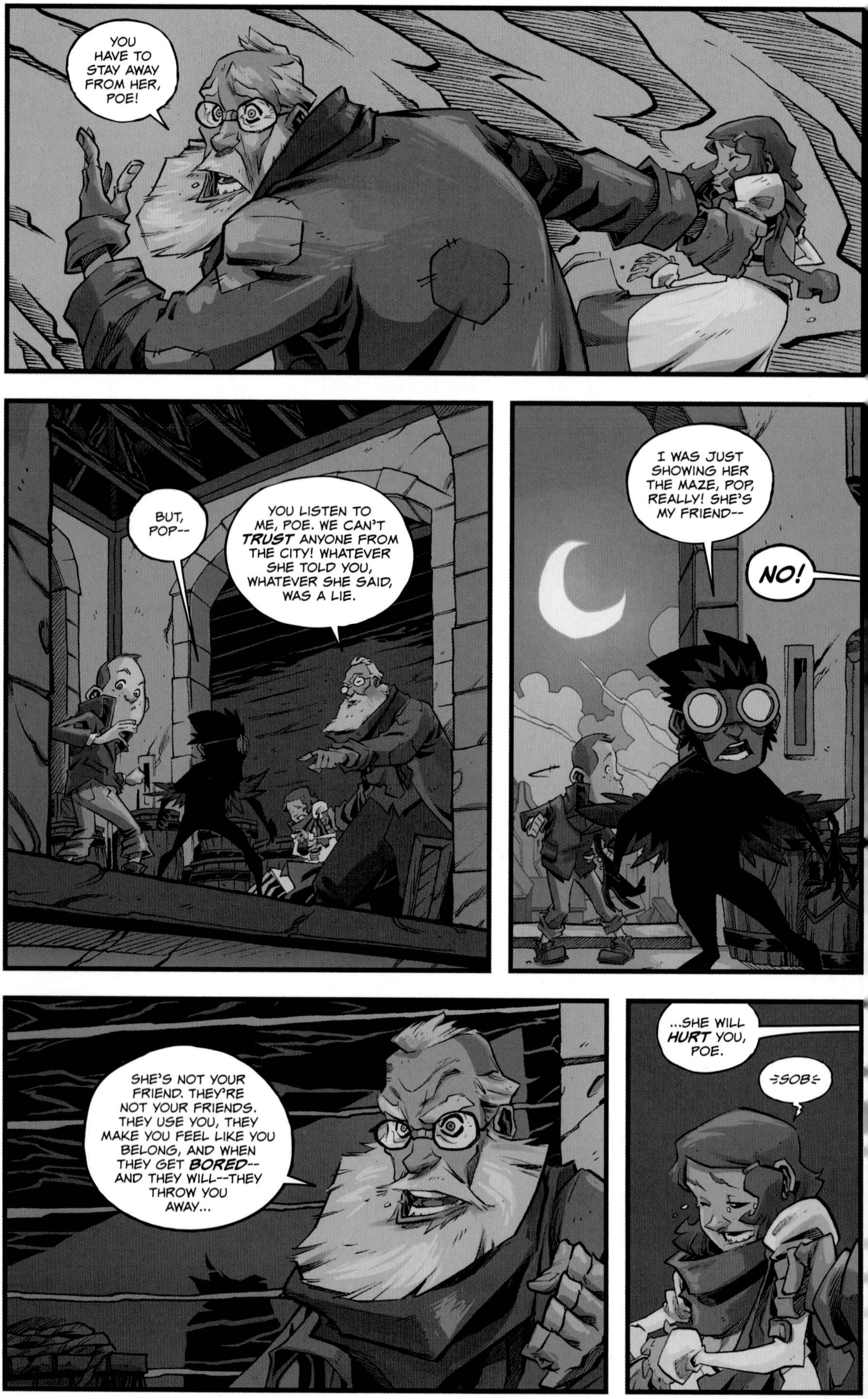
YOU HAVE TO STAY AWAY FROM HER, POE!
BUT, POP--
YOU LISTEN TO ME, POE. WE CAN'T **TRUST** ANYONE FROM THE CITY! WHATEVER SHE TOLD YOU, WHATEVER SHE SAID, WAS A LIE.
I WAS JUST SHOWING HER THE MAZE, POP, REALLY! SHE'S MY FRIEND--
NO!
SHE'S NOT YOUR FRIEND. THEY'RE NOT YOUR FRIENDS. THEY USE YOU, THEY MAKE YOU FEEL LIKE YOU BELONG, AND WHEN THEY GET **BORED**-- AND THEY WILL--THEY THROW YOU AWAY...
...SHE WILL **HURT** YOU, POE.
SOB

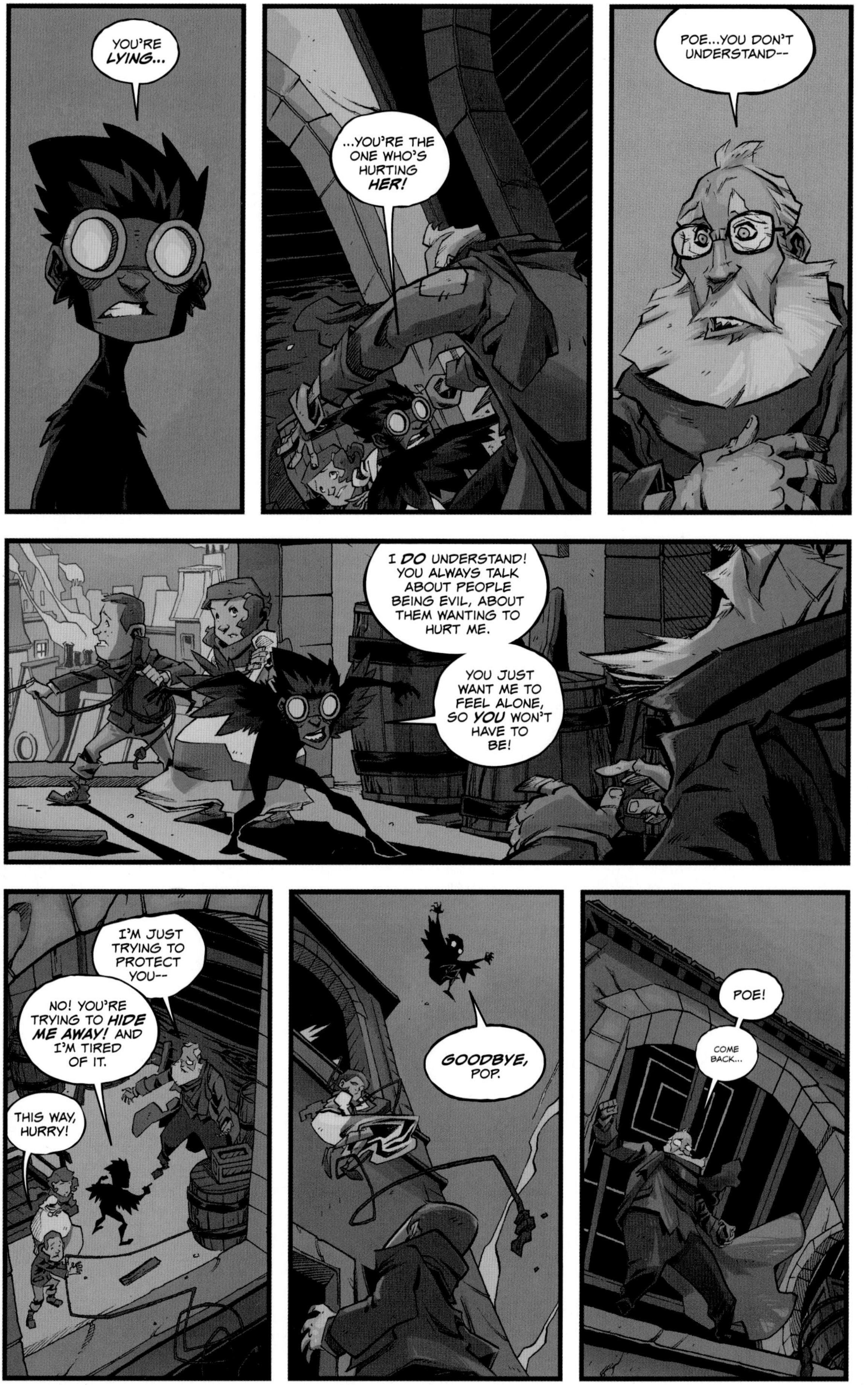
YOU'RE *LYING...*
...YOU'RE THE ONE WHO'S HURTING *HER!*
POE...YOU DON'T UNDERSTAND--
I *DO* UNDERSTAND! YOU ALWAYS TALK ABOUT PEOPLE BEING EVIL, ABOUT THEM WANTING TO HURT ME.
YOU JUST WANT ME TO FEEL ALONE, SO *YOU* WON'T HAVE TO BE!
I'M JUST TRYING TO PROTECT YOU--
NO! YOU'RE TRYING TO *HIDE ME AWAY!* AND I'M TIRED OF IT.
THIS WAY, HURRY!
GOODBYE, POP.
POE!
COME BACK...

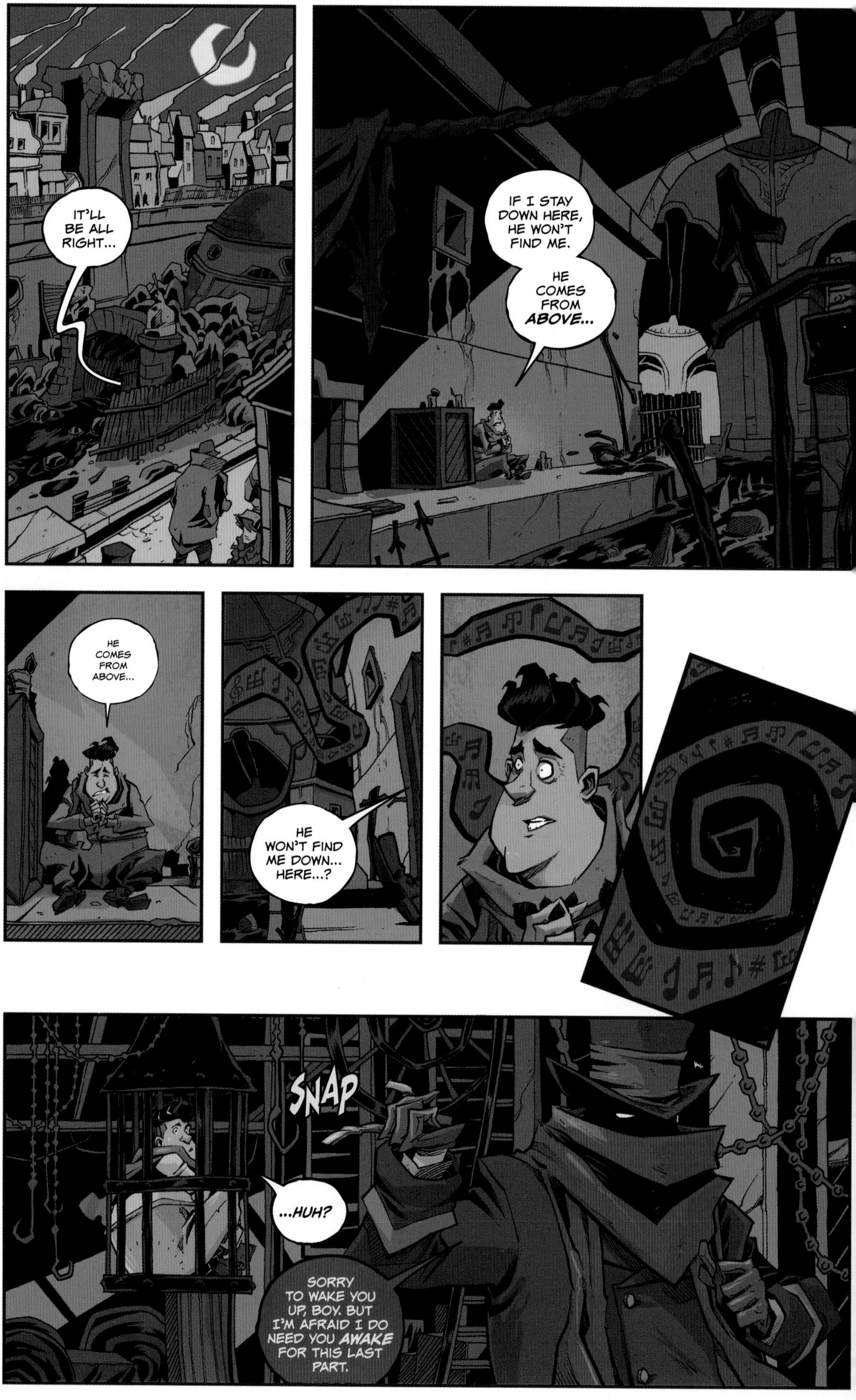
IT'LL BE ALL RIGHT...
IF I STAY DOWN HERE, HE WON'T FIND ME.
HE COMES FROM *ABOVE*...
HE COMES FROM ABOVE...
HE WON'T FIND ME DOWN... HERE...?
SNAP
...HUH?
SORRY TO WAKE YOU UP, BOY. BUT I'M AFRAID I DO NEED YOU *AWAKE* FOR THIS LAST PART.

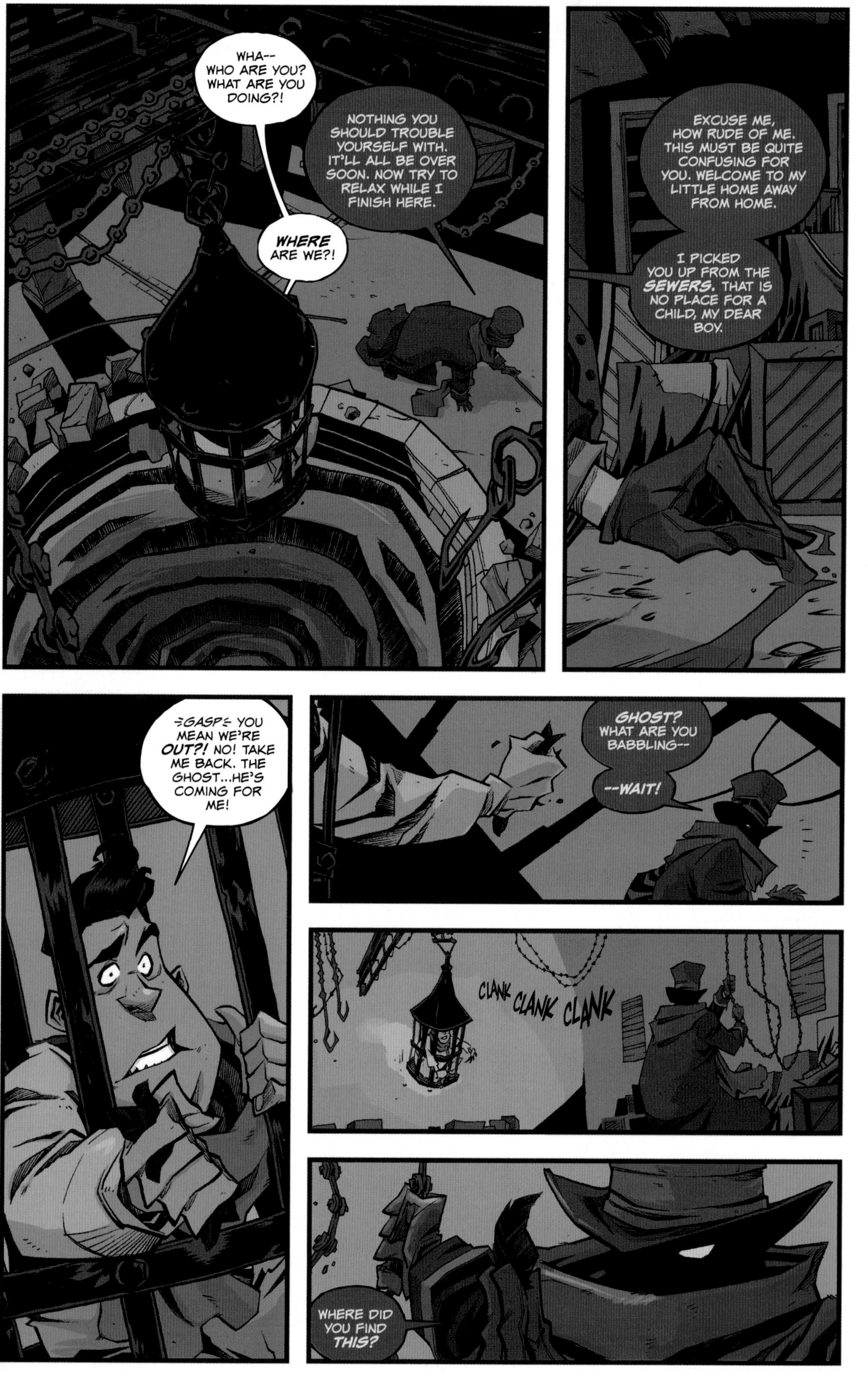
WHA-- WHO ARE YOU? WHAT ARE YOU DOING?!
NOTHING YOU SHOULD TROUBLE YOURSELF WITH. IT'LL ALL BE OVER SOON. NOW TRY TO RELAX WHILE I FINISH HERE.
WHERE ARE WE?!
EXCUSE ME, HOW RUDE OF ME. THIS MUST BE QUITE CONFUSING FOR YOU. WELCOME TO MY LITTLE HOME AWAY FROM HOME.
I PICKED YOU UP FROM THE SEWERS. THAT IS NO PLACE FOR A CHILD, MY DEAR BOY.
=GASP= YOU MEAN WE'RE OUT?! NO! TAKE ME BACK. THE GHOST...HE'S COMING FOR ME!
GHOST? WHAT ARE YOU BABBLING--
--WAIT!
CLANK CLANK CLANK
WHERE DID YOU FIND THIS?

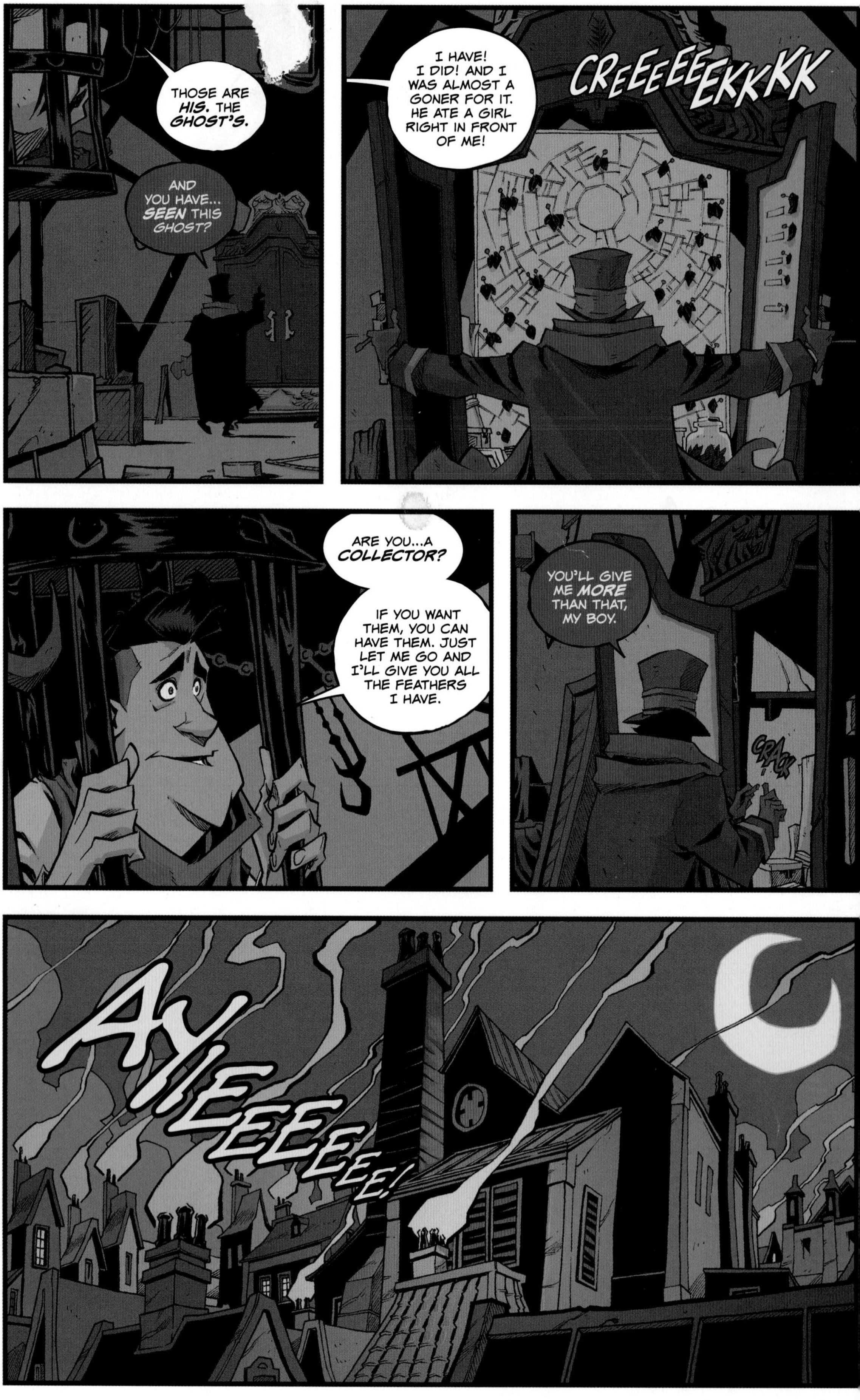
THOSE ARE HIS. THE GHOST'S.
AND YOU HAVE... SEEN THIS GHOST?
I HAVE! I DID! AND I WAS ALMOST A GONER FOR IT. HE ATE A GIRL RIGHT IN FRONT OF ME!
CREEEEEEEKKKKK
ARE YOU...A COLLECTOR?
IF YOU WANT THEM, YOU CAN HAVE THEM. JUST LET ME GO AND I'LL GIVE YOU ALL THE FEATHERS I HAVE.
YOU'LL GIVE ME MORE THAN THAT, MY BOY.
CRACK
AYIEEEEEEE!

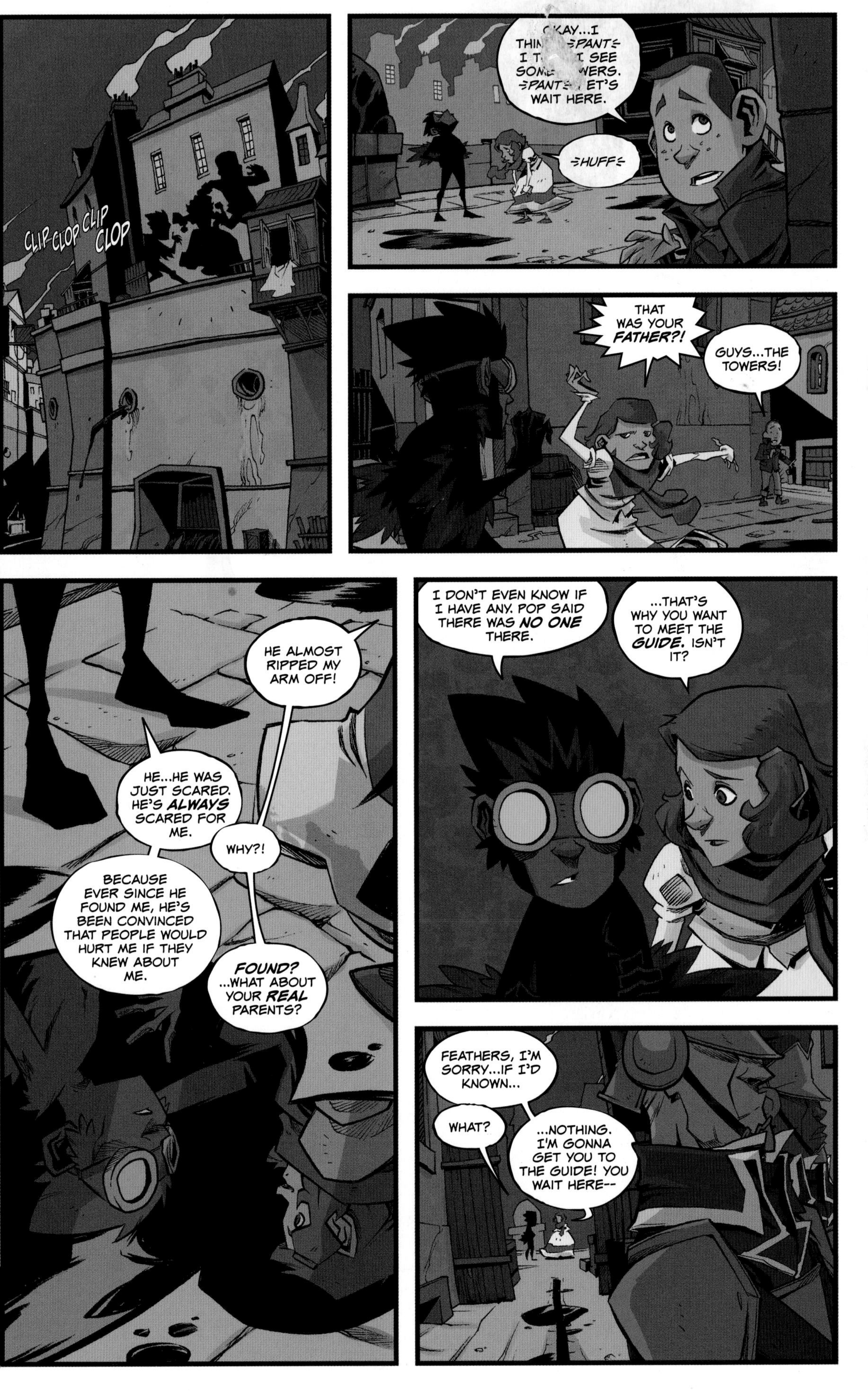
CLIP CLOP CLIP CLOP
KAY...I THIN =PANT= I T SEE SOM WERS. =PANT= ET'S WAIT HERE.
=HUFF=
THAT WAS YOUR ***FATHER?!***
GUYS...THE TOWERS!
HE ALMOST RIPPED MY ARM OFF!
HE...HE WAS JUST SCARED. HE'S ***ALWAYS*** SCARED FOR ME.
WHY?!
BECAUSE EVER SINCE HE FOUND ME, HE'S BEEN CONVINCED THAT PEOPLE WOULD HURT ME IF THEY KNEW ABOUT ME.
FOUND? ...WHAT ABOUT YOUR ***REAL*** PARENTS?
I DON'T EVEN KNOW IF I HAVE ANY. POP SAID THERE WAS ***NO ONE*** THERE.
...THAT'S WHY YOU WANT TO MEET THE ***GUIDE.*** ISN'T IT?
FEATHERS, I'M SORRY...IF I'D KNOWN...
WHAT?
...NOTHING. I'M GONNA GET YOU TO THE GUIDE! YOU WAIT HERE--

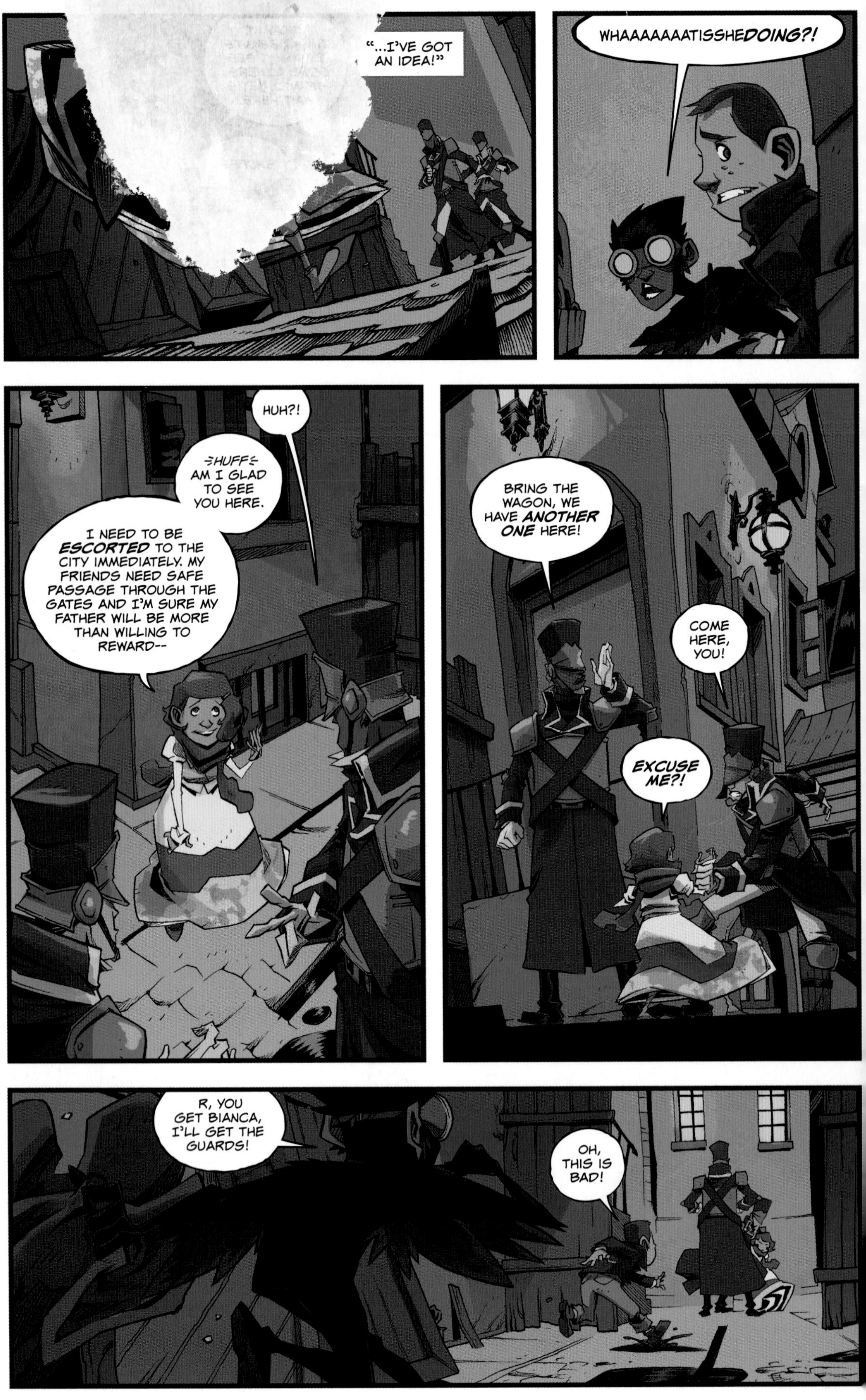
"...I'VE GOT AN IDEA!"
WHAAAAAAATISSHEDOING?!
HUH?!
HUFF AM I GLAD TO SEE YOU HERE.
I NEED TO BE ESCORTED TO THE CITY IMMEDIATELY. MY FRIENDS NEED SAFE PASSAGE THROUGH THE GATES AND I'M SURE MY FATHER WILL BE MORE THAN WILLING TO REWARD--
BRING THE WAGON, WE HAVE ANOTHER ONE HERE!
COME HERE, YOU!
EXCUSE ME?!
R, YOU GET BIANCA, I'LL GET THE GUARDS!
OH, THIS IS BAD!

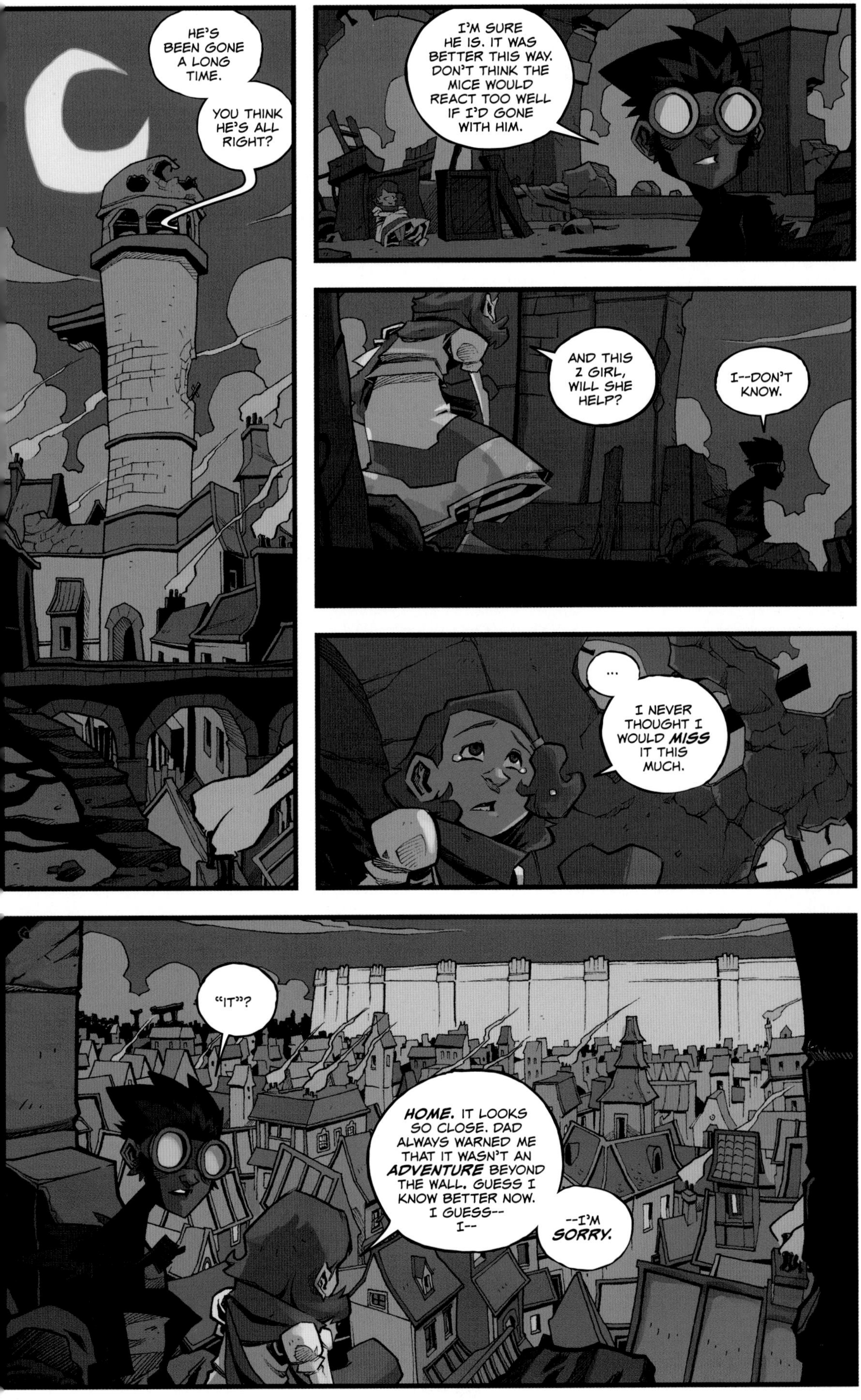
HE'S BEEN GONE A LONG TIME.
YOU THINK HE'S ALL RIGHT?
I'M SURE HE IS. IT WAS BETTER THIS WAY. DON'T THINK THE MICE WOULD REACT TOO WELL IF I'D GONE WITH HIM.
AND THIS Z GIRL, WILL SHE HELP?
I--DON'T KNOW.
...
I NEVER THOUGHT I WOULD MISS IT THIS MUCH.
"IT"?
HOME. IT LOOKS SO CLOSE. DAD ALWAYS WARNED ME THAT IT WASN'T AN ADVENTURE BEYOND THE WALL. GUESS I KNOW BETTER NOW. I GUESS-- I--
--I'M SORRY.

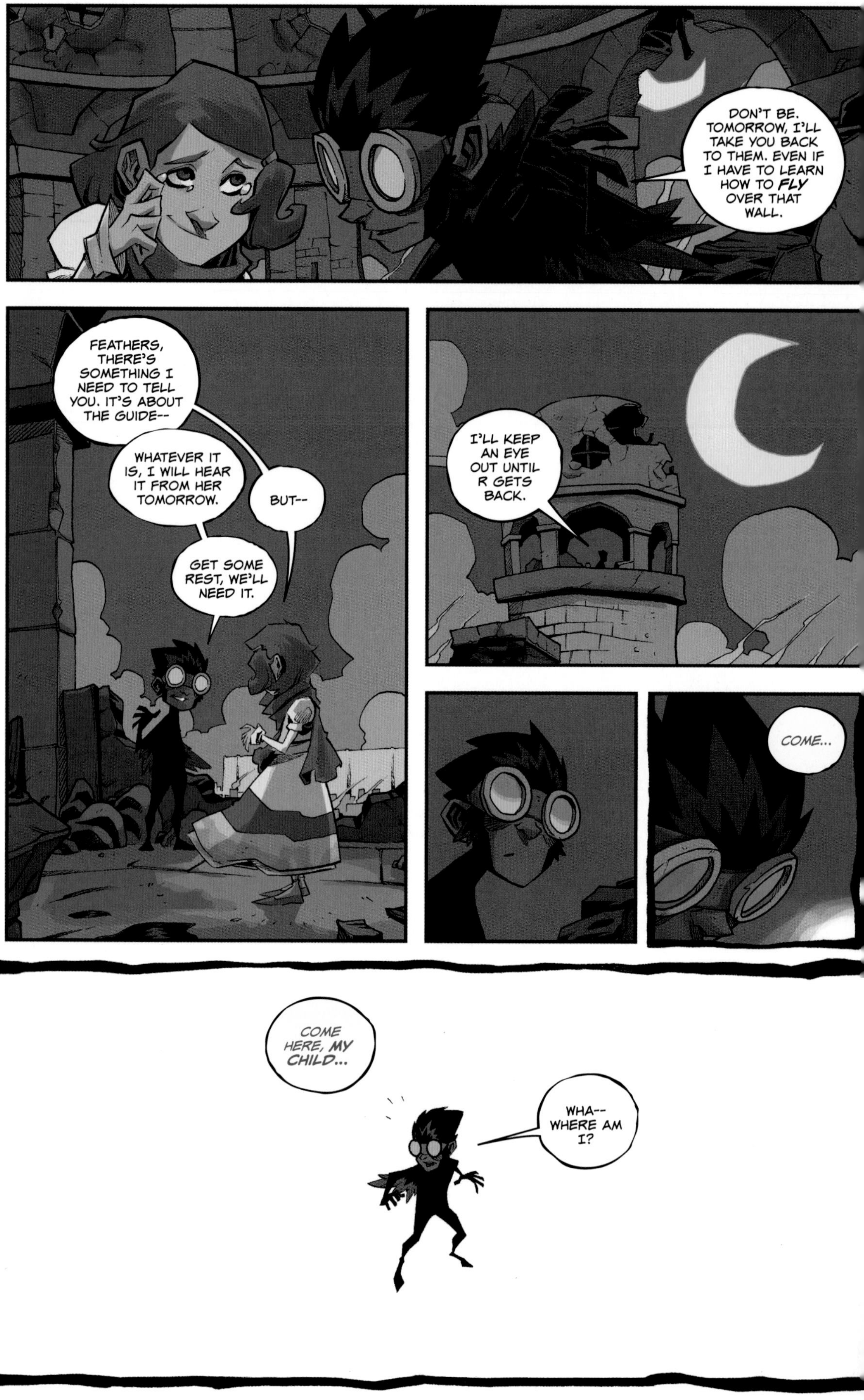
DON'T BE. TOMORROW, I'LL TAKE YOU BACK TO THEM. EVEN IF I HAVE TO LEARN HOW TO FLY OVER THAT WALL.
FEATHERS, THERE'S SOMETHING I NEED TO TELL YOU. IT'S ABOUT THE GUIDE--
WHATEVER IT IS, I WILL HEAR IT FROM HER TOMORROW.
BUT--
GET SOME REST, WE'LL NEED IT.
I'LL KEEP AN EYE OUT UNTIL R GETS BACK.
COME...
COME HERE, MY CHILD...
WHA-- WHERE AM I?

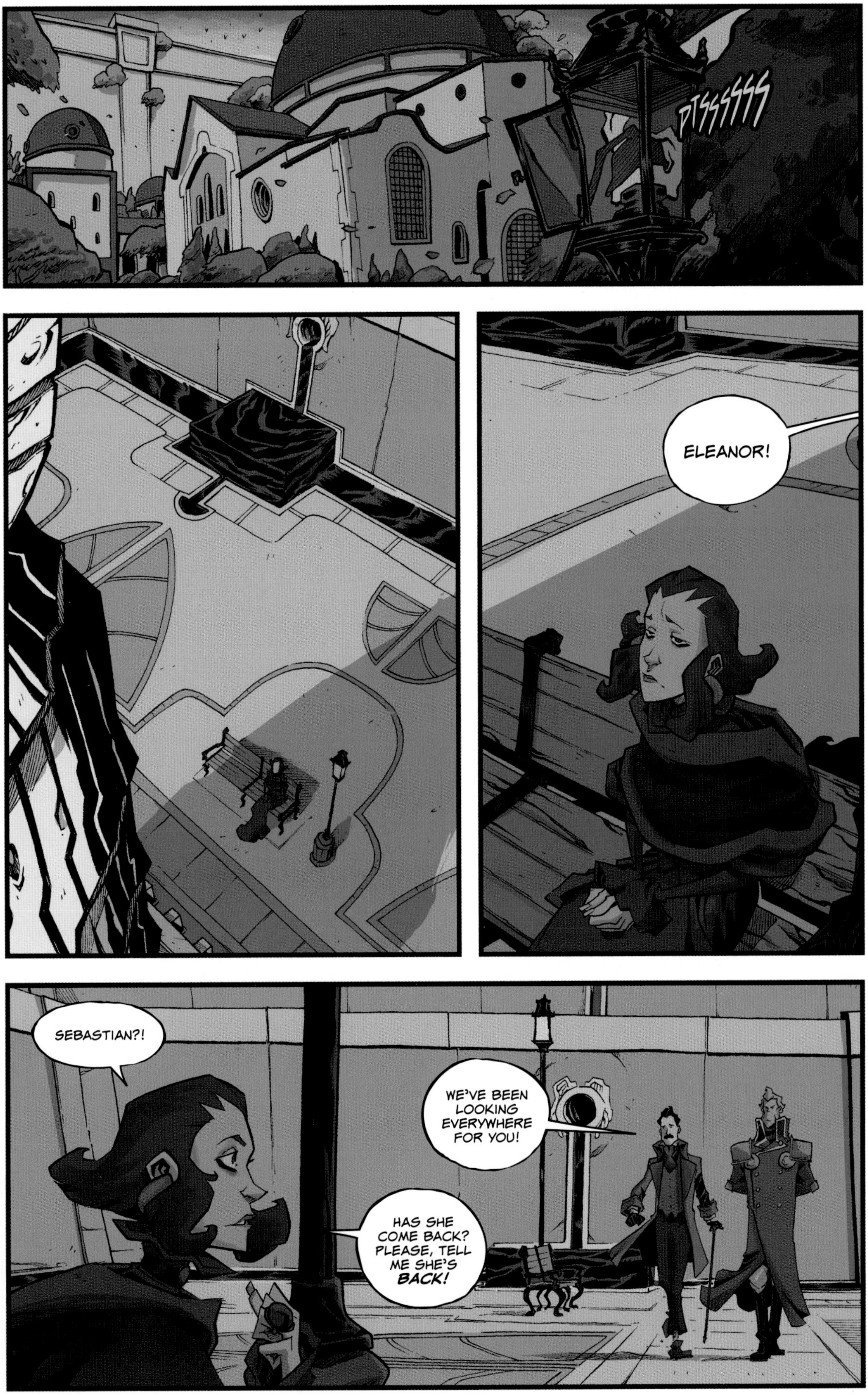
PTSSSSSS
ELEANOR!
SEBASTIAN?!
WE'VE BEEN LOOKING EVERYWHERE FOR YOU!
HAS SHE COME BACK? PLEASE, TELL ME SHE'S *BACK!*

I'VE BEEN WAITING TOO LONG FOR THIS DAY.

HEH-- WHAT'S WITH ALL THE MICE, Z?

I'M UP FOR GETTING ALL THE HELP WE NEED, BUT DON'T YOU THINK THIS MAY BE A BIT TOO MUCH?

THEY'RE NOT HERE TO HELP, R.

WHAT?

NO, THEY'RE HERE TO SEE *HIM.* THE *GHOST.* TO SHOW THAT THEY'RE NOT AFRAID ANYMORE.

AFRAID OF LOOKING THEIR WORST NIGHTMARE--

--RIGHT IN THE *FACE!*

WHAT ARE YOU DOING?!

WAIT YOUR TURN, *WALLER!* I HAVE A BONE TO PICK WITH YOU, TOO!

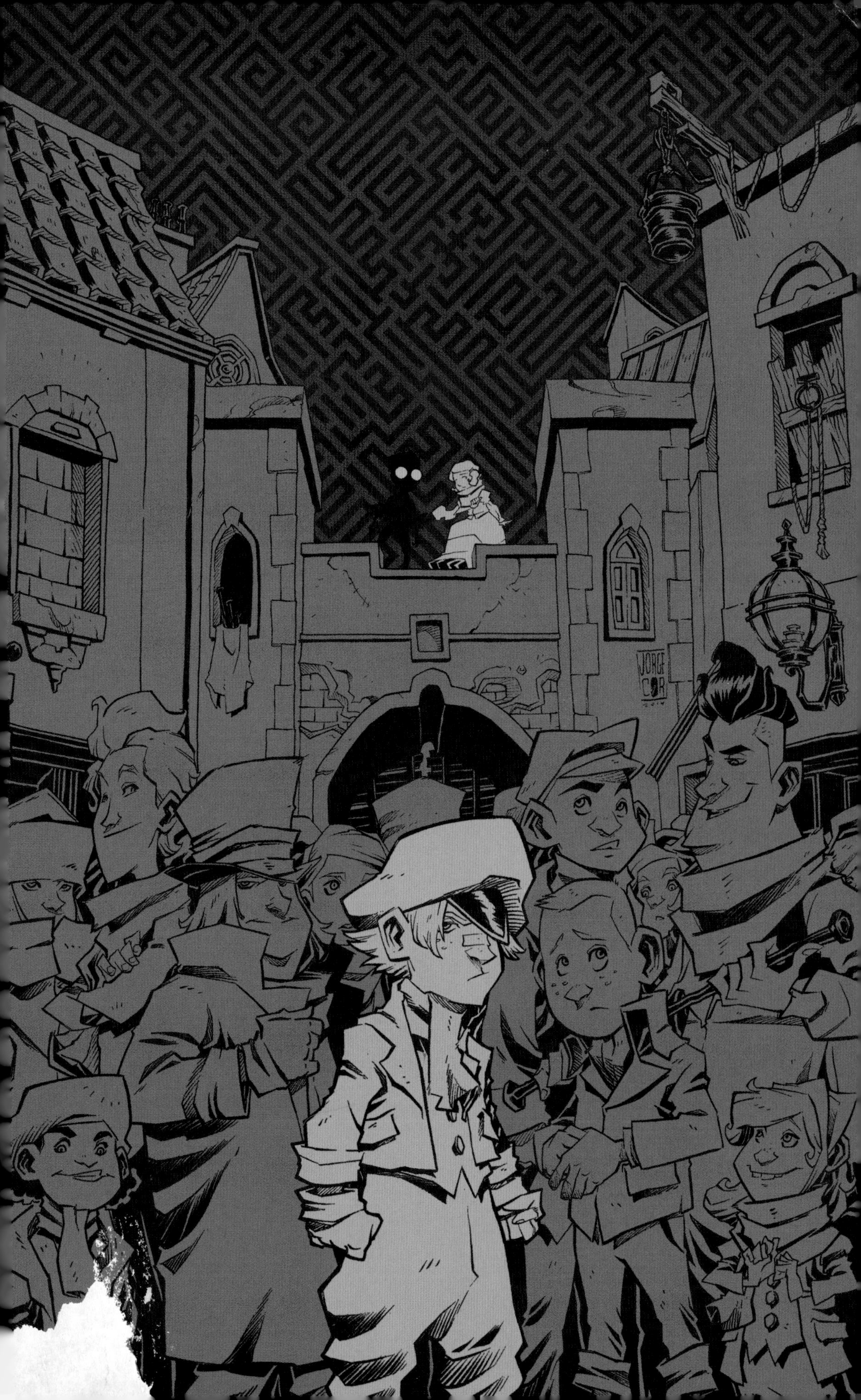
JORGE COR
2014

CHAPTER
FOUR

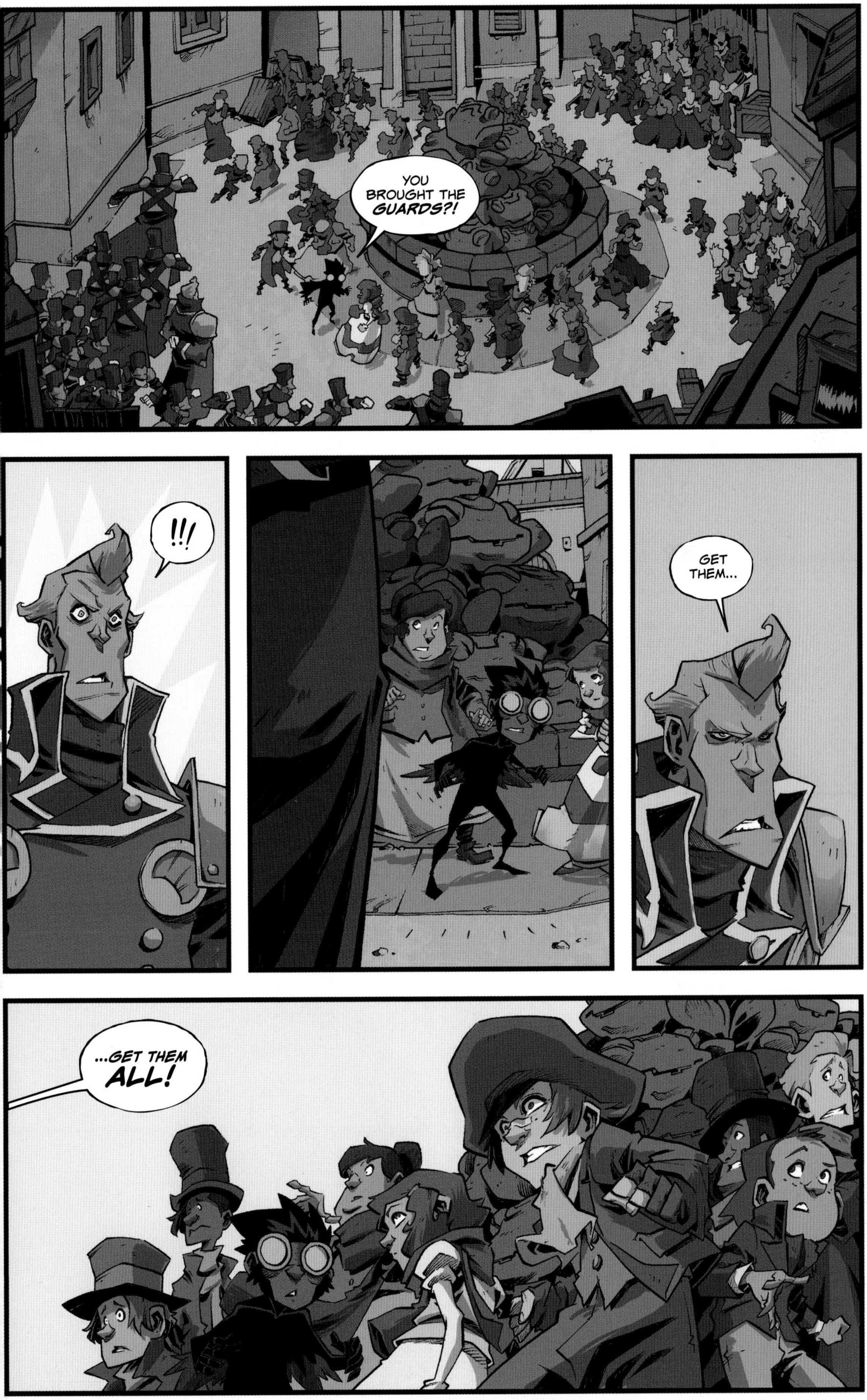
YOU BROUGHT THE GUARDS?!
!!!
GET THEM...
...GET THEM ALL!

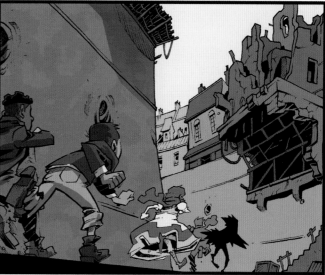

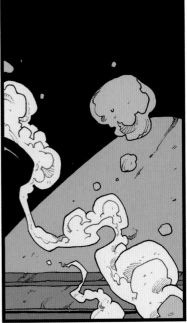

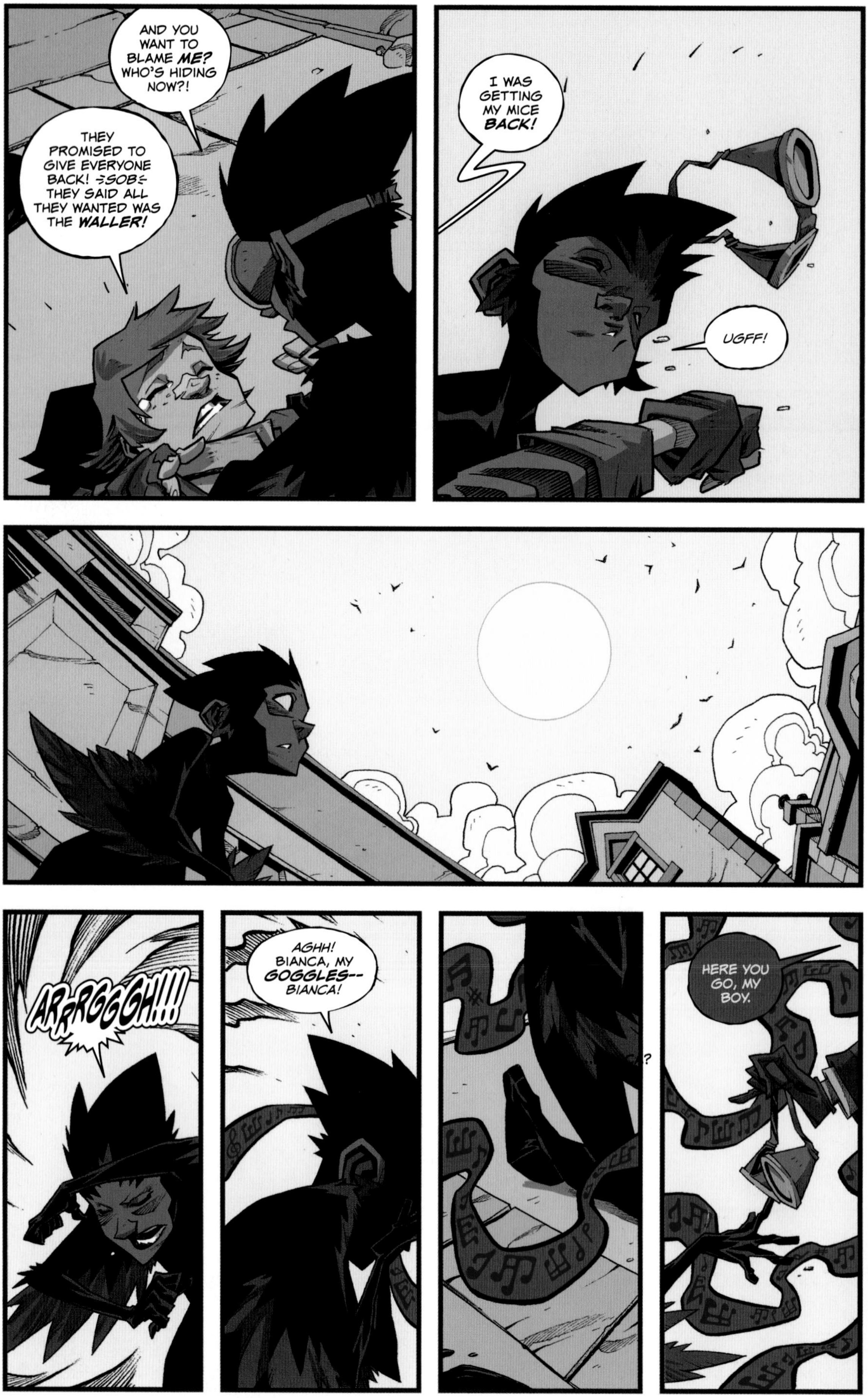
AND YOU WANT TO BLAME ME? WHO'S HIDING NOW?!
THEY PROMISED TO GIVE EVERYONE BACK! =SOB= THEY SAID ALL THEY WANTED WAS THE WALLER!
I WAS GETTING MY MICE BACK!
UGFF!
ARRRGGGH!!!
AGHH! BIANCA, MY GOGGLES-- BIANCA!
?
HERE YOU GO, MY BOY.

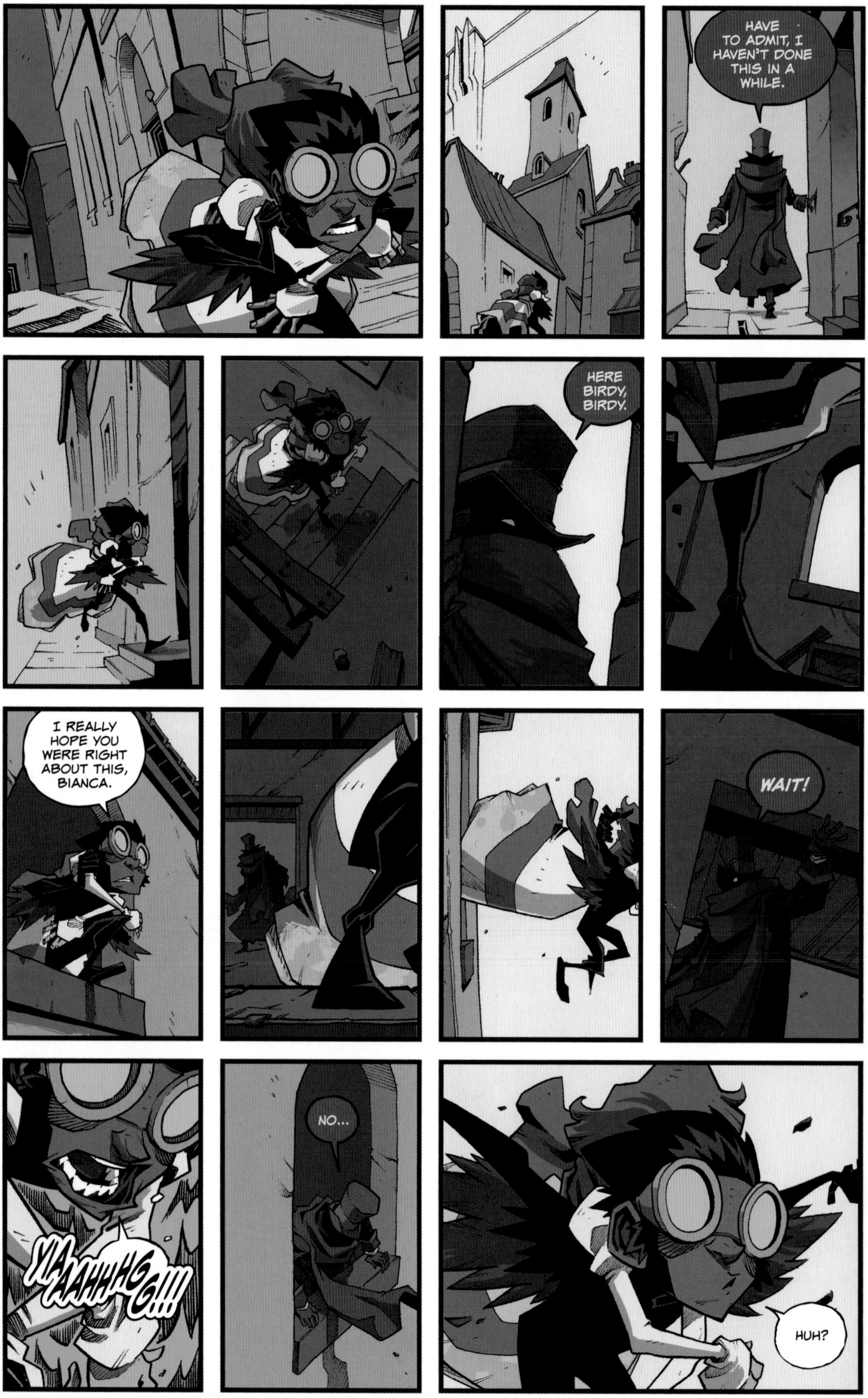
HAVE TO ADMIT, I HAVEN'T DONE THIS IN A WHILE.
HERE BIRDY, BIRDY.
I REALLY HOPE YOU WERE RIGHT ABOUT THIS, BIANCA.
WAIT!
YIAAAHHHGG!!!
NO...
HUH?

=HMMN=
W-WHAT? WHERE ARE WE?

HOLY--
WOAAA!!

CALM DOWN! YOU'RE GOING TO MAKE US *FALL!*

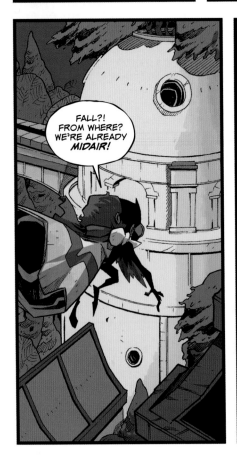

FALL?! FROM WHERE? WE'RE ALREADY *MIDAIR!*

WAIT, HOLD ON.

WHAT WAS THAT?! YOU WERE *FLYING!*

I KNOW! YOU WERE RIGHT!

BUT...WHAT HAPPENED? Z AND THE MICE-- LAST THING I REMEMBER, YOU WERE SCREAMING ABOUT SOMETHING, AND THEN... *MUSIC...*

IT WAS *HIM,* THE MAN WHO'S BEEN TAKING THE MICE. I SAW HIM. HE ALMOST TOOK YOU, TOO. WE BARELY MADE IT OUT.

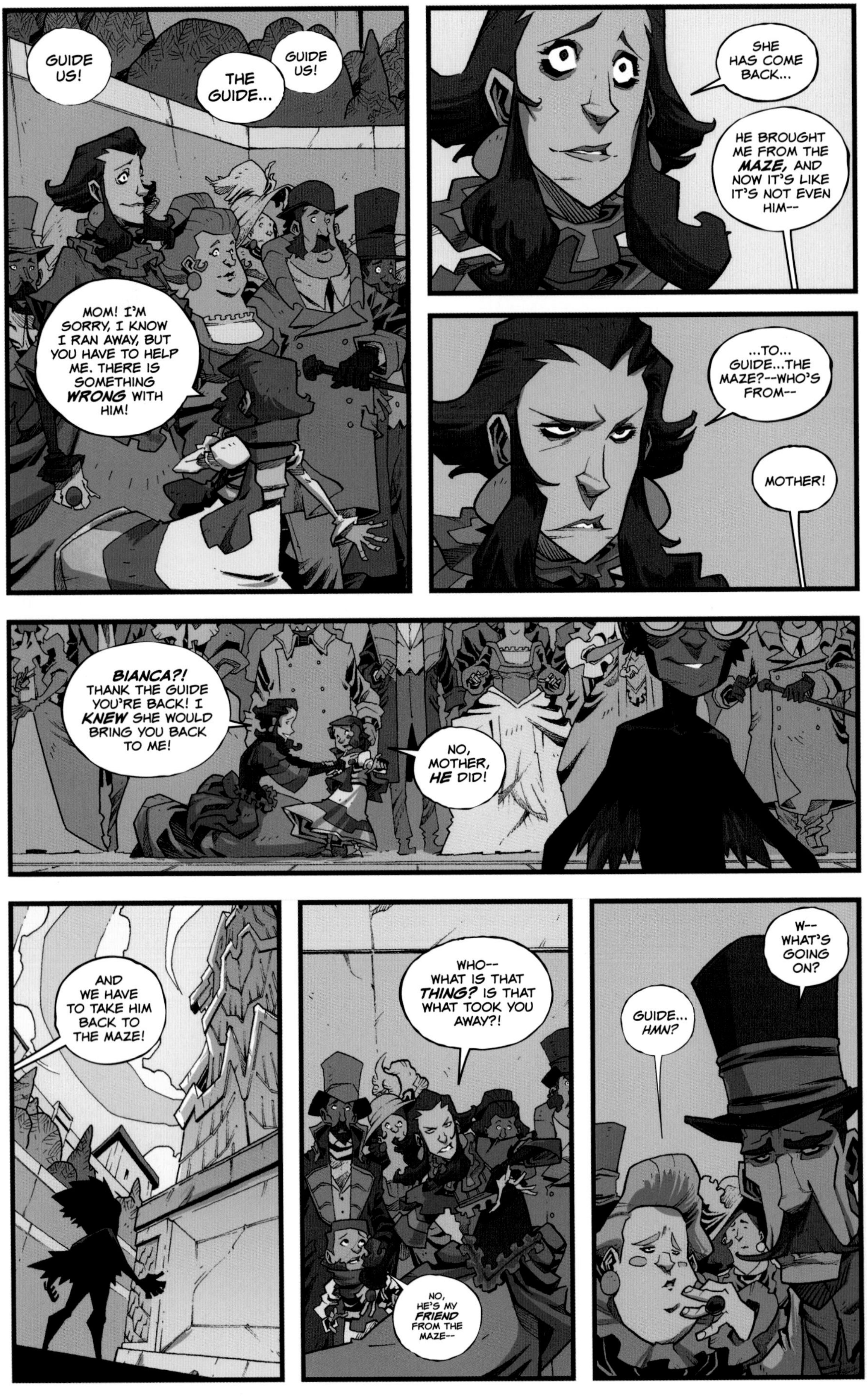
GUIDE US!
THE GUIDE...
GUIDE US!
MOM! I'M SORRY, I KNOW I RAN AWAY, BUT YOU HAVE TO HELP ME. THERE IS SOMETHING WRONG WITH HIM!
SHE HAS COME BACK...
HE BROUGHT ME FROM THE MAZE, AND NOW IT'S LIKE IT'S NOT EVEN HIM--
...TO... GUIDE...THE MAZE?--WHO'S FROM--
MOTHER!
BIANCA?! THANK THE GUIDE YOU'RE BACK! I KNEW SHE WOULD BRING YOU BACK TO ME!
NO, MOTHER, HE DID!
AND WE HAVE TO TAKE HIM BACK TO THE MAZE!
WHO-- WHAT IS THAT THING? IS THAT WHAT TOOK YOU AWAY?!
NO, HE'S MY FRIEND FROM THE MAZE--
W-- WHAT'S GOING ON?
GUIDE... HMN?

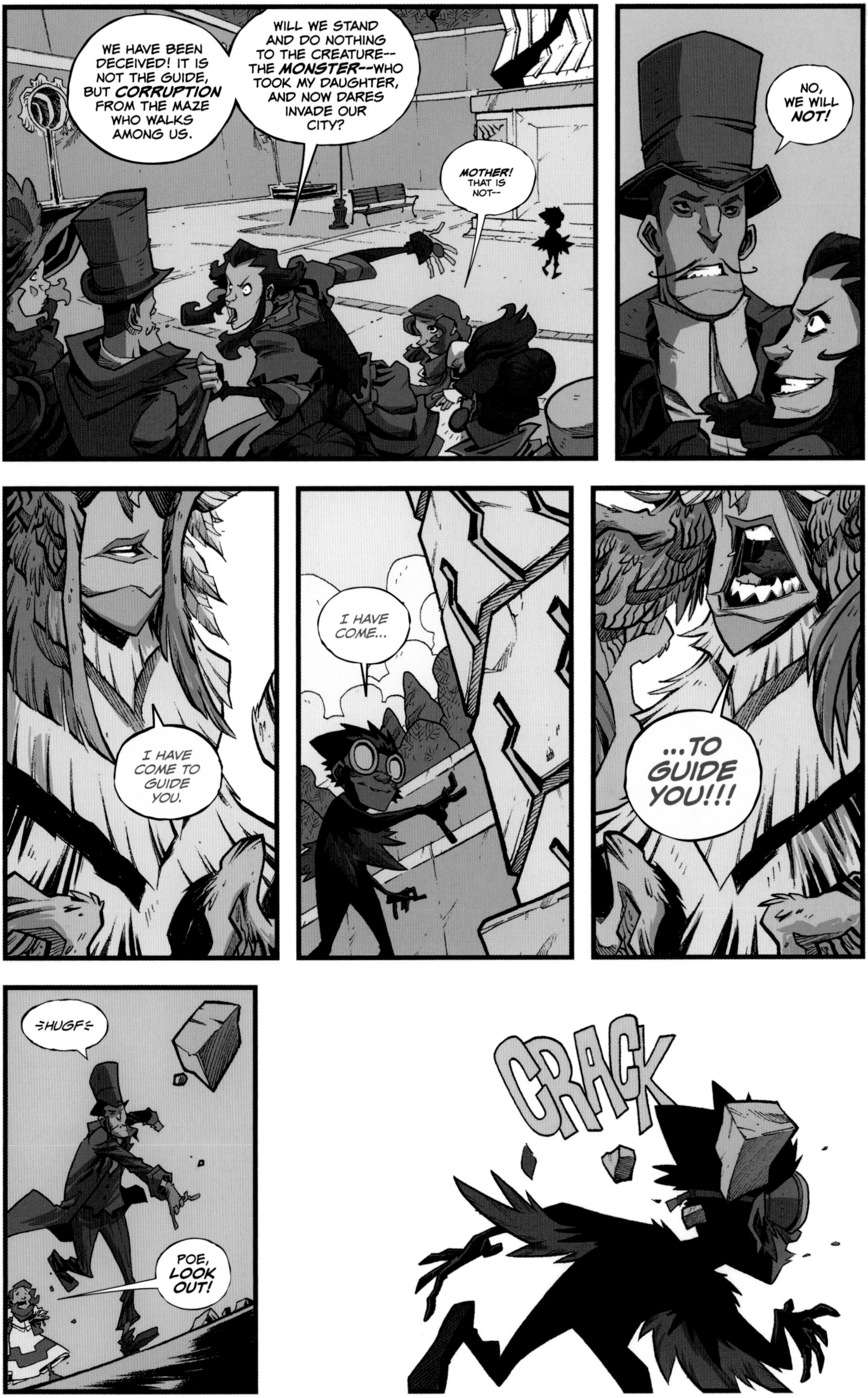
WE HAVE BEEN DECEIVED! IT IS NOT THE GUIDE, BUT CORRUPTION FROM THE MAZE WHO WALKS AMONG US.
WILL WE STAND AND DO NOTHING TO THE CREATURE-- THE MONSTER--WHO TOOK MY DAUGHTER, AND NOW DARES INVADE OUR CITY?
MOTHER! THAT IS NOT--
NO, WE WILL NOT!
I HAVE COME TO GUIDE YOU.
I HAVE COME...
...TO GUIDE YOU!!!
HUGF
POE, LOOK OUT!
CRACK

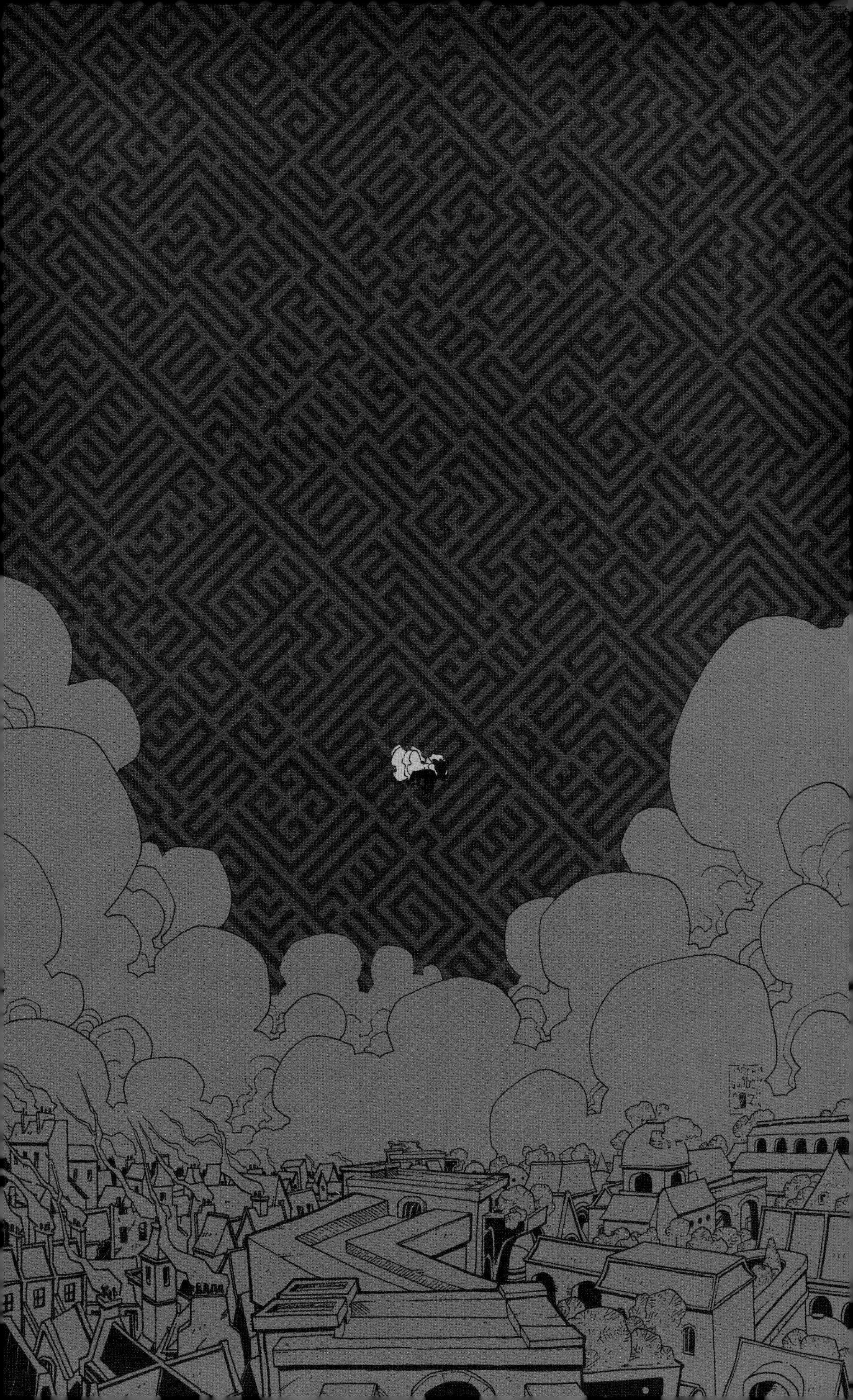

CHAPTER
FIVE

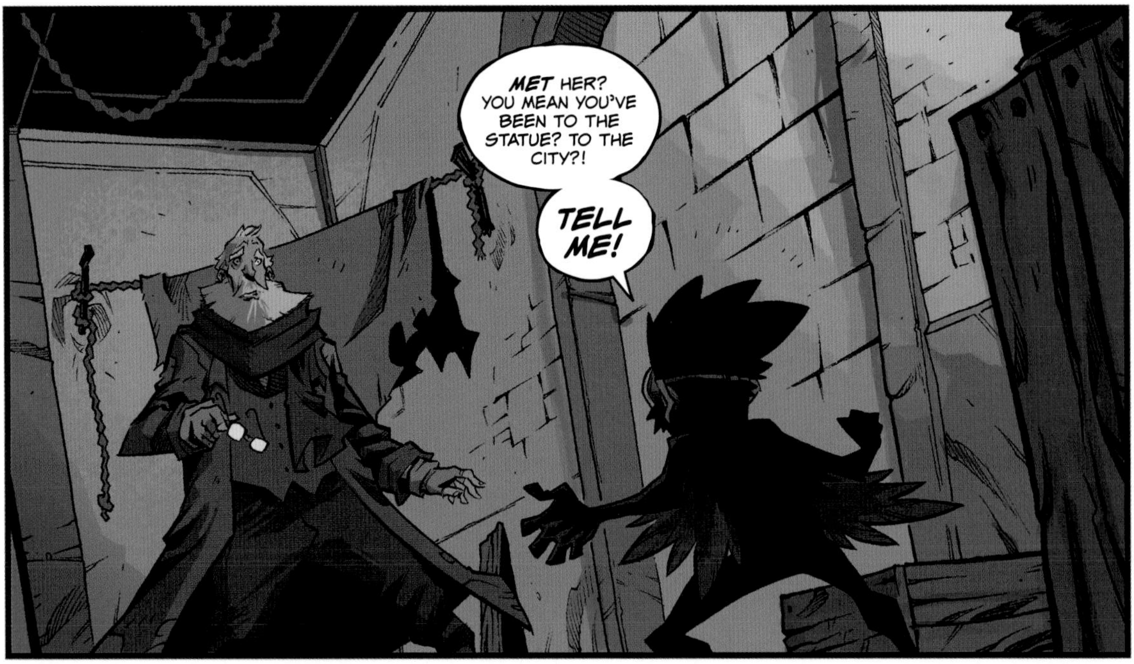
MET HER? YOU MEAN YOU'VE BEEN TO THE STATUE? TO THE CITY?!
TELL ME!

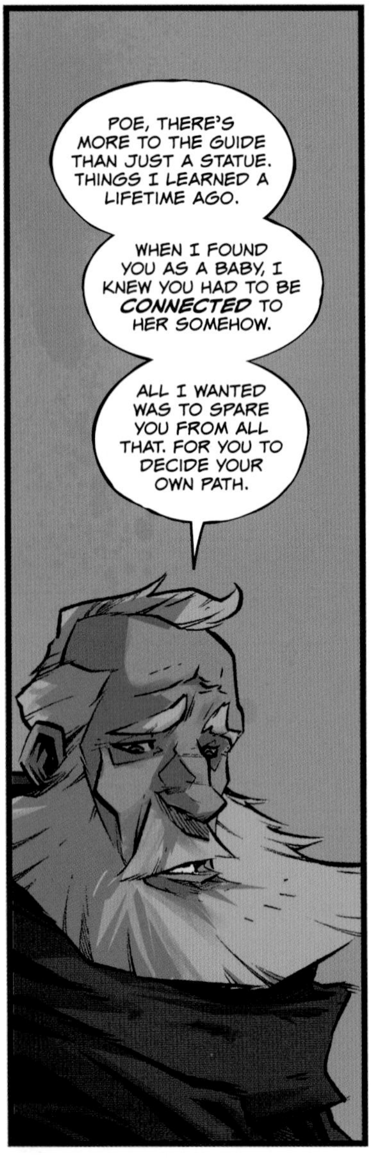
POE, THERE'S MORE TO THE GUIDE THAN JUST A STATUE. THINGS I LEARNED A LIFETIME AGO.
WHEN I FOUND YOU AS A BABY, I KNEW YOU HAD TO BE CONNECTED TO HER SOMEHOW.
ALL I WANTED WAS TO SPARE YOU FROM ALL THAT. FOR YOU TO DECIDE YOUR OWN PATH.

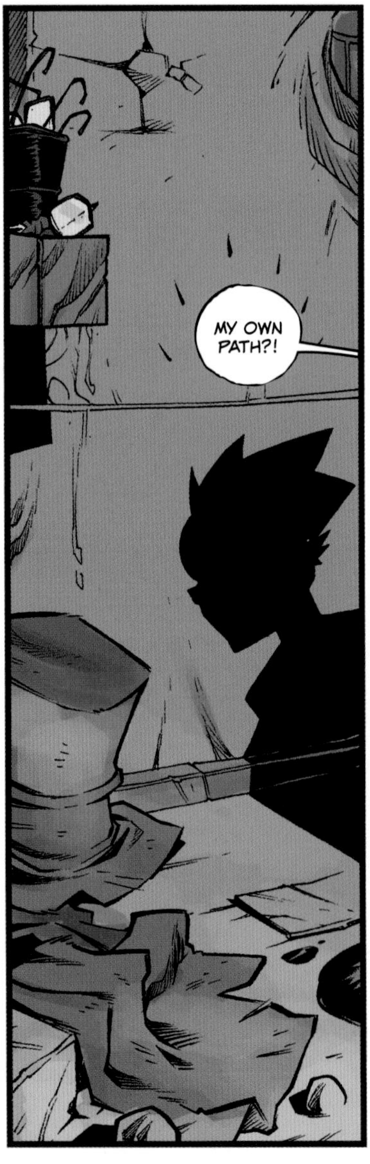
MY OWN PATH?!

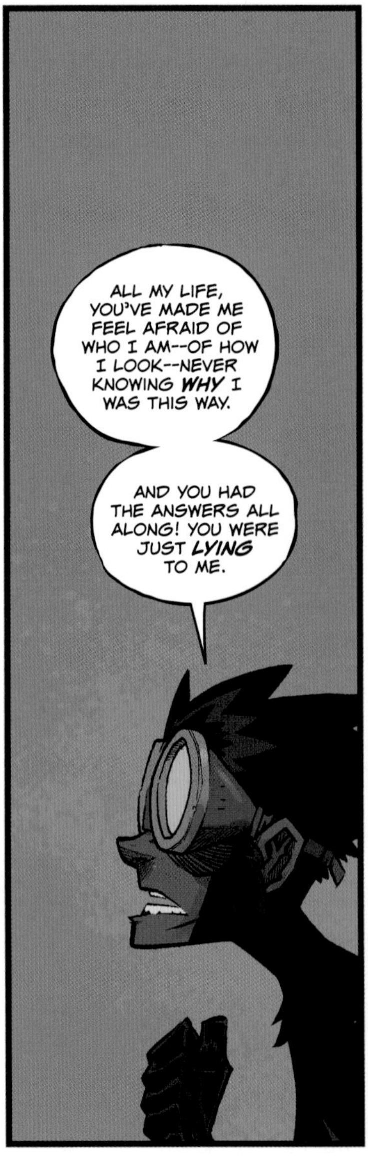
ALL MY LIFE, YOU'VE MADE ME FEEL AFRAID OF WHO I AM--OF HOW I LOOK--NEVER KNOWING WHY I WAS THIS WAY.
AND YOU HAD THE ANSWERS ALL ALONG! YOU WERE JUST LYING TO ME.

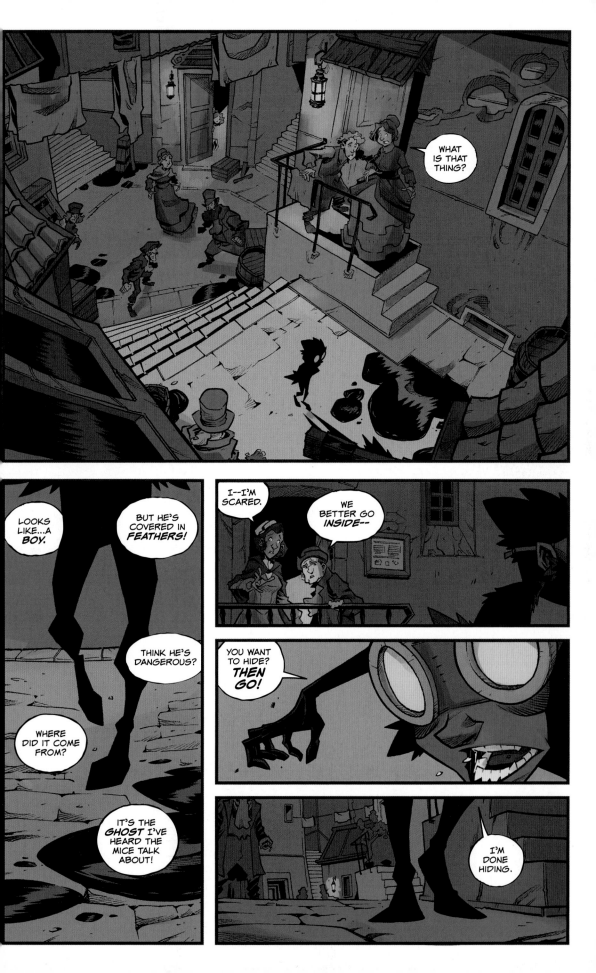

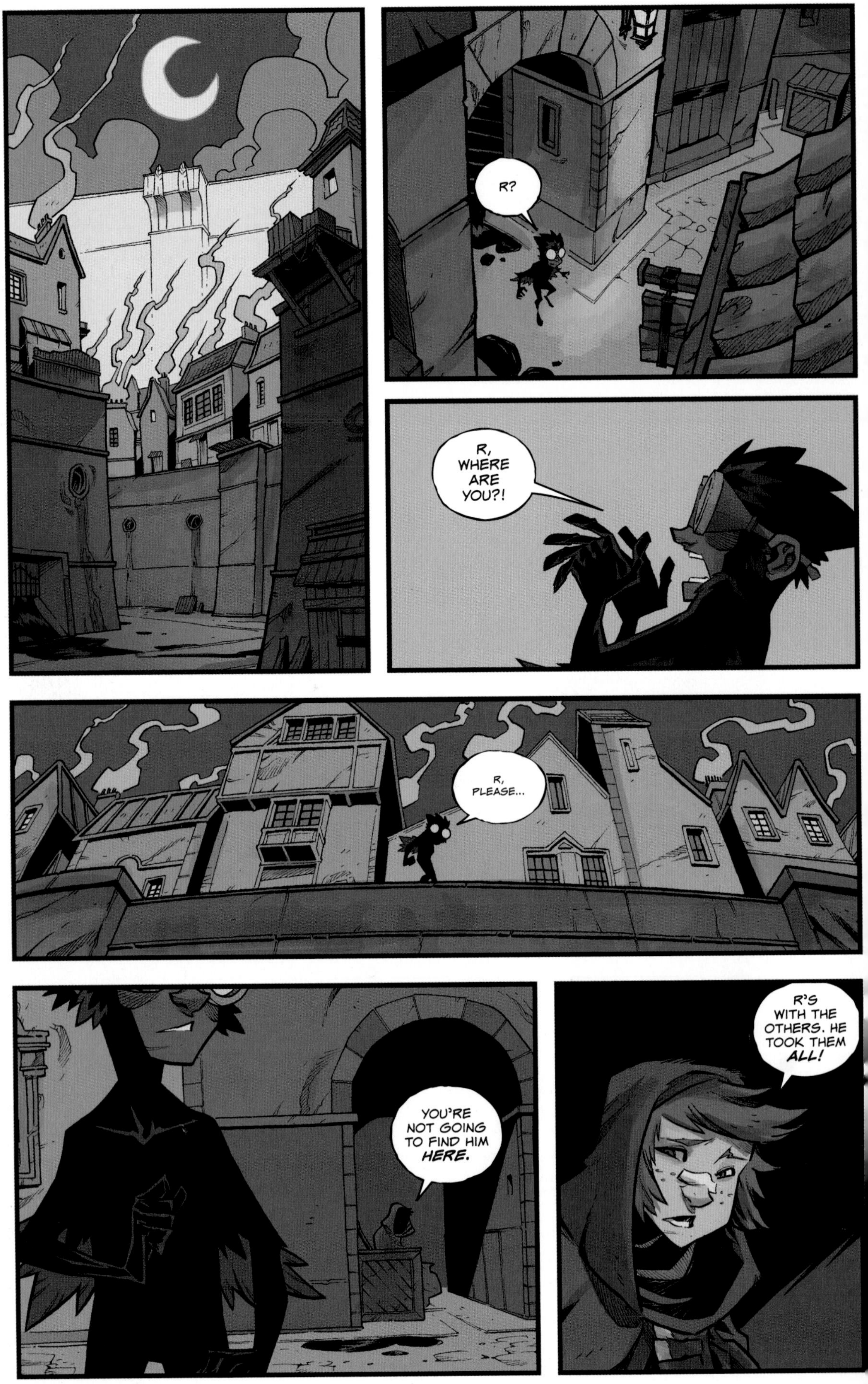
R?
R, WHERE ARE YOU?!
R, PLEASE...
YOU'RE NOT GOING TO FIND HIM HERE.
R'S WITH THE OTHERS. HE TOOK THEM ALL!

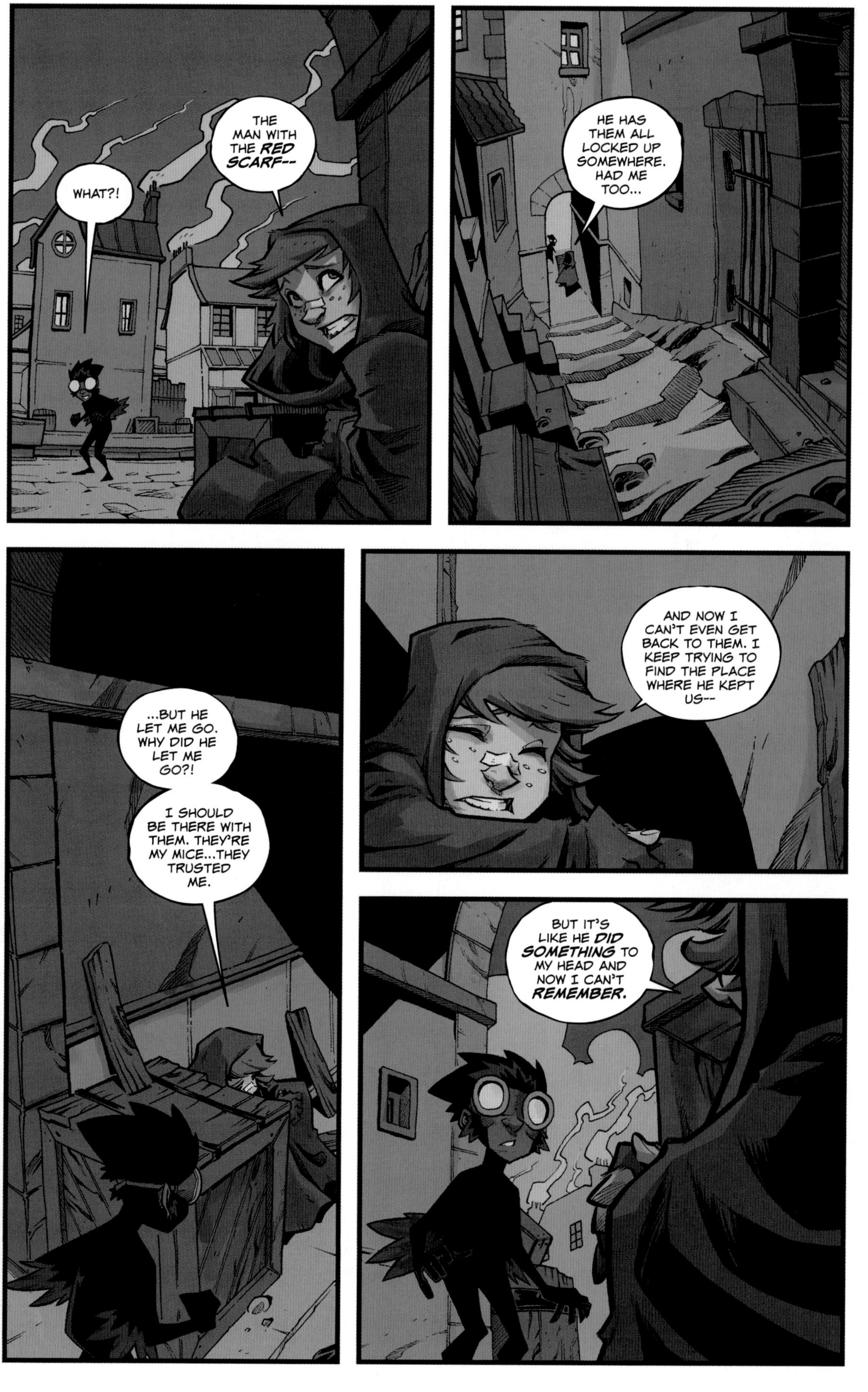
THE MAN WITH THE RED SCARF--
WHAT?!
HE HAS THEM ALL LOCKED UP SOMEWHERE. HAD ME TOO...
...BUT HE LET ME GO. WHY DID HE LET ME GO?!
I SHOULD BE THERE WITH THEM. THEY'RE MY MICE...THEY TRUSTED ME.
AND NOW I CAN'T EVEN GET BACK TO THEM. I KEEP TRYING TO FIND THE PLACE WHERE HE KEPT US--
BUT IT'S LIKE HE DID SOMETHING TO MY HEAD AND NOW I CAN'T REMEMBER.

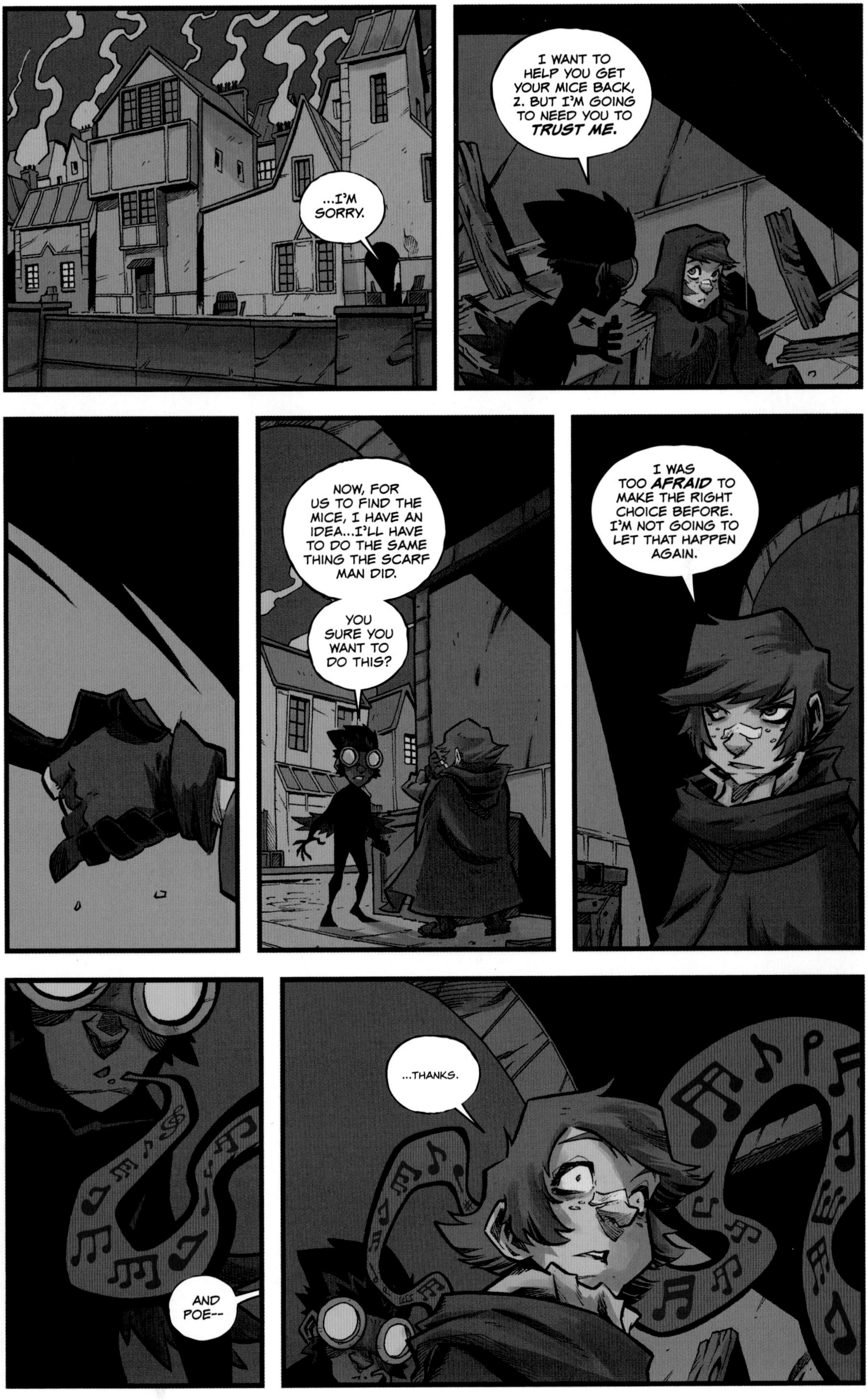
...I'M SORRY.
I WANT TO HELP YOU GET YOUR MICE BACK, Z. BUT I'M GOING TO NEED YOU TO TRUST ME.
NOW, FOR US TO FIND THE MICE, I HAVE AN IDEA...I'LL HAVE TO DO THE SAME THING THE SCARF MAN DID.
YOU SURE YOU WANT TO DO THIS?
I WAS TOO AFRAID TO MAKE THE RIGHT CHOICE BEFORE. I'M NOT GOING TO LET THAT HAPPEN AGAIN.
AND POE--
...THANKS.

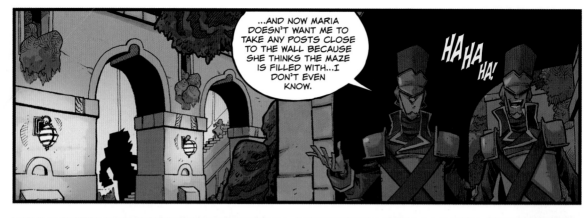

...AND NOW MARIA DOESN'T WANT ME TO TAKE ANY POSTS CLOSE TO THE WALL BECAUSE SHE THINKS THE MAZE IS FILLED WITH...I DON'T EVEN KNOW.

HA HA HA!

⸗HUMPH⸗ HOW DID YOU GET THROUGH THESE?

BIANCA--

WHAT DO YOU THINK YOU'RE DOING?

FATHER!

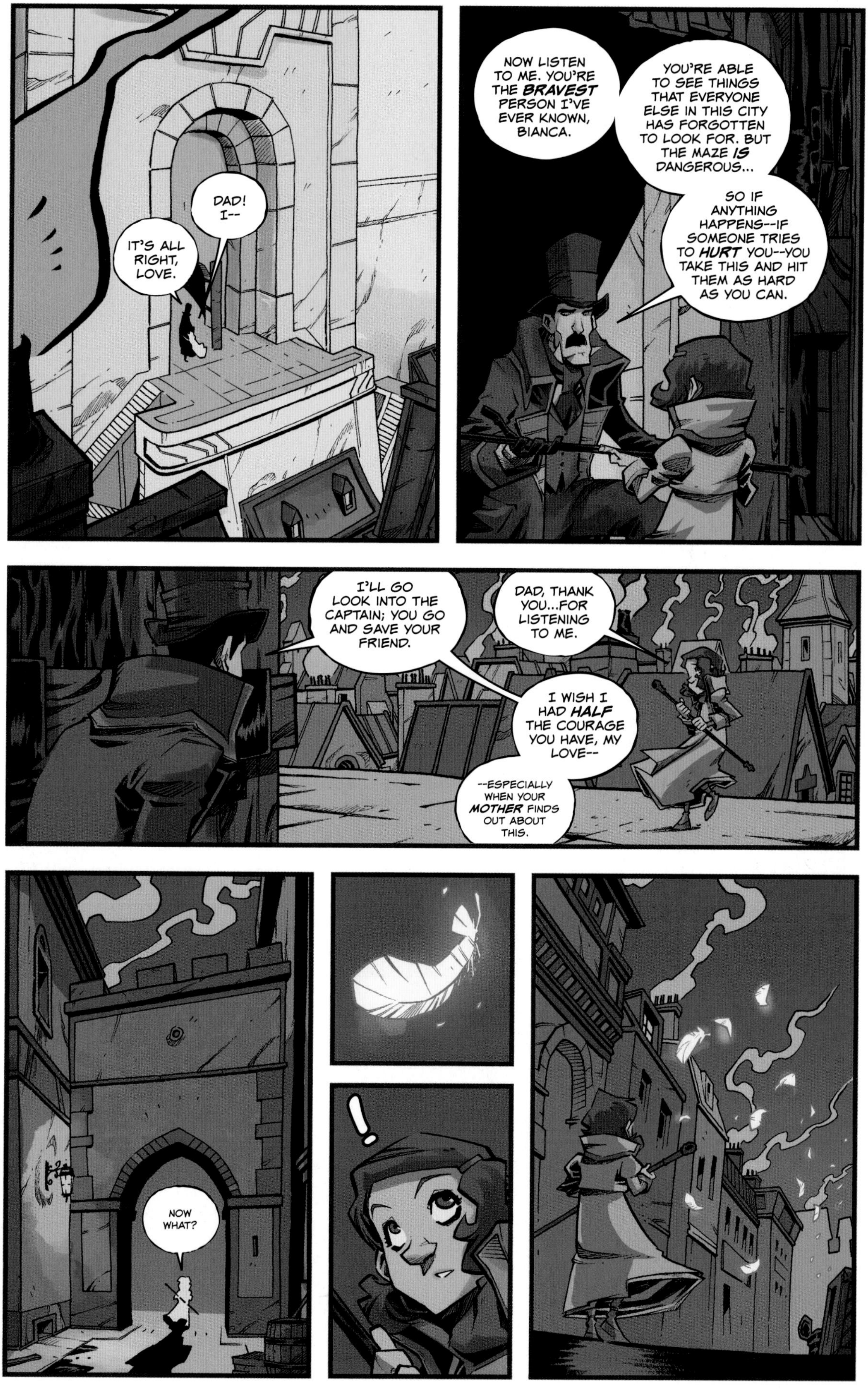
DAD! I--
IT'S ALL RIGHT, LOVE.
NOW LISTEN TO ME. YOU'RE THE BRAVEST PERSON I'VE EVER KNOWN, BIANCA.
YOU'RE ABLE TO SEE THINGS THAT EVERYONE ELSE IN THIS CITY HAS FORGOTTEN TO LOOK FOR. BUT THE MAZE IS DANGEROUS...
SO IF ANYTHING HAPPENS--IF SOMEONE TRIES TO HURT YOU--YOU TAKE THIS AND HIT THEM AS HARD AS YOU CAN.
I'LL GO LOOK INTO THE CAPTAIN; YOU GO AND SAVE YOUR FRIEND.
DAD, THANK YOU...FOR LISTENING TO ME.
I WISH I HAD HALF THE COURAGE YOU HAVE, MY LOVE--
--ESPECIALLY WHEN YOUR MOTHER FINDS OUT ABOUT THIS.
NOW WHAT?
!

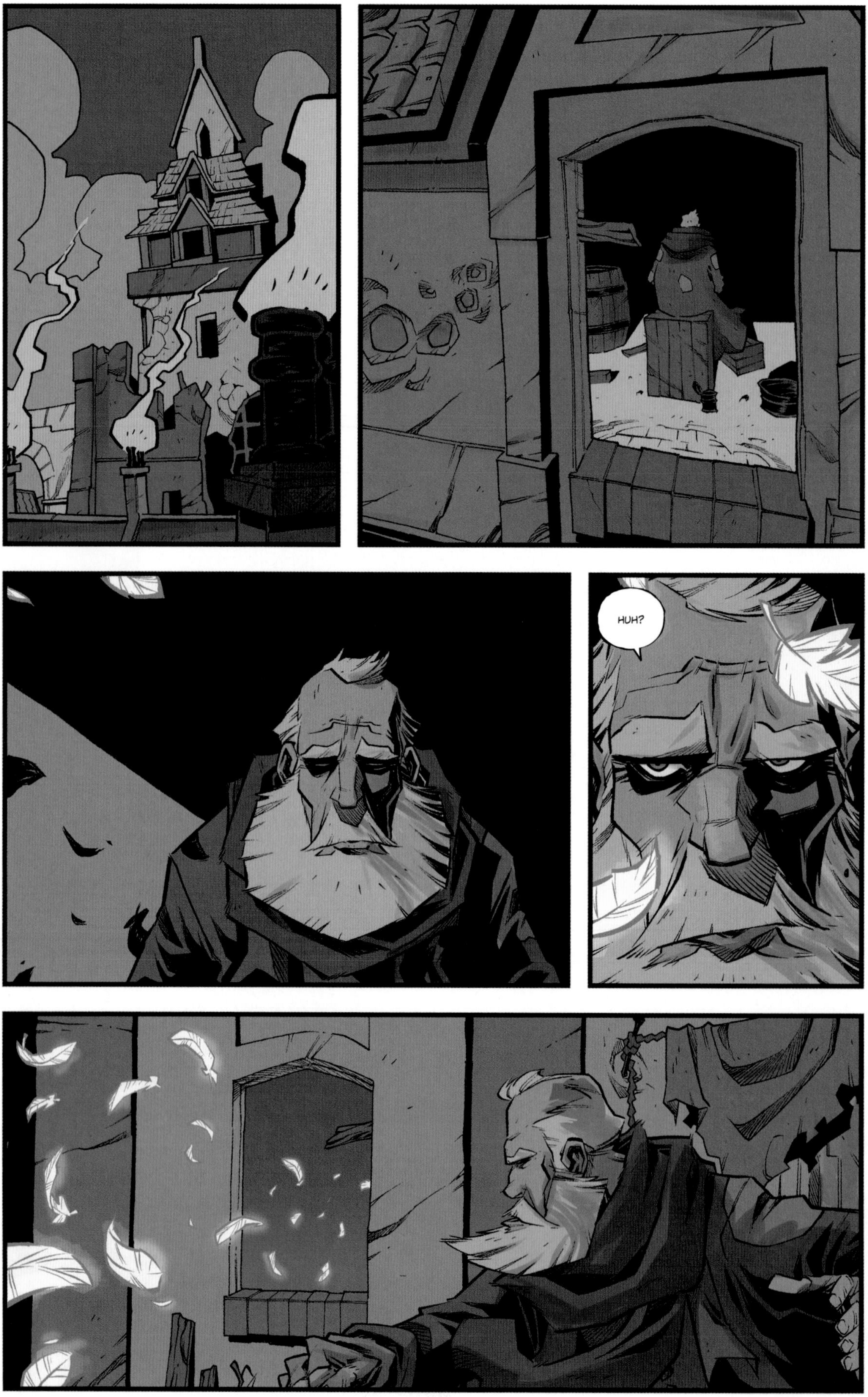
HUH?

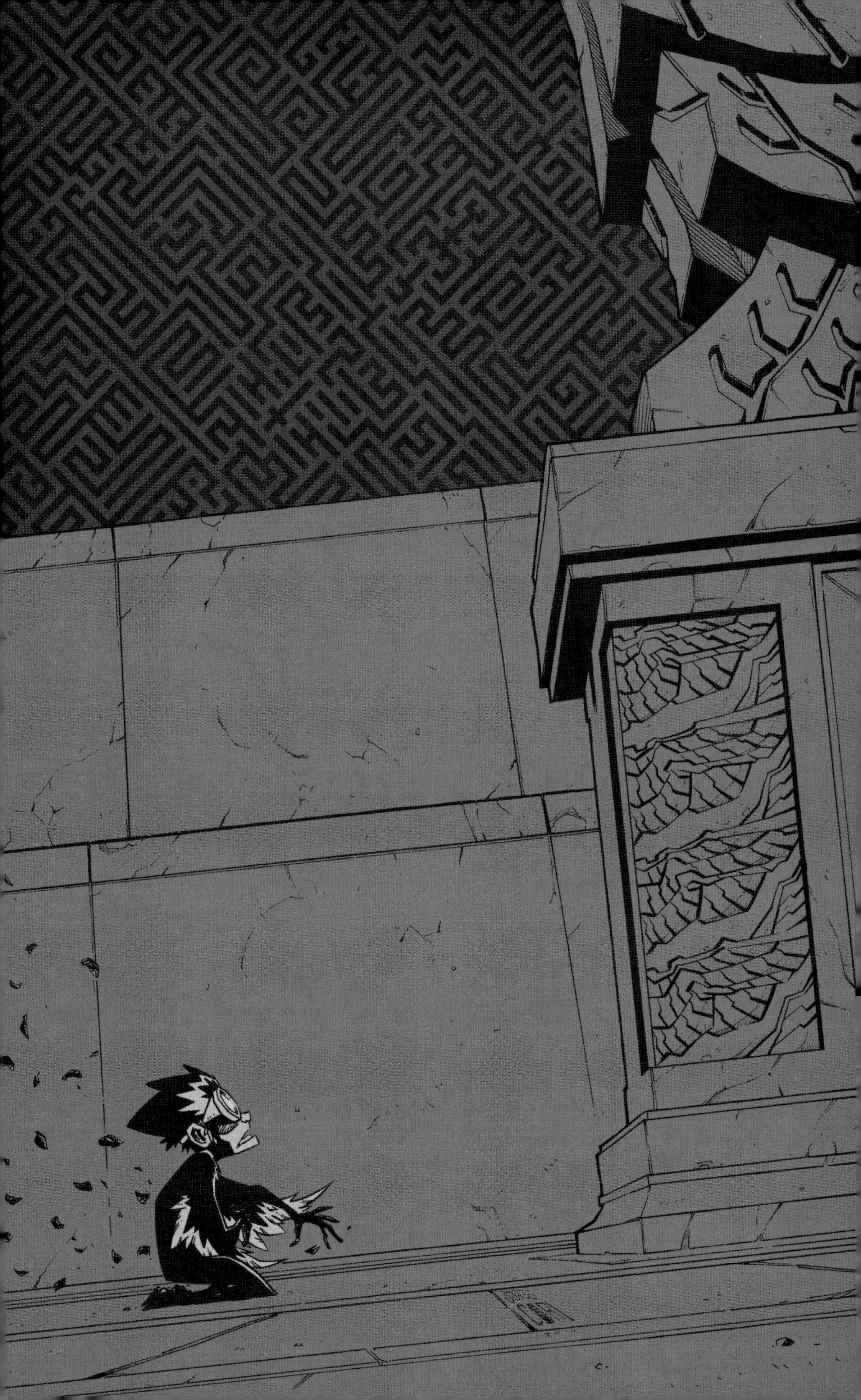

CHAPTER
SIX

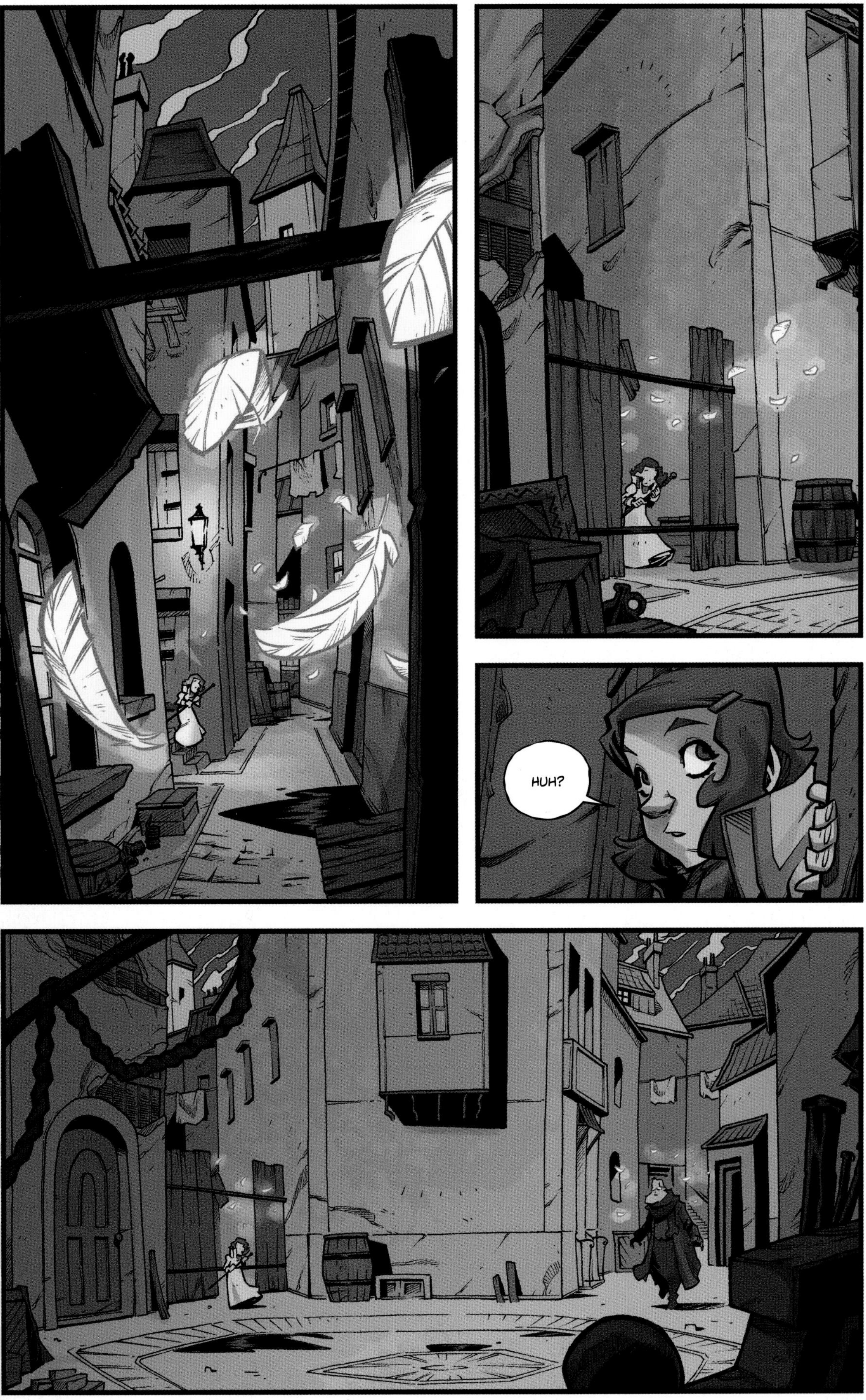
HUH?

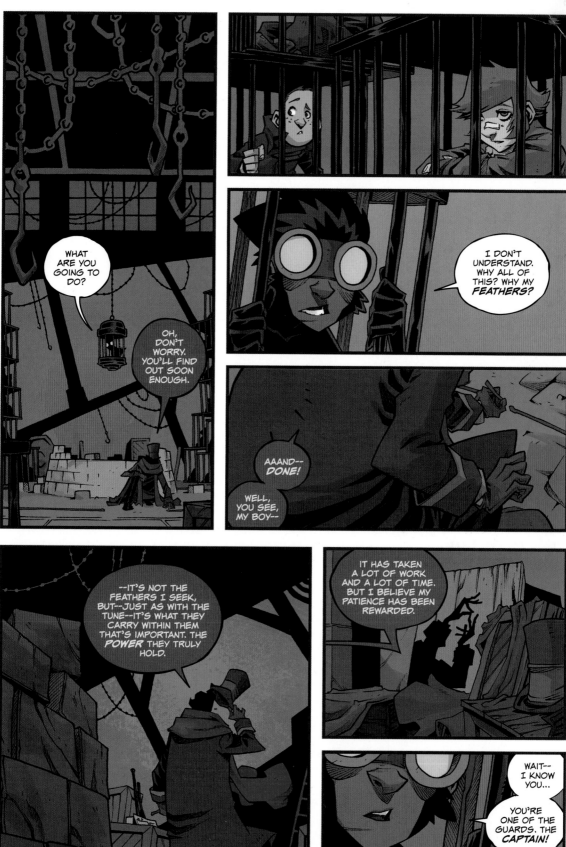

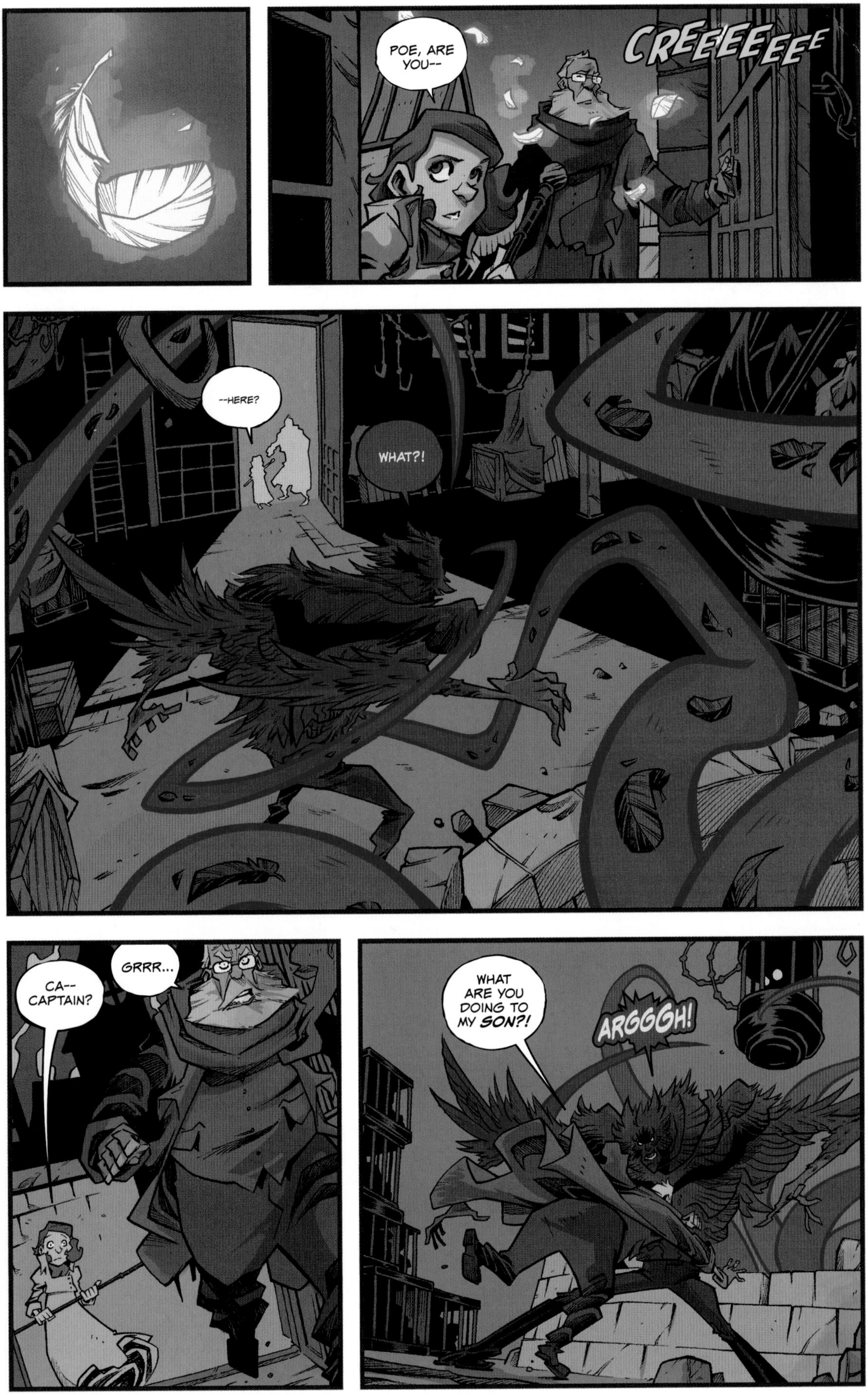
POE, ARE YOU--
CREEEEEEE
--HERE?
WHAT?!
CA-- CAPTAIN?
GRRR...
WHAT ARE YOU DOING TO MY SON?!
ARGGGH!

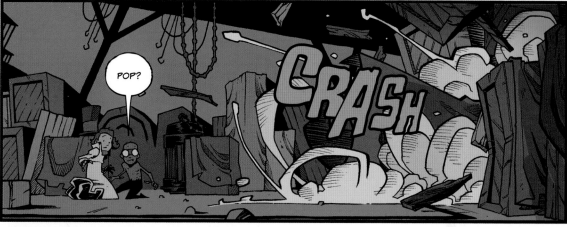

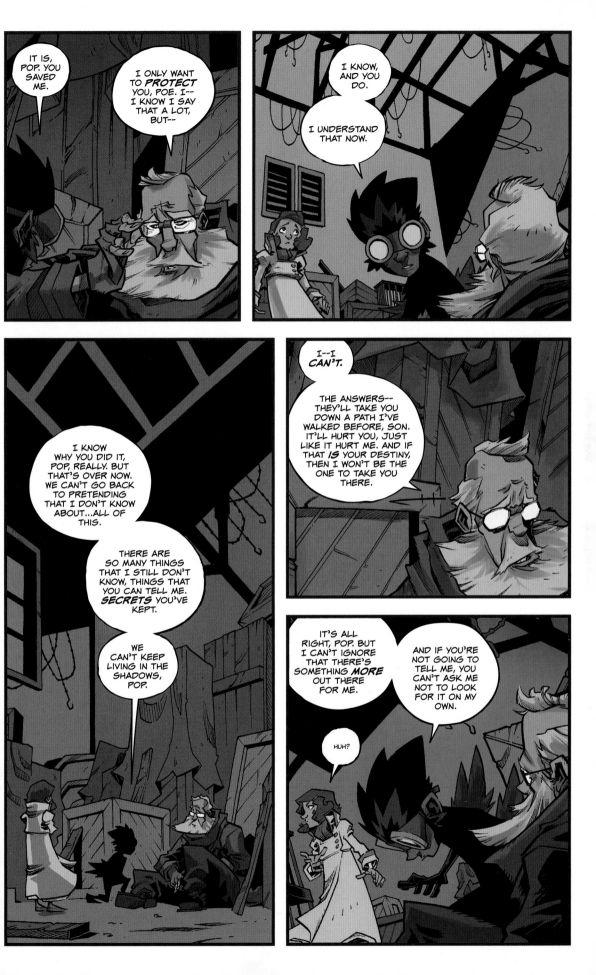

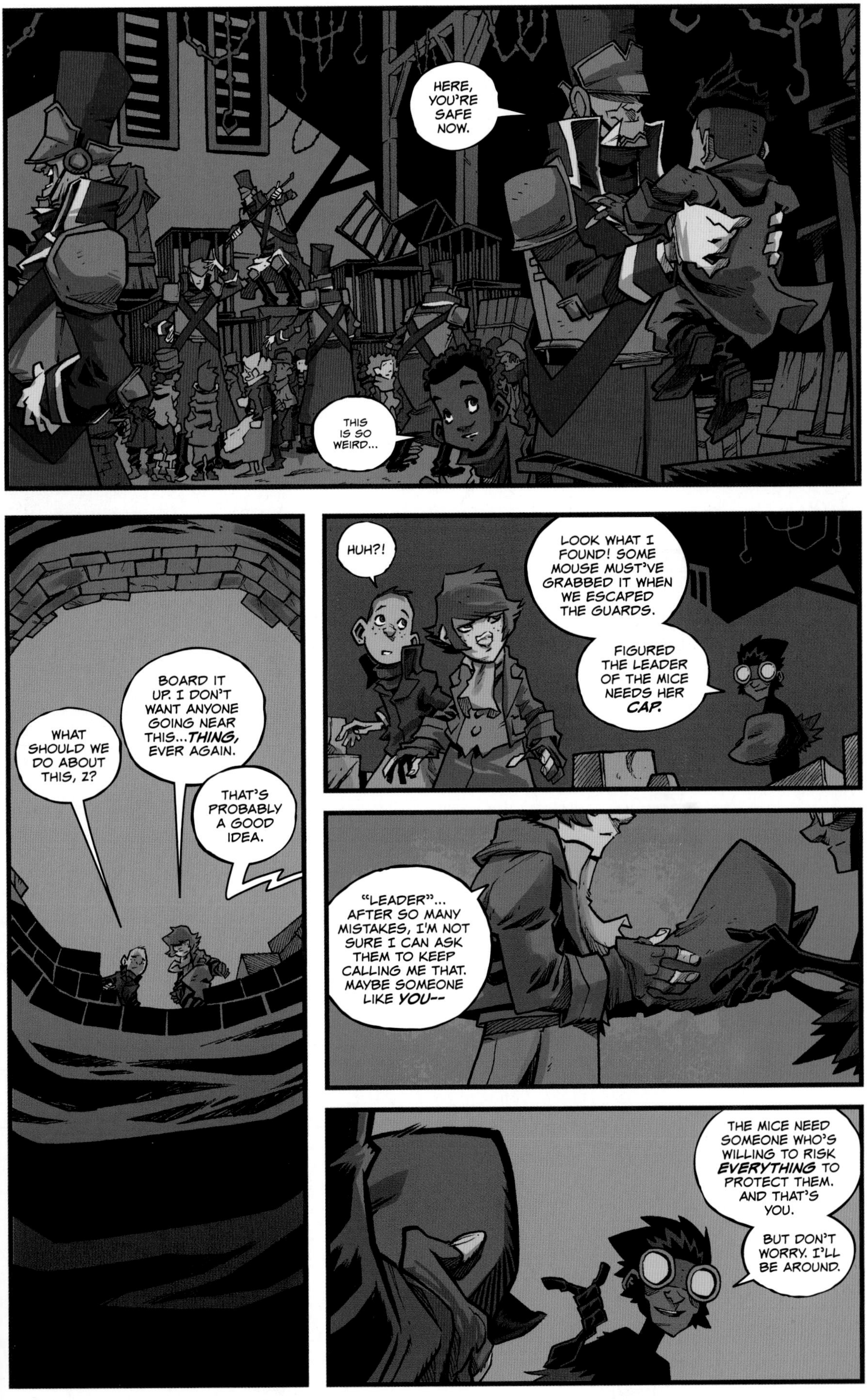
HERE, YOU'RE SAFE NOW.
THIS IS SO WEIRD...
WHAT SHOULD WE DO ABOUT THIS, Z?
BOARD IT UP. I DON'T WANT ANYONE GOING NEAR THIS...THING, EVER AGAIN.
THAT'S PROBABLY A GOOD IDEA.
HUH?!
LOOK WHAT I FOUND! SOME MOUSE MUST'VE GRABBED IT WHEN WE ESCAPED THE GUARDS.
FIGURED THE LEADER OF THE MICE NEEDS HER CAP.
"LEADER"... AFTER SO MANY MISTAKES, I'M NOT SURE I CAN ASK THEM TO KEEP CALLING ME THAT. MAYBE SOMEONE LIKE YOU--
THE MICE NEED SOMEONE WHO'S WILLING TO RISK EVERYTHING TO PROTECT THEM. AND THAT'S YOU.
BUT DON'T WORRY. I'LL BE AROUND.

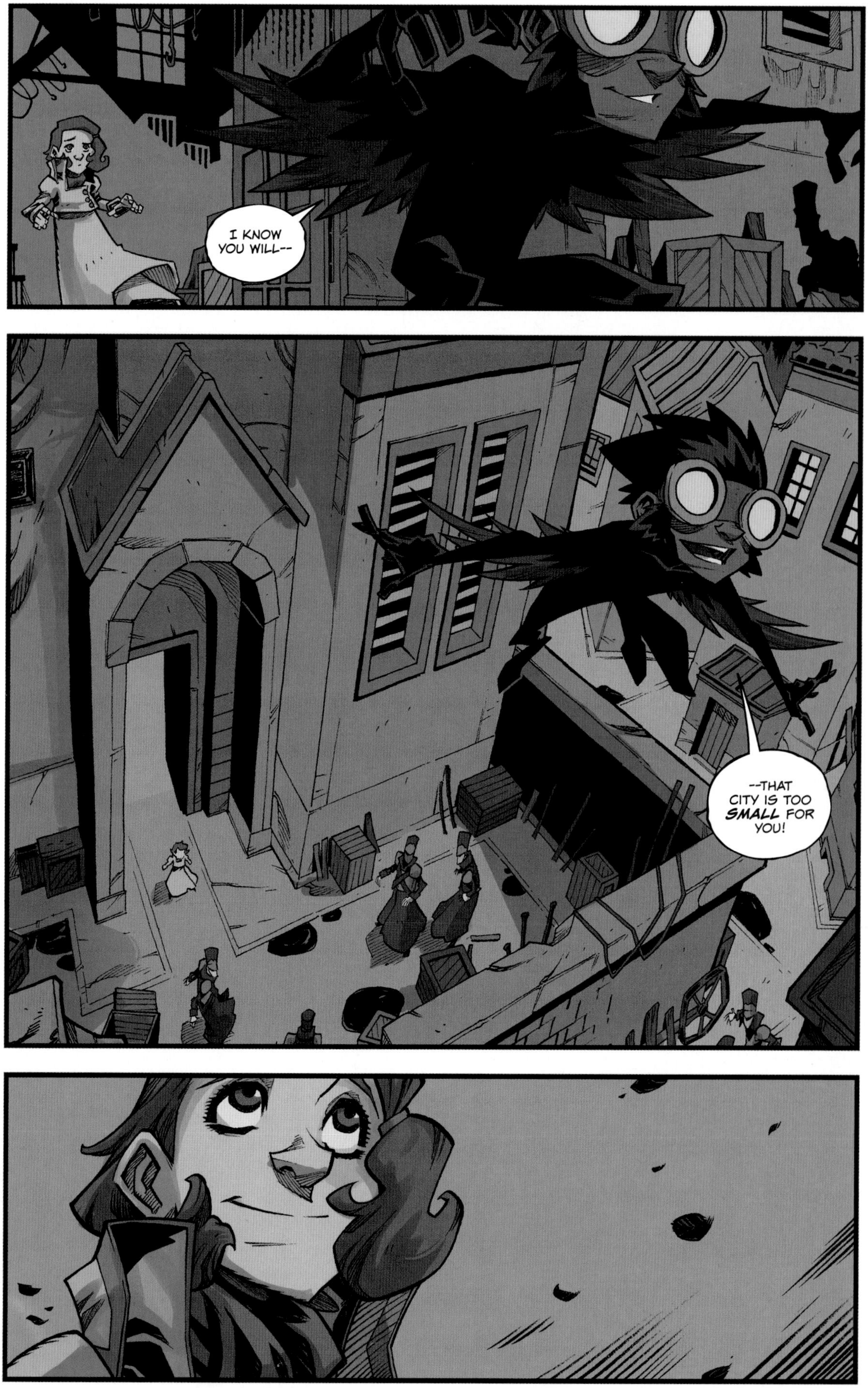
I KNOW YOU WILL--
--THAT CITY IS TOO SMALL FOR YOU!

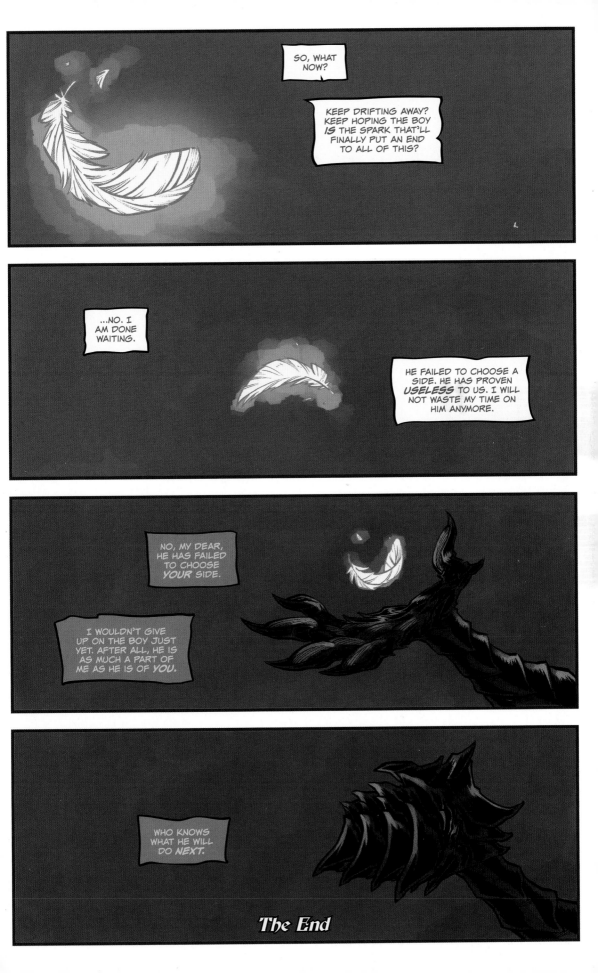

COVER
GALLERY

ISSUE ONE COVER
JORGE CORONA

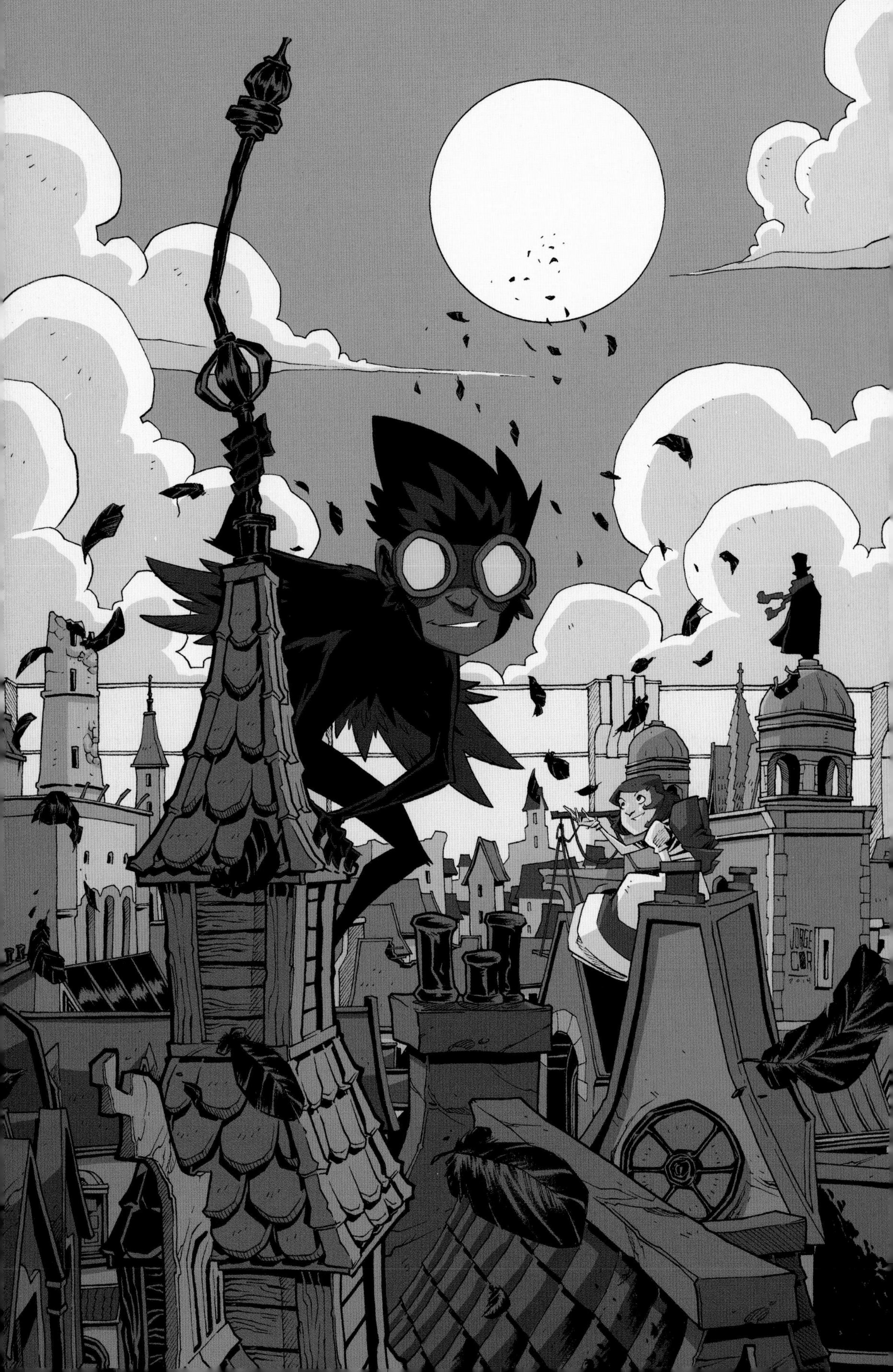

ISSUE ONE BOOM! TEN YEARS VARIANT COVER
RAMÓN K. PÉREZ

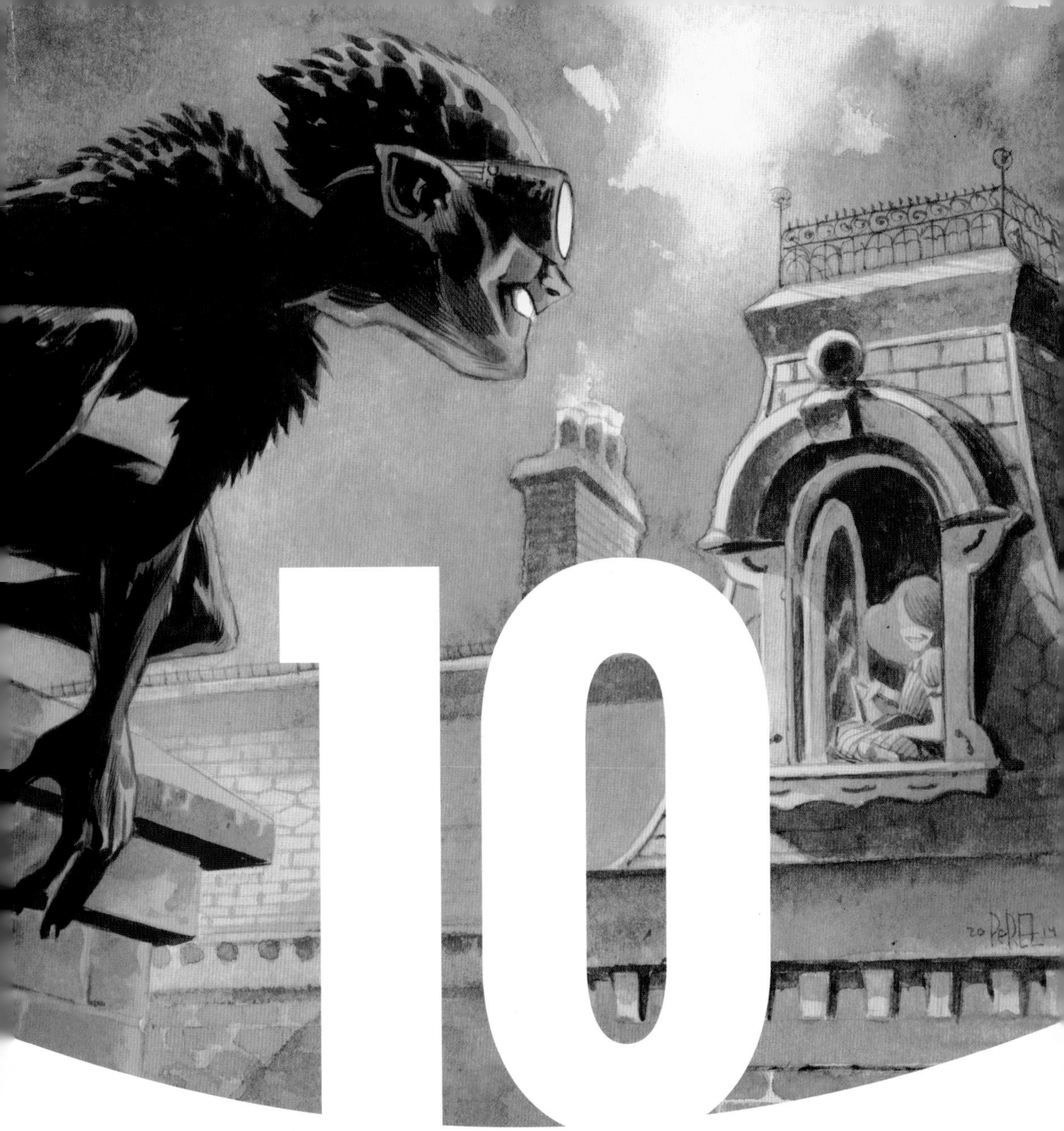

10

ISSUE ONE VARIANT COVER

KEN NIIMURA

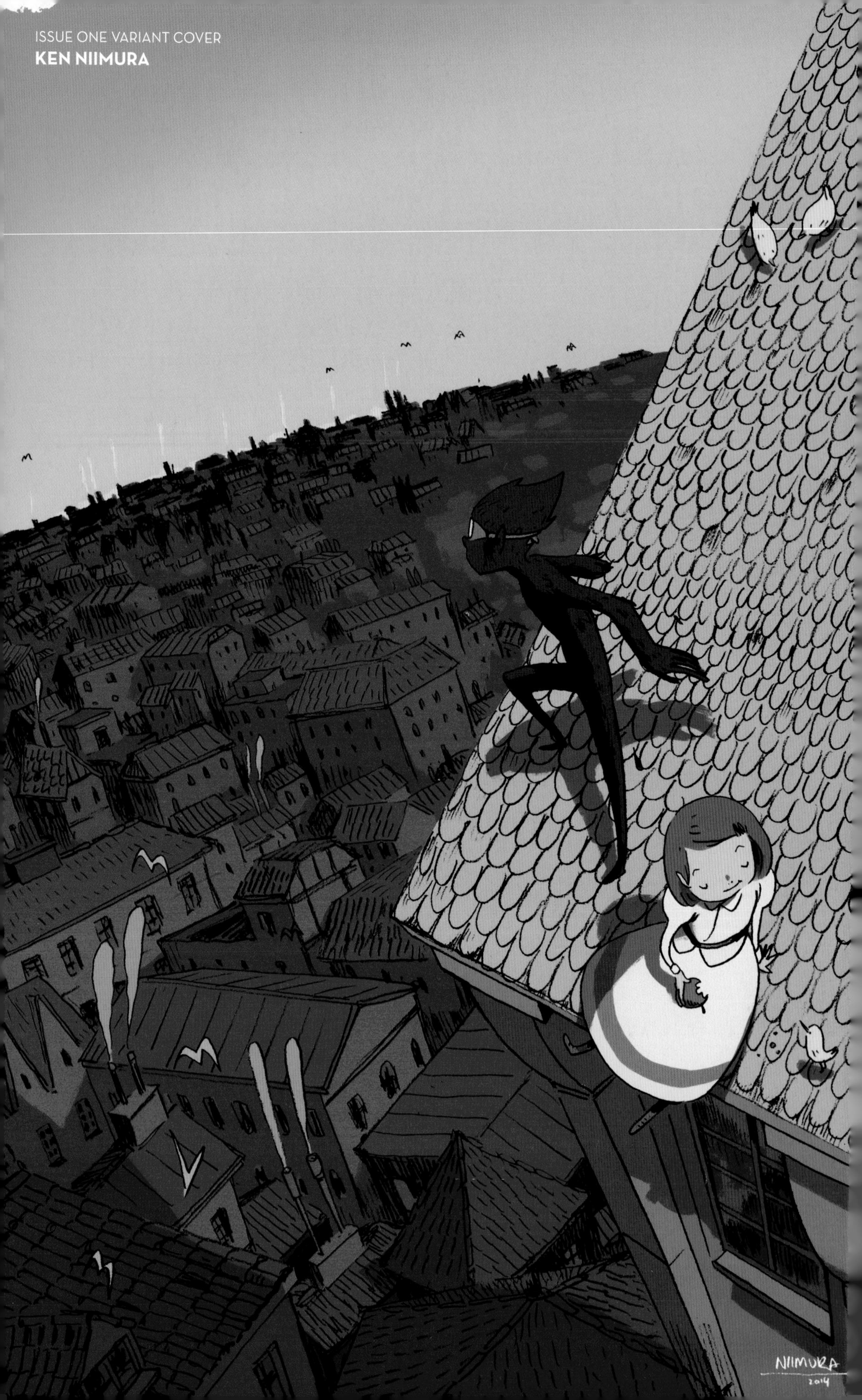

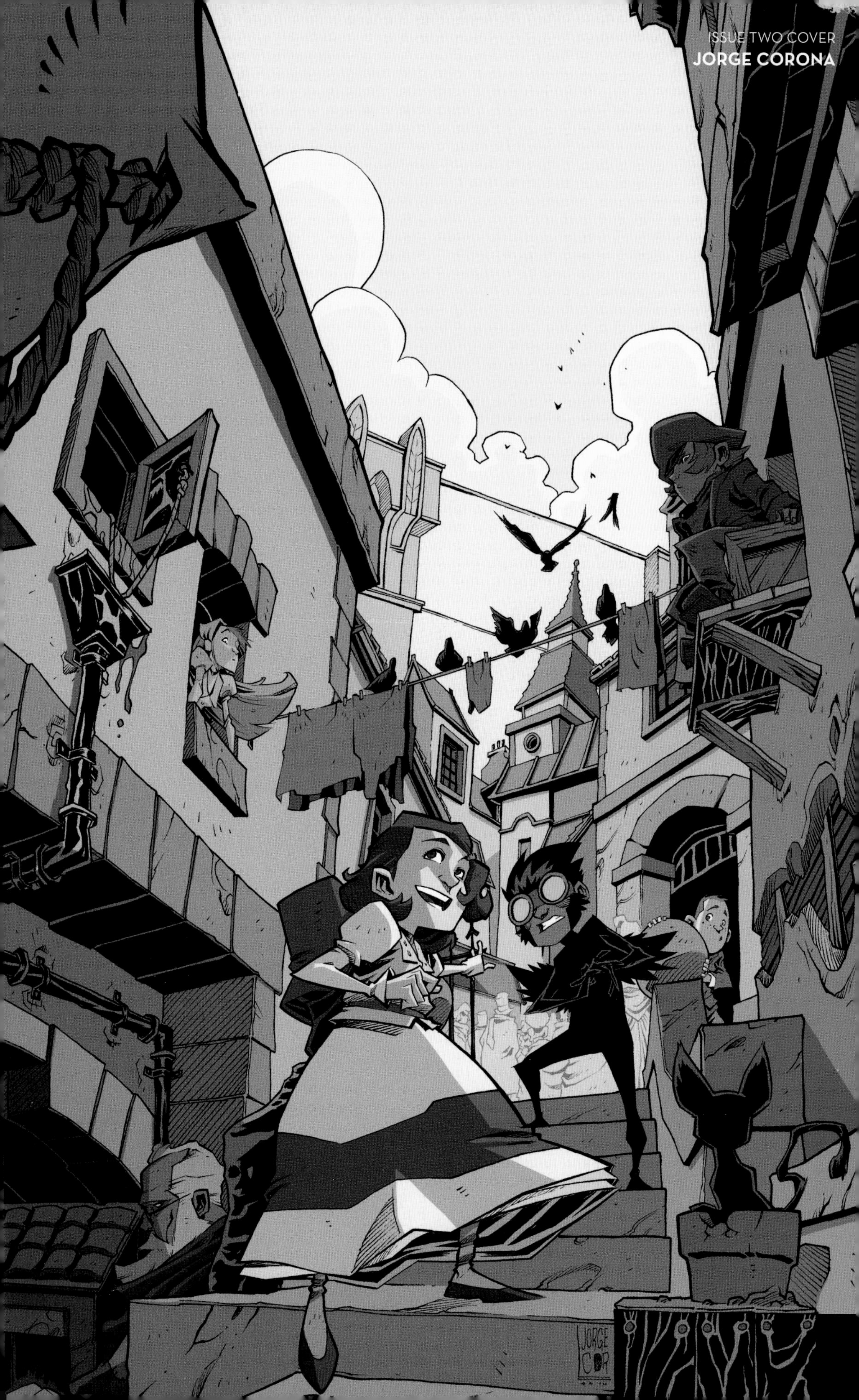
JORGE
COR

ISSUE TWO COVER
JORGE CORONA

ISSUE THREE COVER
JORGE CORONA

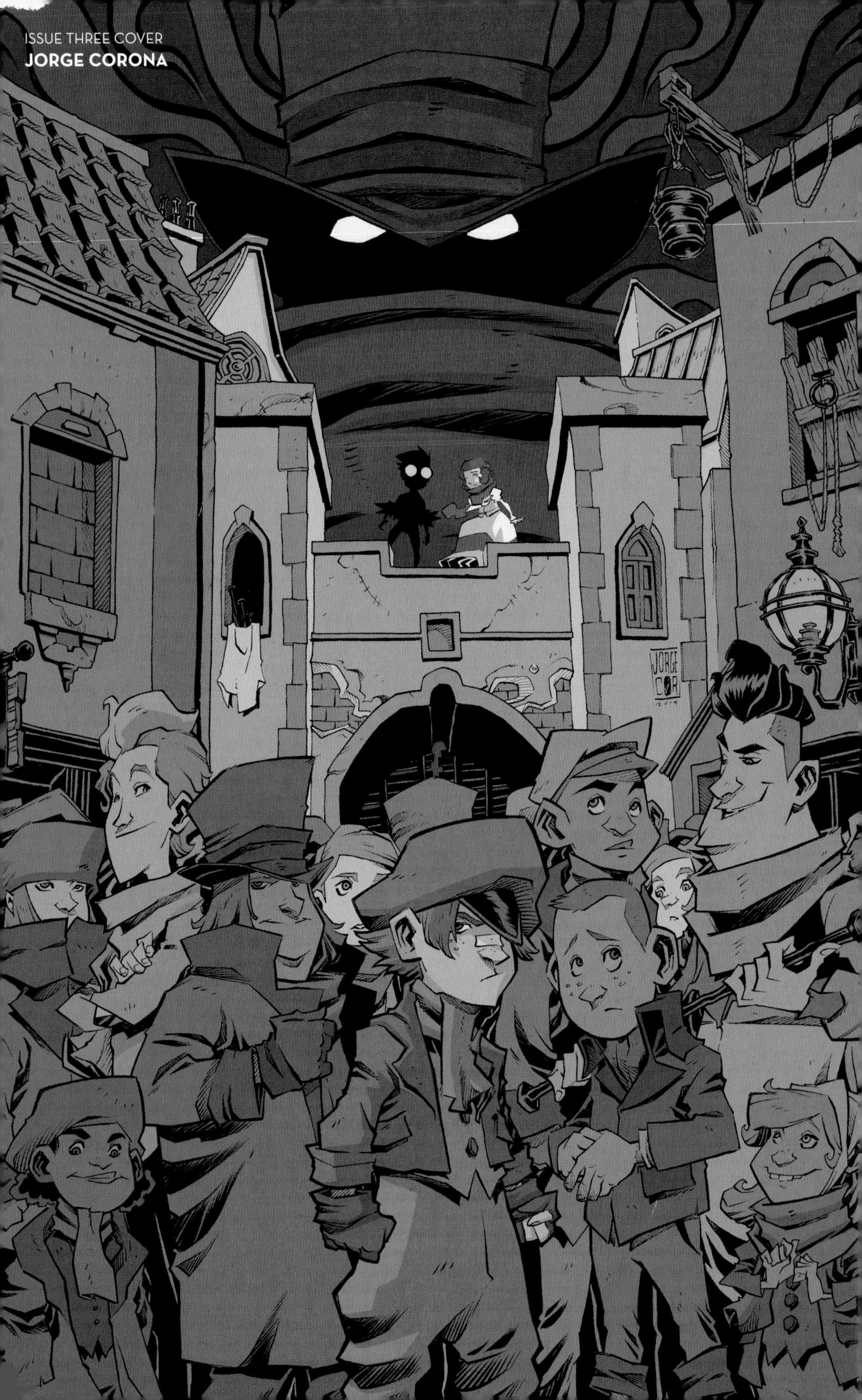

ISSUE FOUR COVER
JORGE CORONA

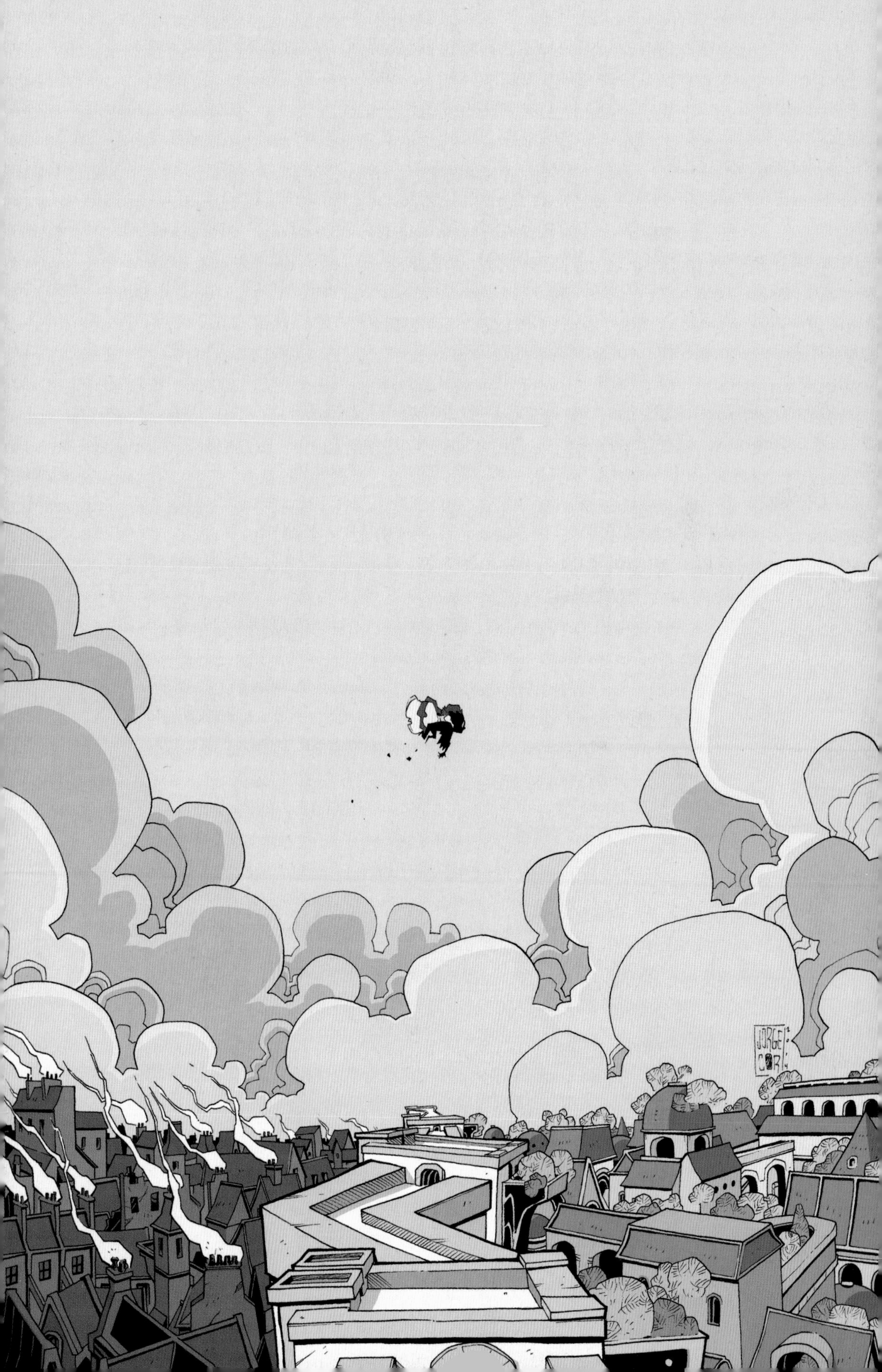

CREATING FEATHERS™

WITH SKETCHES & COMMENTARY
BY **JORGE CORONA**

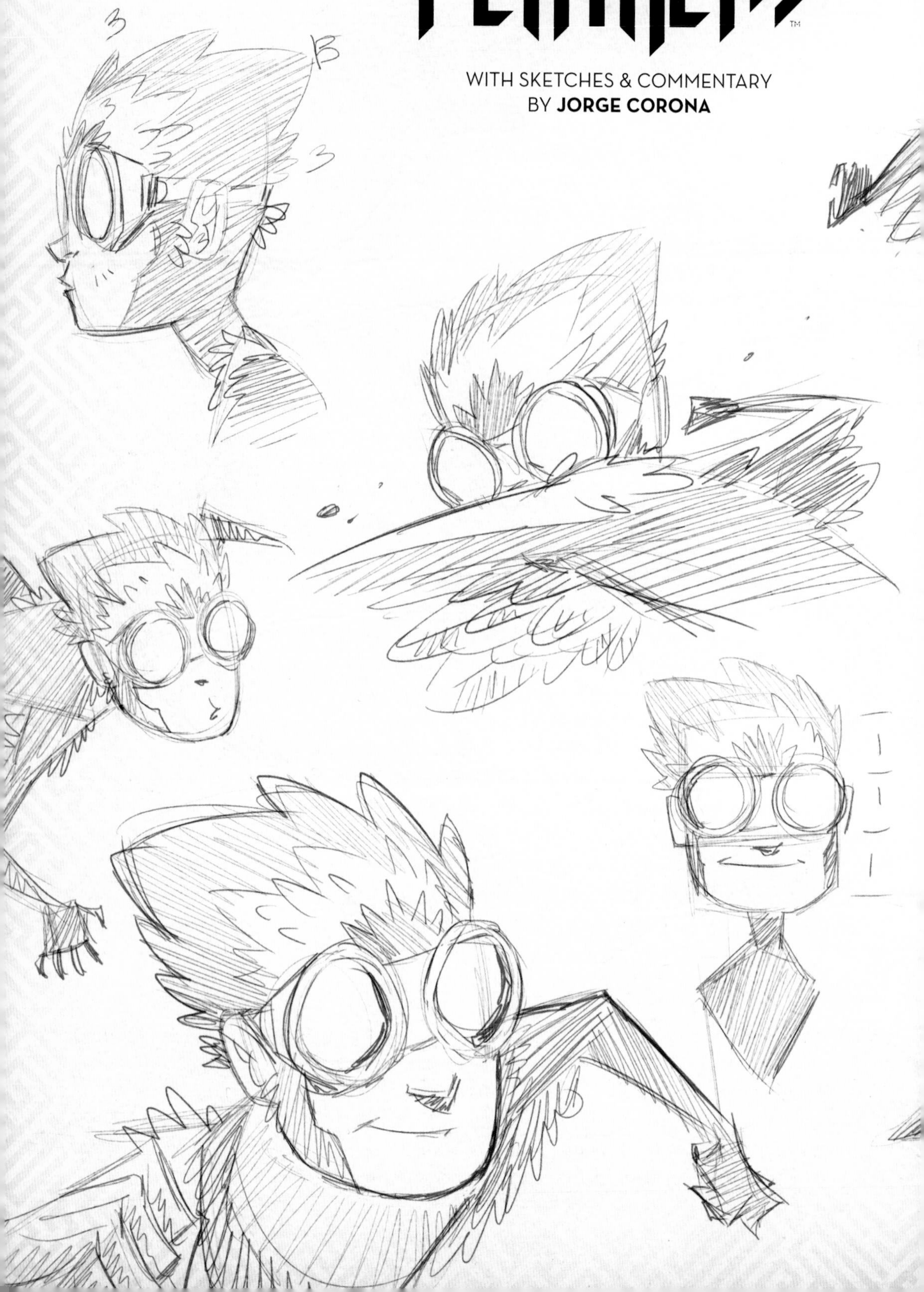

POE

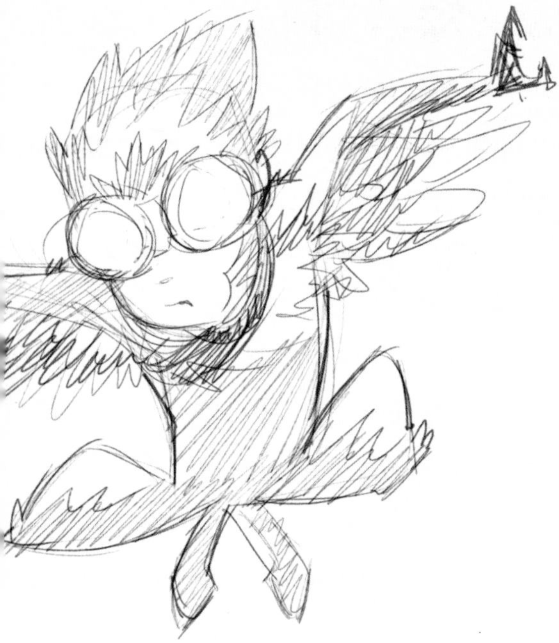

One of the hardest and most important things when first working on the idea for *Feathers* was finding the right voice and design for Poe. It was clear to me since the beginning that I wanted Poe to remain a shadow, a simple silhouette; coming up with it proved harder than expected.

"A boy covered in feathers." That was Poe's description from the get-go, but the first problem I encountered was to determine how different he would actually be from a "regular" boy. Was he a bird? Did he have a beak? Was it just a skin condition? The only thing I knew for sure was that I wanted something to break the silhouette, and that I really didn't like Poe's human face. The goggles were the solution to all that.

There was a lot of exploration into different aesthetics. Some rendered too cartoony, parting from what I wanted the mood of the book to be, other directions were more stylized, going for a more distinctive graphic approach. The thing about feathers (actual feathers, not the title of the book) is that they can be rendered very organically, but also very synthetic and finding that sweet spot in the middle took searching far in both directions.

At the end, it was almost taken down to a formula, one that I could play with so that the silhouette was constant but also allowed some room to bring an organic feel to it.

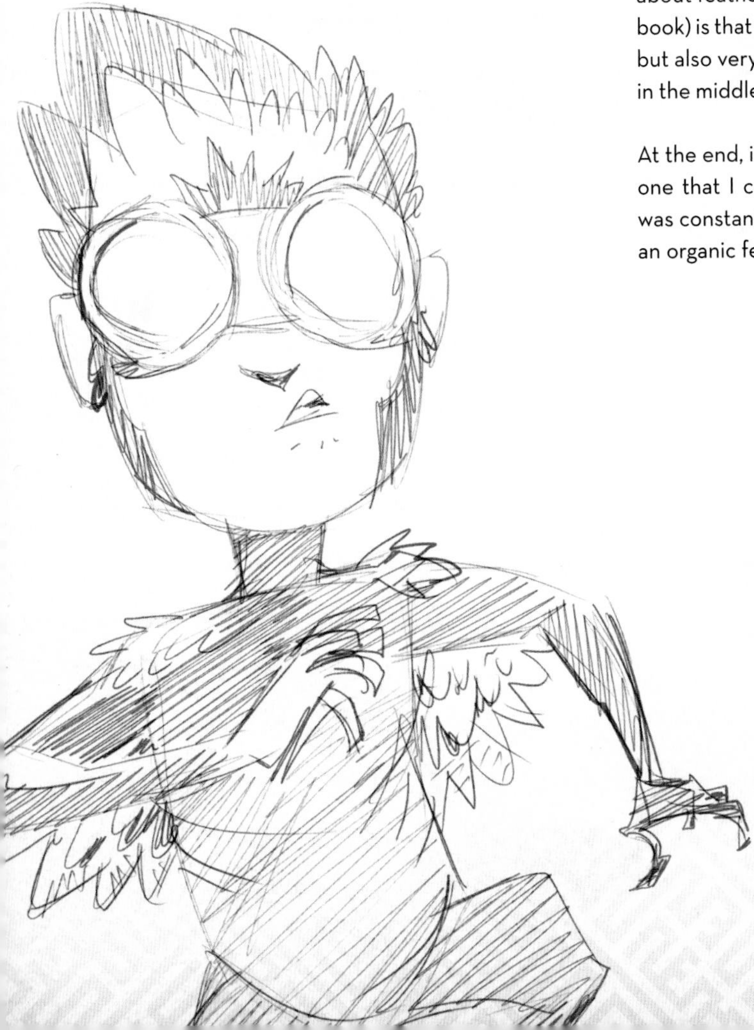

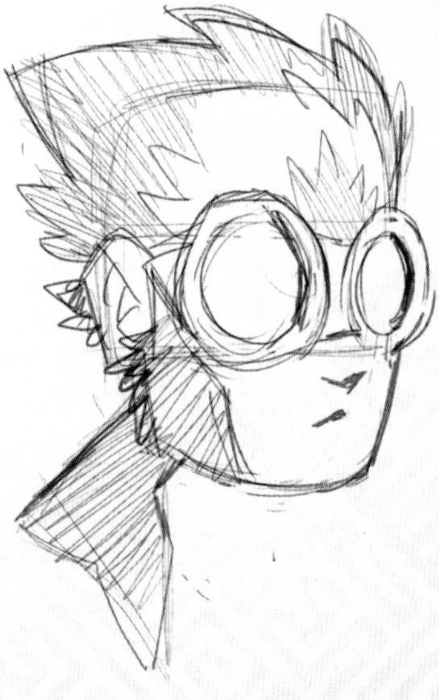

CHARACTER DESIGNS

Bianca's design had a wonderful challenge to it. The nature of the character was that of wealth and comfort on the outside, but a much more adventurous spirit on the inside. Bianca's strong personality had to come through, and that rebel strand of hair constantly getting in her face was the perfect balance to her otherwise princess-like appearance.

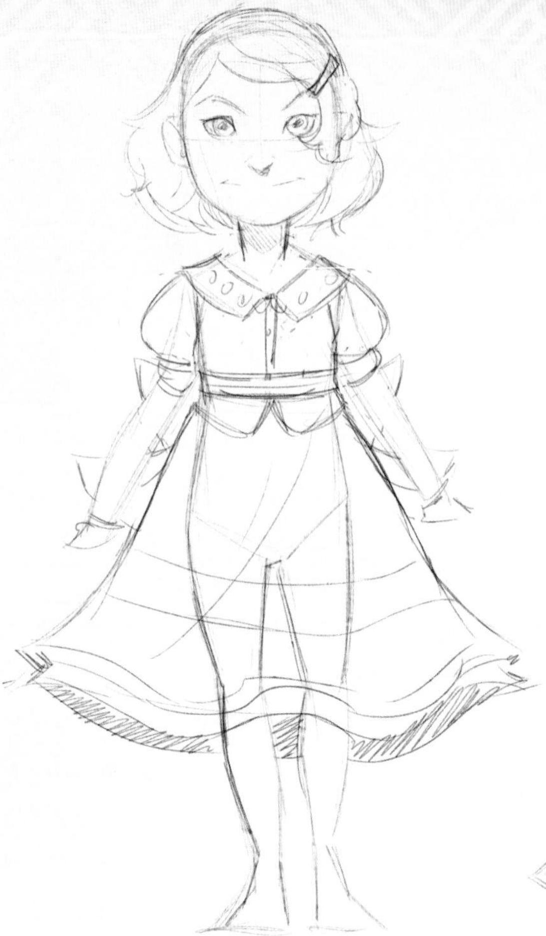

Another side of the character's journey that I wanted to reinforce was that, in contrast with some of the other characters, Bianca never compromises her nature. Her motivations and desires change throughout the story, but I never wanted her to feel like she needed to change in order to grow. When standing next to the rest of the cast, Bianca has her own voice. Next to Poe, she's a softer visual, a contrast to Poe's sharpness; ironically, the contrary is true when it comes to their personalities.

There was one particular character that I wanted Bianca to play against in terms of design. When it came to her family, Bianca was the black sheep in the eyes of her mother; **Eleanor** had to be a colder version of what Bianca could have been. After coming up with Bianca's design, it was just a matter of sharpening edges and we had Eleanor Chappelle.

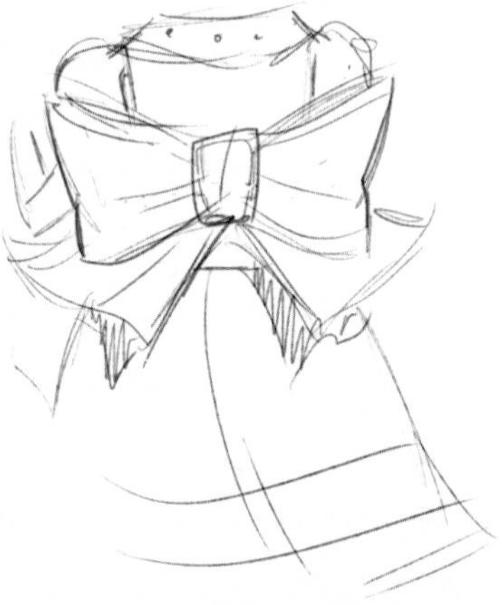

Two sides of the same coin, **Sebastian** and Eleanor are two different products of the City. Both accustomed to their way of life, they each have different views of their coexistence with the world beyond the Wall. Opulent in the way they dress, Sebastian had to project a bit of warmth that was definitely lacking in Eleanor's demeanor.

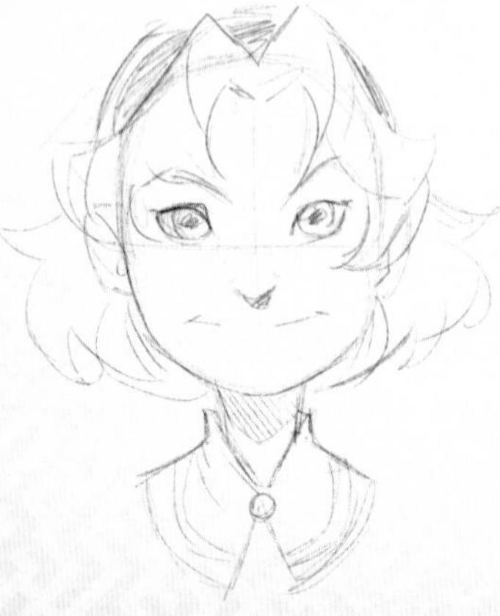

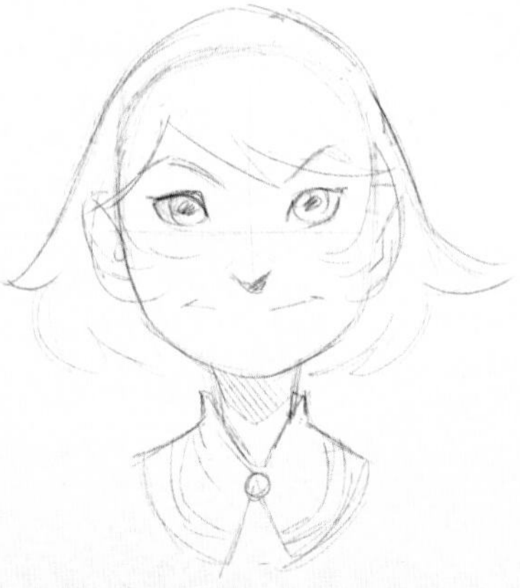

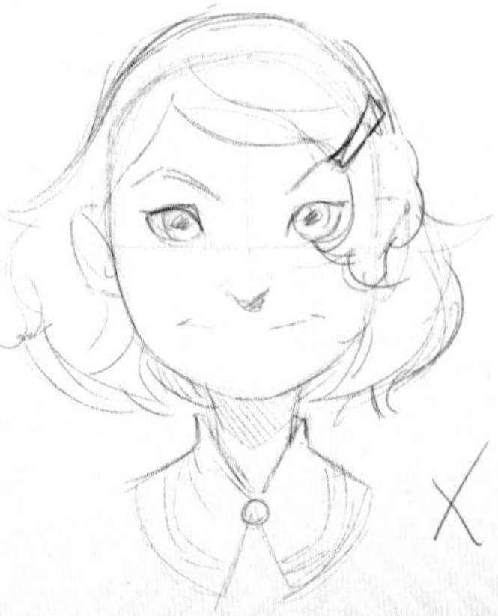

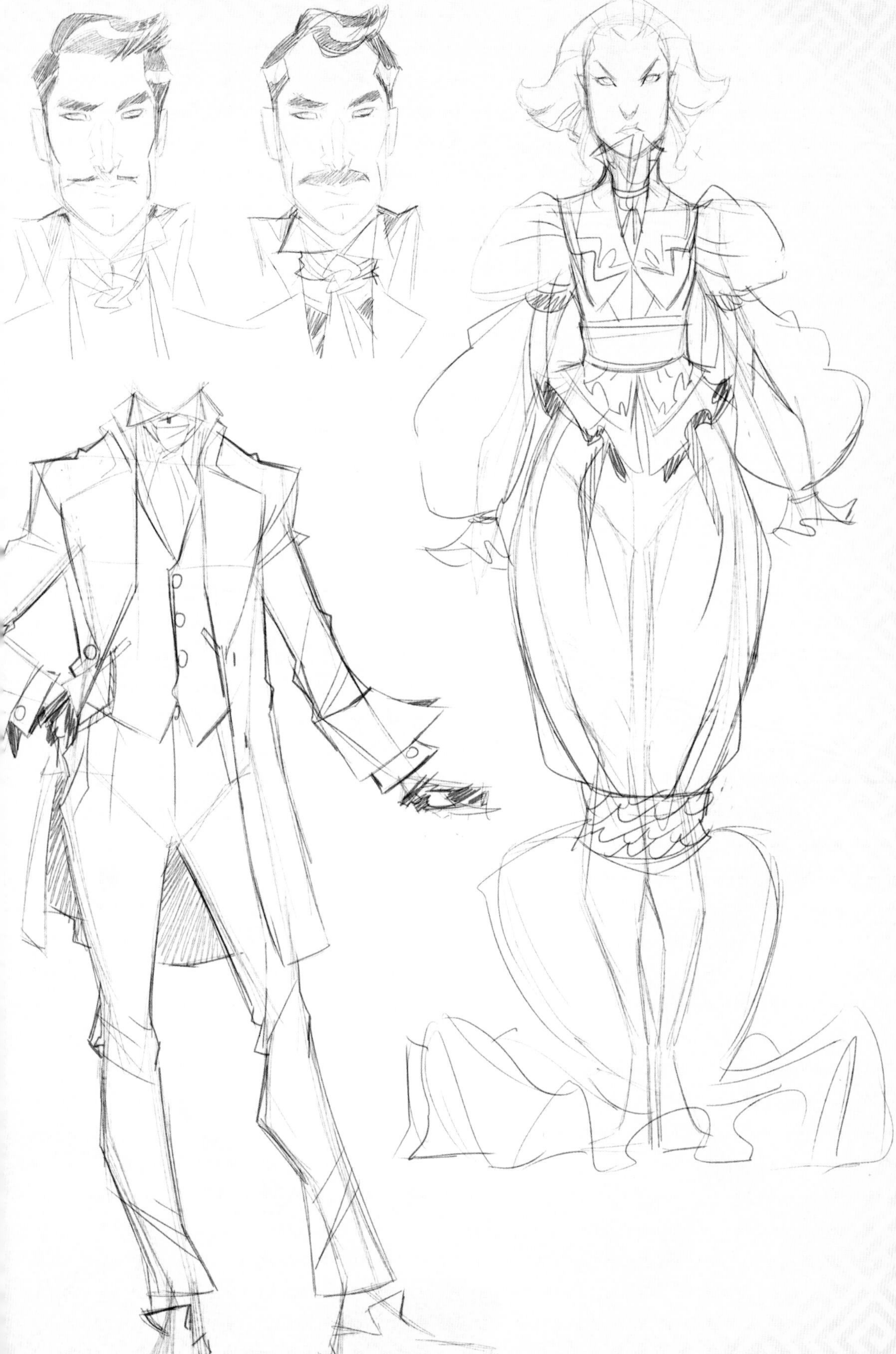

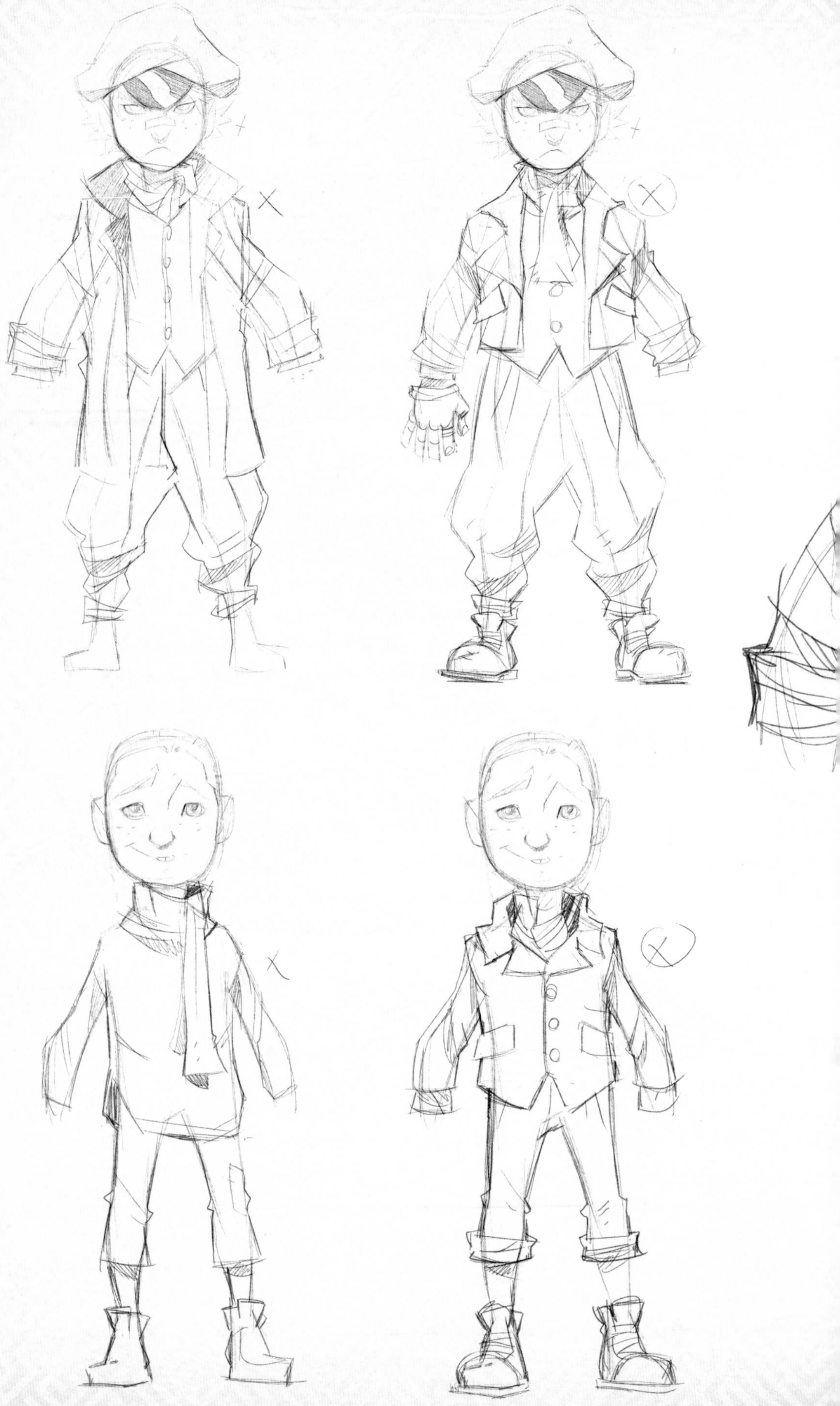

Z and **R** are the most prominent Mice within the story and, just like Eleanor and Sebastian, they are two outcomes of a similar environment. Z's harsh and tough personality had to be contrasted by R's more innocent nature. Z is the general, and the cap serves to embody that idea: everything in her outfit is meant to evoke the idea of militia. R, on the other hand, was straight out a Dickens story, the archetypal street boy. His silhouette, though, had to play against Poe's and Bianca's. As the third party in the main cast, he had to be the midpoint between Bianca's rounded features and Poe's spikier ones.

The **Guard**'s uniform was another one of the main challenges when designing the look of the book. I definitely wanted a bit of a Stormtrooper quality to them, a group mentality, with just enough room for individuality. The other main influence was the traditional tin soldier, and the only problem with that was referencing such a specific "real world" figure. The result was an amalgamation of different military uniforms from different ages. The **Captain** was an extension of that: streamlining the uniform and giving him a bulkier frame gave him enough presence to stand out as a figure of authority no matter the context.

Gabriel was one of the characters that I knew, from the very beginning, how I wanted him to look. A troubled soul with a painful past, Gabriel acts out of love, but sometimes that comes out in the worst possible way. One of the initial traits that I wanted for the character was that, since he's in a never-ending quest to find the perfect prescription for his sight, the frames of his spectacles were supposed to be wildly different from one another. This proved a bit too distracting, so I toned it down in the final pages.

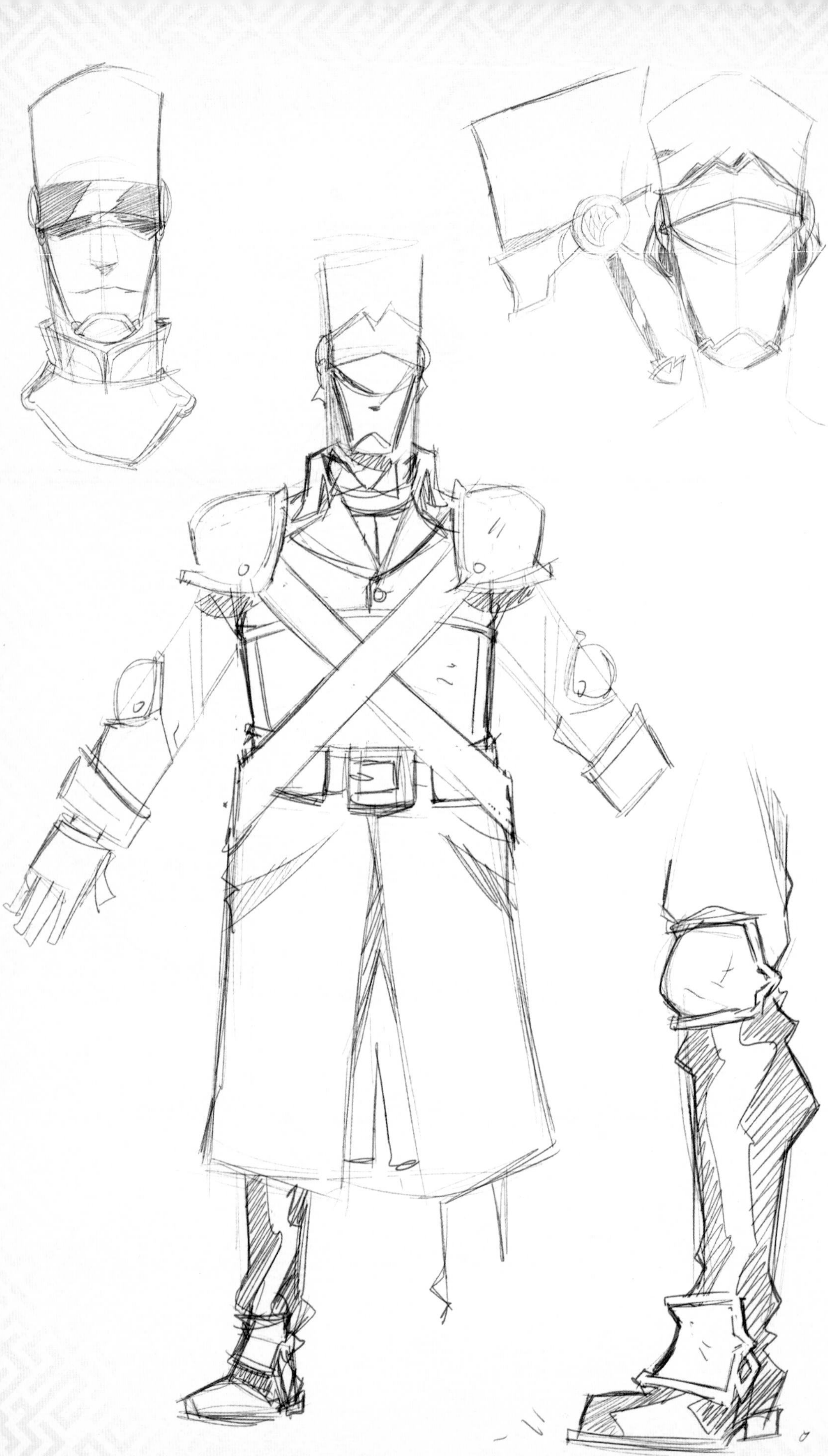

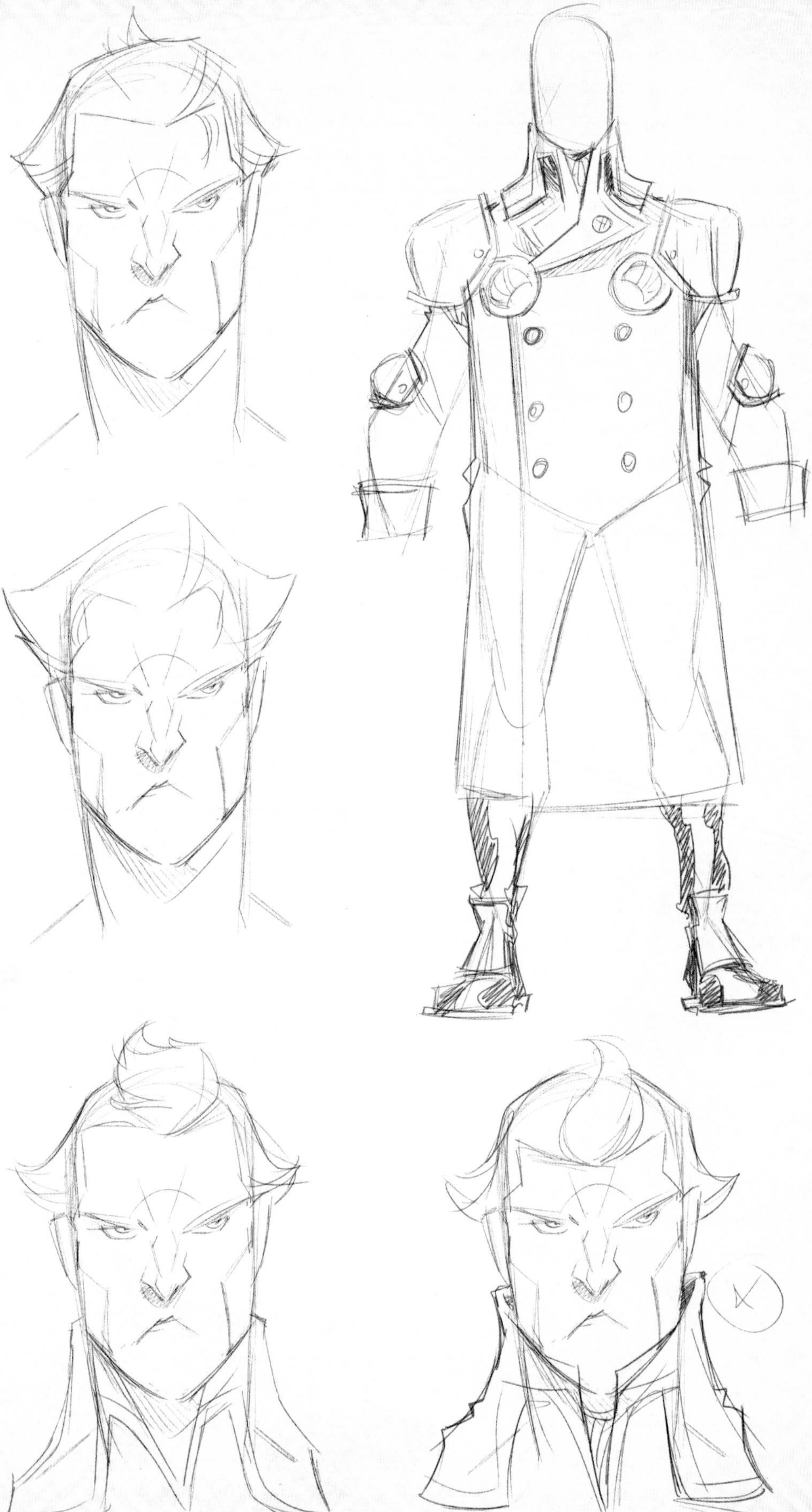

ORIGINAL PITCH

Back in 2013, after many years of only playing with the idea in my head and maybe drawing a handful of sketches, I decided it was time to try and get Poe's story out there. What follows is the original pitch I submitted to Rebecca Taylor and Archaia.

This was the first time I drew the characters in a comic format and, although these pages managed to stay very similar in the final book, the most important change came by the hand of Jen Hickman and the addition of her wonderful color palette, bringing new layers of life to the world of *Feathers*.

During the process of shaping the original idea for Poe and the world of *Feathers* all the way to the final product you now hold in your hands, some of its core elements evolved and changed. The wonderful malleability of a story, one that was now being worked on by a larger crew instead of a single mind, was truly enjoyable to experience. *Feathers* became this deceivingly complex world, and it wouldn't be here if it weren't for the extraordinary group of people I had the pleasure of working with.

PROCESS GALLERY

From the get-go, I wanted to maintain a very classic structure for layouts within the pages of *Feathers*, but it was when we needed to expand (due to some changes in format) the scene of Poe and Bianca exploring the Maze that Rebecca asked me to break the mold with the panel layout. The result was one of the most iconic sequences in the book.

THUMBNAILS

After having a general plot breakdown, my first step, before even writing the script, is to tell the story visually. This is where the heavy lifting happens.

The thumbnails for this scene were a challenge for two reasons: first, the idea was to break the panel grid and try to convey the mess that the Maze really was while keeping track of readability and storytelling; and second, we had to deal with the fact that this was a scene where the reader (and the characters) are being shown two different realities at the same time.

On one hand, we had Poe leading Bianca across the Maze, showing her various sites that would speak of the nature of this place. Broken-down buildings, impossible structures, and dark corners would shape the Maze to the eyes of Bianca, but at the same time, she was leading Poe through another exploration. A big part of the world-building was done here in the form of Bianca's story about the first settlers and the White Guide. This, of course, was of great interest for Poe and, instead of just talking about it, the characters were sharing the space with actual imagery from the story being told, pulling them in as much as the actual world of the Maze was.

SCRIPT

After having a concrete idea of how the pages were going to look, the next step was to write the dialogue to go along with it. At this step, it is mostly the individual voice of each character that has to come through. The script also includes notations and descriptions of the panels for Jen and Deron to reference after the page is drawn.

PENCILS

Once I have the layout and the script, the pencil stage is where character acting and details in environments come together. For the most part, I use pencils to define composition and shape, making sure that everything has its place. That's the reason why lately I've been doing most of the penciling digitally. It allows me a faster exploration without losing time with too many redraws.

THUMBNAIL LAYOUTS

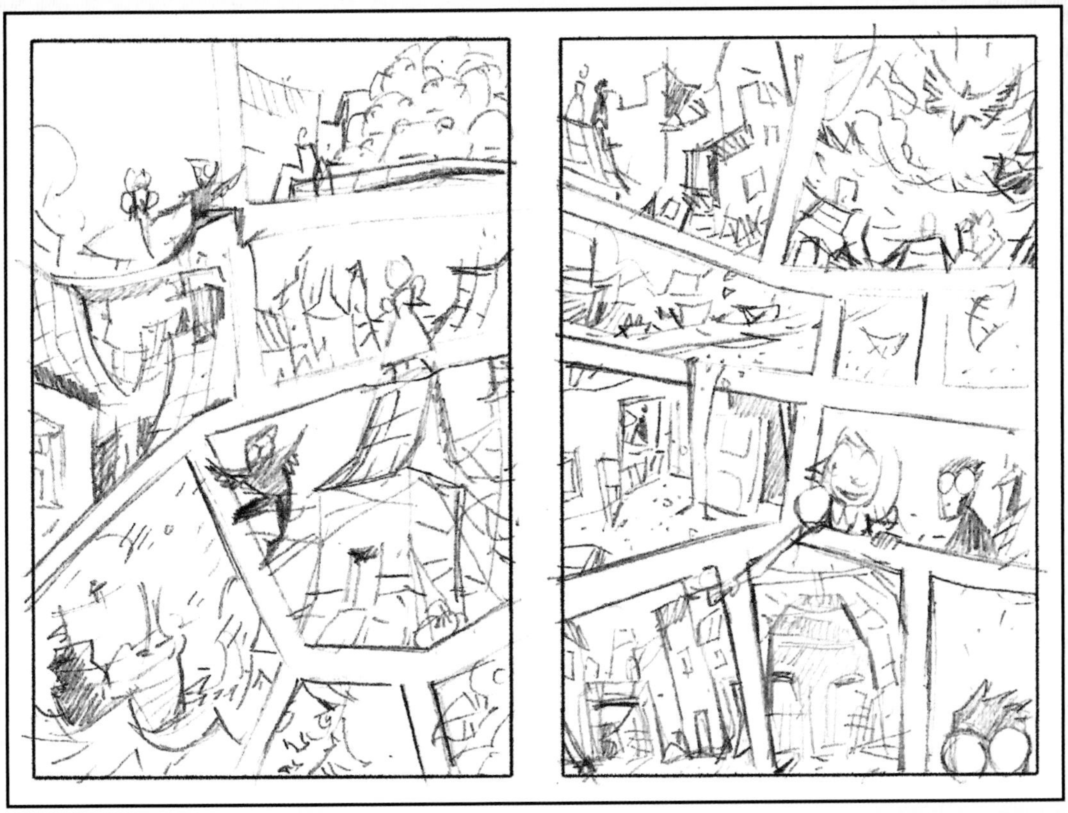

PENCILS

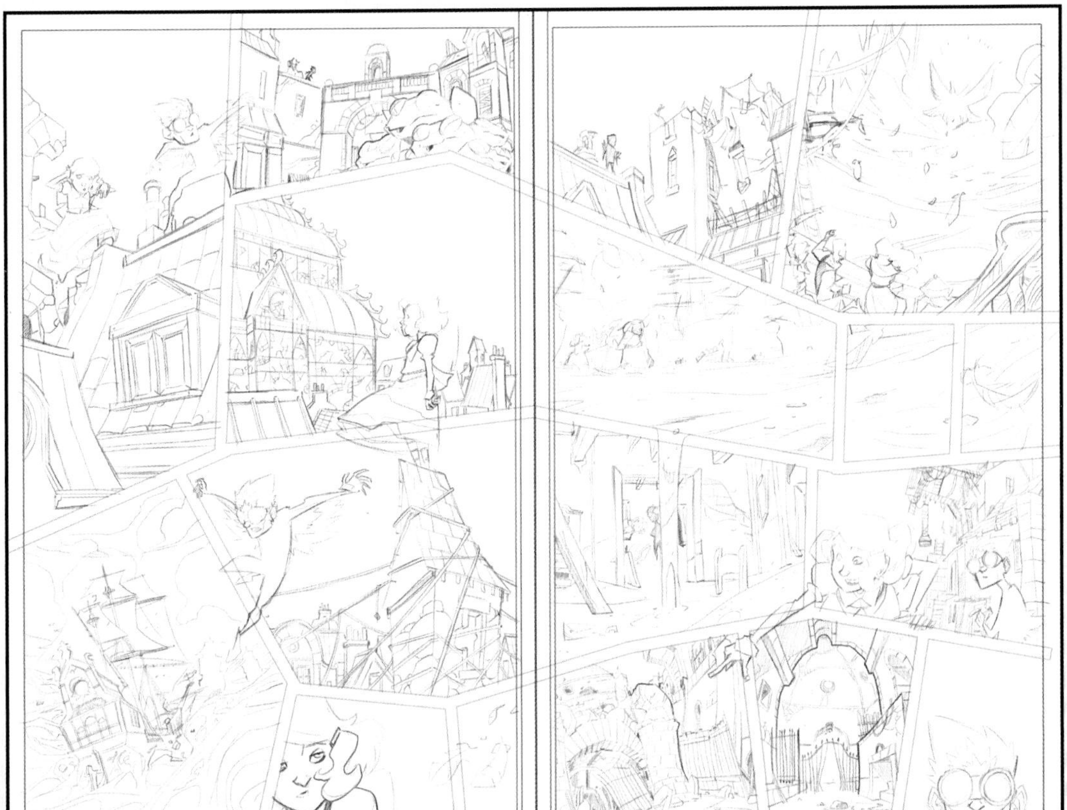

INKS

After having everything down on the page, it is time for inking. While I like to keep the pencils digital, I do prefer to ink traditionally. There is something about the feel of the ink on the paper that I can't seem to find when I ink digitally. It is at this point that I also look for the balance between black and white, making sure that everything is readable but also generating volume and depth where possible. Texture is also a priority when inking.

COLORS AND LETTERS

During the whole process of working on *Feathers*, this had to be my favorite part: waiting to see the pages come to life with Jen's colors and the voices from Deron's letters. And the best part of all? It was always a surprise to me! After spending weeks looking at the pages from thumbs to inks, it was here where I felt like a spectator and witnessed the world I wrote about take shape on its own. It was really a magnificent job these two did, and for which I will always be grateful.

For this specific sequence, the challenge came in keeping everything clear. Jen did a few versions of colors where the segments of backstory were treated differently in order to isolate them from the present time. It was a good trial-and-error approach that ended up defining the style we'd use for all sequences that parted from the "current" events.

Deron was the one who kept everything together, helping the reader to follow the dialogue in the right order. With a sequence where panels break the page in odd ways, and the traditional "left to right" way of reading can be compromised, he did an outstanding job making sure the eye followed each balloon, giving room for the reader to also experience the environments the kids were traveling through.

INKS

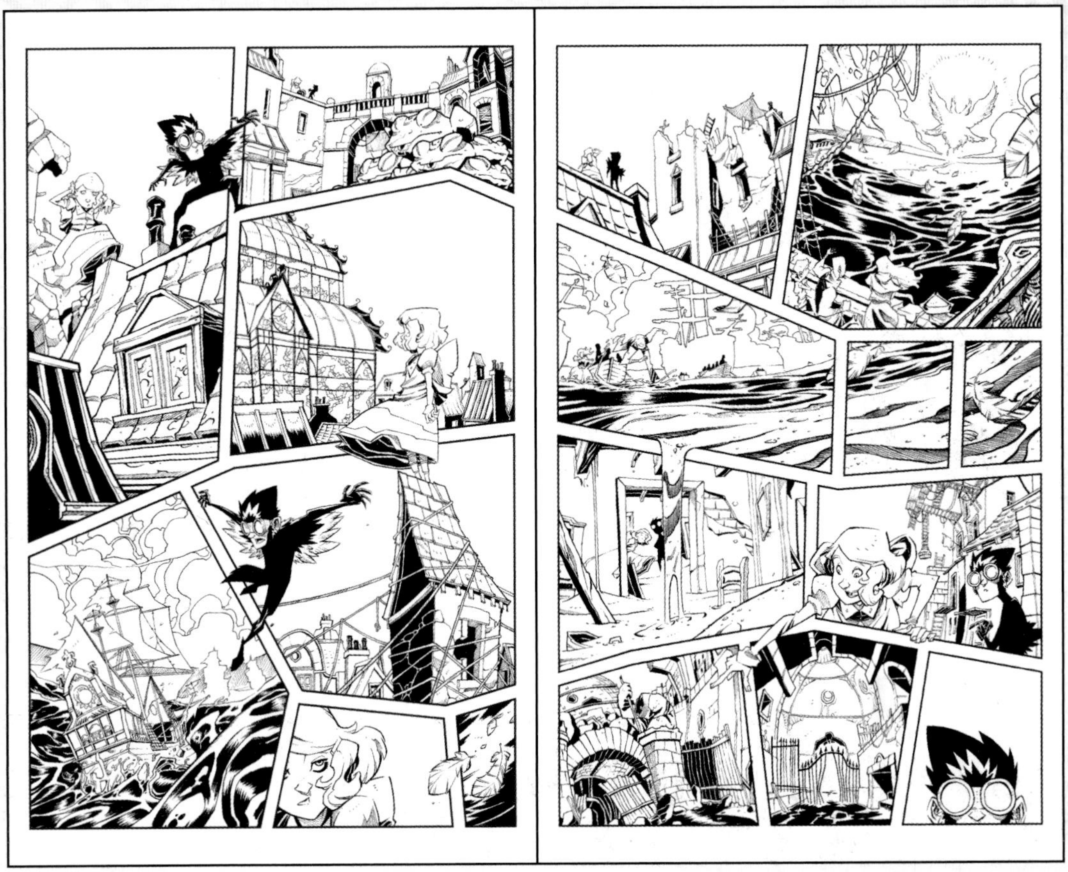

COLORS

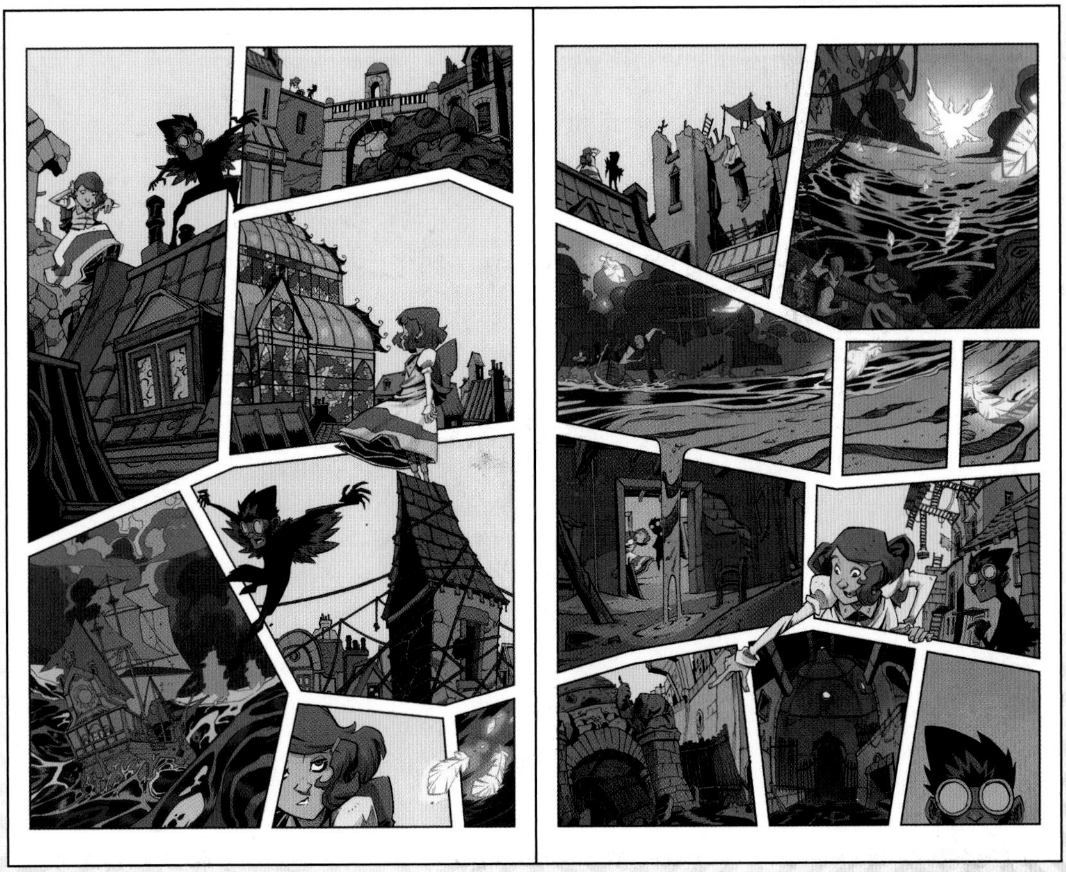

Jorge Corona was born in Maracaibo, Venezuela. After years of working as a Graphic Designer and Art Director for several companies back home, he was awarded the Fulbright Scholarship and attended the Savannah College of Art and Design, where he followed his lifelong dream of becoming a Sequential Artist. A fan of cartoons, comics, movies, and all things *Batman*, Jorge has worked on a diverse group of titles and genres, always with a fascination for superheroes and fantasy. In 2015, he received the Russ Manning Promising Newcomer Award.

Jen Hickman is a Californian illustrator who drinks too much coffee and loves making comics more than most other things. She recently self-published, with writer James Maddox, a graphic novel called *The Dead*, and had a short story in the paranormal anthology *Then It Was Dark*. Jen's work can be found at umicorms.com.

Eisner and Harvey Award-nominated letterer, **Deron Bennett** has been providing lettering services for various comic book companies for over a decade. His body of work includes the critically acclaimed *Jim Henson's Tale of Sand*, *Jim Henson's The Dark Crystal*, *Mr. Murder is Dead*, *The Muppet Show Comic Book*, *Darkwing Duck*, and *Richie Rich*. He has also ventured into writing with his creator-owned book, *Quixote*. You can learn more about Deron by visiting his website www.andworlddesign.com or following @deronbennett on Twitter.